Blackstone and the Rendezvous with Death

An Inspector Blackstone Mystery

SALLY SPENCER

LUME BOOKS

LUME BOOKS

First published by Severn House Publishers Ltd in 2003

Copyright © Alan Rustage 2014

This edition published in 2022 by Lume Books

The right of Sally Spencer to be identified as the author of
this work has been asserted by them in accordance with the
Copyright, Design and Patents Act, 1988.

ISBN 978-1-83901-405-5

www.lumebooks.co.uk

CONTENTS

'I have a rendezvous with Death
at some disputed barricade.'

Alan Seeger *(1888-1916)*

PROLOGUE

The fog had begun to descend just before nightfall, and within minutes it had covered the whole of the area north of the river. It was a thick, clogging fog, more yellow than grey. And it stank—not just of smoke and sulphur, but also of the decay and desperation it absorbed from the crumbling houses as it slid menacingly along them.

To the shabbily dressed young man who was making his way with cautious speed down Burr Street, this fog seemed more than just an inconvenience. It was, to him, nothing less than a malevolent force that was doing all it could to detain him—to prevent him from reaching that part of the city where he could be reasonably sure he would be safe.

He had been too rash, he thought. Far too rash. He should have ended his investigation earlier, at the point when he had *already* discovered enough to sketch out a rough picture of the terrible, terrible thing that was about to happen. But instead, he'd stuck doggedly at it, collecting extra details, refining the picture—putting himself more and more at risk. And finally, that night, he was paying the price, because—though he could not swear to it—he was almost certain he had been spotted. Which made it vital that he got all he knew down on paper before...before...

Suddenly, he realized he was not alone! He could hear footfalls behind him. And not ordinary footfalls. They didn't make the same sound as his scuffed dress boots, nor did they have the angry clump of a working man's sturdy clodhoppers. No, these steps were muted, swishing like a slithering serpent.

In a panic, he glanced over his shoulder, but could see nothing except the fog. He increased his pace, and behind him the swish-swishing grew faster, too. He felt his heart begin to pound, and could taste raw, naked fear in his throat.

He tried to calculate exactly where he was. It was a good ten minutes since he'd turned on to Burr Street, so even moving at the slow pace the fog dictated, he should be almost at the end of that street by now. If the public house on the corner were open— if, by some happy chance, the landlord had chosen to disobey the licensing laws—then he would be safe, at least for a while. True, the rough men inside—the dockers and the watermen—might see through his disguise and ridicule him. They might even rob him. But perhaps they would believe what he had to say, too. So that even if this was to be his last night on earth, his death might at least have some purpose.

He reached the corner, and his heart sank as he saw that the pub was shuttered and in total darkness. Where could he go now? he wondered, as his panic increased with every passing second. Where was there left to run to?

Head along Lower East Smithfield, towards Aldermans Stairs!

counselled the tiny grain of rational thought still left in his brain.

Yes, that was it! There was another pub on that corner, and even if it was also closed, there was always the chance that there would be a waterman on duty at the Stairs, willing to take him across the Thames—to carry him to safety.

You're fooling yourself! he thought angrily.

There would be no watermen. Not on a filthy night like this. Yet there was no choice but to cling to that slim hope, because now he was convinced that there was not one set of slithering footsteps behind him, but two.

He turned the corner, and was confronted by a black shape, looming in the darkness. An ambush! Naturally! Why had he ever imagined these people would leave anything to chance?

Perhaps if he could somehow manage to overpower the one ahead, then make a dash for it before the ones behind...

'Lookin' fer a good time, duckie?' asked a cracked female voice.

He could now see the shape for what it was. Nothing but a common prostitute, so desperate to earn her gin money that she was touting for custom even in this weather.

Or was it simply a trick? Was she, in reality, one of *them*?

He approached the woman cautiously, aware, even as he was doing so, that it would enable the men behind him to gain some ground. She was a small woman, well past her prime, and dressed in other people's cast-offs. It was hard to believe that she could be part of any conspiracy against him.

The woman lifted her skirt to show that she was wearing no drawers, then turned her back and presented him with her naked, mottled rear.

'Eivver end,' she said. 'I'm not fussy. Long as yer've got a tanner, yer can 'ave me any way yer want.'

'I'm...I'm not here for...for...' the young man stuttered.

'Yer won't get a better offer than that nowhere,' the woman said, a note of irritation creeping into her voice.

But the young man was already brushing past her and plunging once more into the swirling fog.

Surely he would come across a policeman on duty soon, he told himself. Surely, somewhere on his route, he would find a bobby who could protect him. But would any solitary man—even one wearing a blue uniform—be able to do anything against his ruthless pursuers?

He increased his pace again, but he did not run, because he knew that they would only do the same: and he wanted to have a little energy left in reserve for when he finally reached the desperate conclusion of this chase.

The swishing sound was still hauntingly behind him, but despite his encounter with the prostitute, it did not seem any closer. They were holding back, he decided—waiting until they could catch him in an even more secluded place than this achingly empty street. And he was leading them right to such a place! He knew that. But that same place, as dangerous as it might be, was where his only remaining hope lay.

Like a drowning man, he felt his whole life flash in front of him. The school his parents had sent him—a school he'd hated and where he'd continued to be bullied long beyond the age at which bullying should have stopped. He thought about his stern, unyielding father, his cowed mother, and his baying, opinionated older brother. And he thought about his loving, gentle sister, who had provided the few moments of happiness in his grim existence, and who was—indirectly—responsible for the situation in which he now found himself.

The pub at the edge of Aldermans Stairs was as dark and empty as the one outside which the prostitute had been lurking. And here there were fewer street lamps, so that he was moving in almost total darkness.

He stretched out his foot and felt for the edge of the Stairs.

'Hello, is there anyone down there?' he called out, thinking how squeaky and immature his voice sounded.

There was no answer, save for the gentle whoosh of the river.

He cleared his throat. 'Is there anybody down there?' he repeated, in a much deeper voice this time.

Once again, there was only silence in response.

He made his way groping down the Stairs. Perhaps he could swim for it, he thought. But he had never been a strong swimmer—never a strong *anything* if he was honest about it—and he was sure that before he was even half-way across the broad river he would succumb to exhaustion, and sink into oblivion.

He had reached the bottom of the Stairs, and his shin banged against something hard. A boat! By some miracle, one of the watermen—probably too drunk to know what he was doing—had left his boat moored where anyone could take it.

He felt along the edge of the boat until he came to the mooring rope. A miracle, he thought again—the possibility of escape when all such hope had seemed to be gone.

Working in almost total darkness—and with trembling hands— he clawed at the professionally tied knot that kept the boat tethered to the landing stage. As he worked, one small corner of his mind registered the fact that the swishing sound behind him had stopped. But there was no time to consider such matters now, when all his energy—all his will—had to be directed to getting the boat free.

He felt one of the fingernails on his right hand break, but ignored the short, inevitable, stab of pain. He twisted and tugged at the knot, knowing he should he more methodical, yet being unable to discipline himself into adopting a more rational approach. And finally, after what seemed a lifetime, the knot slid apart in his hands.

He put a tentative foot into the boat, and felt it move. But of course it moved! Now that he had untied it, what was there to *stop* it from moving? He lifted his other leg, lost his balance, and fell clumsily on to the floor of the craft.

Something was digging into his side, and he realized that it must be one of the oars. He picked it up, and poked it blindly into the darkness in the general direction of the landing stage. He felt the oar make contact, and then the prow of the boat swung away from the shore and towards the middle of the Thames.

But the stern stayed where it was!

The boat was tied up at both ends! He should have checked on that before he got in. He awkwardly manoeuvred himself round until he was in the right position to find the second mooring rope. Yes, there it was, and there was the knot holding it.

He wished he had brought a knife with him, so he could have sliced through the rope with one smooth movement. But he hadn't thought to bring a knife. There were *so many* things he hadn't thought to bring. Perhaps that was why he found himself in the position he was in now—because he hadn't planned ahead, but had relied solely on instinct.

Even as he grappled with the second knot, he could picture his father, watching the whole process and shaking his head in a gesture of censure and despair.

Yes, Father, he thought, I've failed again.

Except that this time it wasn't just the Earl he was letting down—this time it went far, far beyond the bounds of his narrow, censorious family.

The knot finally started to give at the same moment as he heard the violent crash behind him and felt the boat lurch violently. And then, almost before he'd had time to register what was happening, a pair of powerful hands had pinned his arms behind his back, and something cold and sharp was being drawn across his throat.

He wondered how they had managed to get so close to him without his hearing them. Wondered, too, how he could know he was in pain and yet not really feel hurt. Then he stopped wondering—and everything went black.

PART ONE

ALDERMANS STAIRS

ONE

The small crowd had formed almost as soon as the police rowing boat landed. At first it had been all of a huddle, and there was a real danger of the two Wet Bobs being forced down Battle Bridge Stairs and into the river. Then the senior of the two Thames policemen had ordered the mob to step back, and—reluctantly—it had. Now it formed a broad semicircle, so that those people who were at either end were perched perilously on the edge of the wharf, while those in the centre had their backs pressed up against the wall of the nearest warehouse.

From their various vantage points, the individuals who made up the crowd—costermongers who kept one of their eyes on the scene and the other on their barrows, trading company clerks with manifests tucked under their arms, watermen who spent most of the day rowing customers across the river, and the ne'er-do-wells who habitually hung around hoping to earn a dishonest shilling—all strained their necks to get the best view of what was happening.

There wasn't a great deal to see. The two policemen stood almost like statues, and the sausage-shaped object they'd pulled out of the river was completely shrouded in a tarpaulin.

The sergeant swept his eyes over the restive mob, then leaned towards his partner. 'I'll be glad when somebody from Scotland Yard finally gets 'ere,' he whispered.

'Yer can say that again,' the constable agreed.

And almost as if he had been waiting in the wings for his cue, a 'somebody' from Scotland Yard *did* appear. The new arrival was at least a head taller than anyone else on the wharf. He looked around him, assessed the situation, and then—seemingly effortlessly—induced the tightly packed mob to crush together even tighter in order to create a path for him.

A bit like Moses partin' the Red Sea, thought the sergeant, who had had the Bible—and very little else—thoroughly knocked into him when he was a pupil at the Lant Street board school.

The tall man reached the front of the crowd, and came to a halt in the open space between it and the tarpaulin sausage. It was not just his height that made him stand out, the sergeant realized, although someone nearly six feet tall was a bit of a novelty. The man's face, too, was striking. The sergeant ran his eyes over it quickly, taking in the details just as he'd been trained to. Bushy eyebrows formed two arches over sharp, penetrating eyes. The nose below them was large and almost a hook. The mouth was wide; the chin solid and square. The impression of Moses had been spot-on—though if the man really had been Jewish it would have been most unlikely he'd have been working for the Met.

The Scotland Yard man looked at the two river policemen in turn. 'Inspector Blackstone,' he said crisply.

The sergeant saluted. 'I'm Sergeant Roberts, sir. An' this 'ere is Constable Watts.'

The Inspector nodded, as if he had already known that, and was only testing their truthfulness. 'Are you the ones that found him?' he asked the sergeant.

'That's right, sir,' Roberts agreed.

'When and where?'

'We were on the six o'clock shift,' Roberts explained. 'We start out from Wappin' an' go up river—'

'Get to the point,' Blackstone said—though not unkindly.

'As we was drawin' level wiv Battle Bridge Stairs, we saw this thing caught up in the ropes of a barge that was moored in the middle of the river. We didn't know what it was at first, but as we got closer, we could see it was a body.' Roberts shrugged his broad shoulders. 'An' that's about it, sir. We pulled 'im on board, rowed to the shore, and 'ere we are.'

'Let's have a look at him then,' Blackstone said.

The sergeant glanced first at the crowd, and then back at the Inspector. 'What about all these people, sir?' he asked.

'It's a shame to disappoint them after they've waited so long,' the Inspector told him.

If you're sure, sir...' the sergeant said tentatively. Blackstone raised his head and looked into the crowd in such a way that almost every member of it blinked.

'We're taking the tarpaulin off now,' he said in a large, authoritative voice he had not used previously, 'and if any of you moves so much as an inch forward, I swear I'll have you.

Understand?'

Several heads nodded to indicate belief and acceptance. Satisfied, Blackstone turned back to the sergeant. 'Let the dog see the rabbit, then.'

The two river policemen knelt down and rolled the corpse out of the tarpaulin. Then, when they'd straightened up again, the Inspector bent down in their place.

Blackstone frowned. 'This isn't good,' he said. 'This is trouble.'

'What is, sir?'

'We're not looking at one of your average dockland murders here. This man isn't even a local.'

Roberts ran his eyes over the corpse's clothes—jacket fraying at the cuffs, trousers that had seen better days, boots scuffed at the toecaps. 'He's dressed like a local, sir.'

'Agreed. But look at his face.'

The sergeant examined the dead man's features. 'I see what you mean, sir,' he admitted.

The murder victim was probably twenty-three or twenty-four, Blackstone estimated, but his was not the early-twenties face usually seen in the area—a face that was already showing signs of starting to lose the struggle for existence, and proclaimed, more eloquently than words ever could, that the owner of the face was no more than twelve or fourteen years from the grave.

No, there was none of pinchedness of growing up in poverty on this face. None of the lines earned by working long hours from the age of twelve or thirteen. What he had here, the Inspector decided reluctantly, was the corpse of one of the Quality.

He let his eyes travel down to the throat, and examined the deep jagged gash that ran the whole length of the jawbone. 'Nasty,' he said, more to himself than to anyone else.

And the killer hadn't been satisfied to merely half-sever the head. The chest was pitted with at least a couple of dozen stab wounds as if the assassin couldn't quite accept he'd already accomplished what he'd set out to do.

'So what d'yer make of it, sir?' asked Sergeant Roberts.

'Well, it's either murder or the most determined case of suicide I've ever seen,' Blackstone told him.

Roberts raised an eyebrow. 'Beg pardon, sir?'

Blackstone sighed. 'If you want to get on in the police force, Sergeant, then the first thing you have to learn is to laugh at your superiors' jokes—however bad they happen to be.'

The sergeant grinned. 'Right, sir, I'll remember that.'

The Inspector lifted one of the dead man's limp hands, and examined it critically. 'Any thoughts on this, Sergeant?'

Roberts peered down at the hand. 'Broken finger nails,' he said after a few seconds' scrutiny. 'But 'e doesn't look to me like the kind of bloke 'oo'd 'ave broken 'em at work.'

'Agreed.'

'An' there seems to be a strand of somefink caught under one of 'em.'

'Rope fibre,' Blackstone said firmly. 'And where was a young gent like him likely to have come into contact with rope?'

'Dunno, sir,' the sergeant confessed.

'By the river. The broken nails indicate haste, the rope points to a boat. I would suggest he was trying to free a boat from its moorings when he was murdered.'

'You might be right, sir,' Roberts admitted.

'How long do you think he's been in the water?'

The sergeant turned his gaze to the face again. 'Not much sign of 'im swellin' up yet. I'd say it couldn't be more than a few hours.'

Blackstone nodded his agreement. 'In other words, he was murdered sometime in the early hours, right by the riverside. Have you got a tide timetable on you?'

'Don't need one, sir,' the sergeant said confidently. 'Down at Wappin', we know the tides better'n we know our own names. It started to ebb at twelve minutes past three precisely.'

'So assuming we're right about when the body entered the water, it would have been carried up river for a short time. Then, if it hadn't been caught up in the mooring ropes, it would have been swept out to sea.'

'That's about the size of it, sir.'

Blackstone let the corpse's hand drop back to his side, and was just on the point of standing up when he noticed the dead man's left eye.

'What do you make of that, Roberts?' he said, pointing. 'It's bruised.'

'You're right. But I don't think that happened when he was getting his throat cut. Do you?'

Roberts shook his head. 'From the way it's healed, I'd say he got that particular injury at least a couple of days ago.'

The black eye might—or might not—be connected to the

murder, Blackstone thought. Only time would tell.

He stood up. 'When you get back to Wapping, have a word with your comrades who were on night duty, Sergeant,' he said. 'Find out if they saw anything suspicious.'

'I'll do that, sir,' Roberts promised.

Blackstone nodded. He was sure that the sergeant—who seemed a conscientious officer—would make every effort to follow his instructions. But though he had made the request himself, the Inspector doubted that Roberts' inquiries would turn up anything remotely useful—because he already had the feeling that this was a crime in which *nothing* would come easy.

*

There were inspectors attached to the Yard who took a hansom cab to travel a few hundred yards, but Blackstone was not one of them. There had been no money for cabs when he'd been growing up—no money for much of anything—and walking had become a habit. Besides, walking helped him to think—and just at that moment, he had a lot on his mind.

Investigating the average murder—the slaying of a costermonger, for example—was easy. You found out who the man's business rivals were, and which of them he'd come to blows with recently. Then you went to the rival's local pub—where you would inevitably finding him drunk—and within five minutes the man would be sobbing that he ''adn't meant to kill ol' Charlie,' and 'I don't know what come over me.' Wives killed by husbands, husbands killed by wives, prostitutes murdered by their pimps as a lesson to the other girls in the stable—these were all commonplace slayings, with a simple, brutal logic to them that surprised nobody.

But occasionally there was a murder that was different. Blackstone remembered a few of those he'd solved. The case of the Canadian wool importer, whose body had turned up in instalments—the torso in the left luggage facility at Victoria railway station, the hands in King's Cross, the head at Euston. The murder of the money lender who had lain in a steamer trunk in Scotland Yard's own lost property office until the smell had alerted the duty constables that something was wrong. And then, of course, the London Bridge Murder, in which a famous racing jockey had been found hanging from a gas mantle. Yes, they had all been challenging cases in their way. But he had already begun to suspect that none of them had been as challenging as this one would be, because *this one* threatened to take him into a world of big houses and fine carriages—a world of which he knew almost nothing.

He had reached the Embankment, and stopped to look at the workmen who were busy stringing bunting between the lampposts. Blackstone gazed at the row after row of vivid red, white and blue Union Jacks, hanging there in homage to the little woman who had sat on the English throne for sixty long years.

How many of her subjects could remember her coronation? he wondered. He would have been surprised to find that there were more than a few thousand in the whole country.

The workmen stepped back to inspect the bunting, then moved their ladder on to the next lamp standard. It was still over a week to the Queen's Diamond Jubilee celebration, but already London was in a state of frenzy. What would it be like when the great day actually came—and the population of what was already a great and vast city had swollen to *three times* its normal size?

Blackstone turned to look at the river. As always, it was teeming with activity. Lighters were making their way downstream. Tugs, pulling a convoy of barges behind them like mother ducks with their young, were chugging towards the Pool of London. There were steamers that had travelled all the way from the Far East and tall sailing ships from Holland. The Thames was the heart of the city—and without that heart, London would die.

The Inspector focused his attention on one of many small dramas being acted out in the river. A steamer was anchored there, dwarfing the lighter moored next to it. A chute connected the two boats, and down that chute rolled chunks of granite. The men armed with rakes who stood on the lighter—trimmers, they were called—had the job of spreading the rock evenly across the deck. It was dangerous work because—time being money—granite continued to spew from the chute as they worked. The trimmers were forced to dodge and spread, spread and dodge. Accidents were common, and a man involved in one would consider himself lucky if he got away with no more than a broken leg or a few crushed ribs.

The lighter Blackstone was watching had completed its task, and began to move away towards the warehouses on Tooley Street.

Immediately, another craft took its place, and more trimmers began the elaborate dance they hoped would save them from an early end.

He was going to have to be a bit like a trimmer himself on this case, the Inspector thought—because if he offended any of the people of quality who were dragged into it, they could crush him as surely as the granite boulders could crush the men on the lighter.

TWO

An army of thick, black clouds hung menacingly over the river, but still the workmen continued to string their bunting between the lampposts along the Embankment. How many flags had they already put up? Blackstone wondered. A thousand, at least. And this wasn't even on the Queen's route. The whole city seemed to have been swept up in the euphoria of the Jubilee celebrations.

The Inspector ran his hand over his chin, feeling the stubble that was already in evidence despite his morning shave. 'We should have heard something about the body by now,' he said.

'It's early days yet, sir,' replied a voice behind him.

Yes, Blackstone agreed silently, under normal circumstances the forty-eight hours that had elapsed since Sergeant Roberts had pulled the body out of the river would indeed have qualified as 'early days'. It was often weeks—or even months—before a corpse found floating in the Thames was identified. Sometimes no one ever claimed it, and it went to a pauper's grave unmourned. But this was not some raddled prostitute or casual labourer with work-hardened hands who'd been drowned. This was a rich man. And the disappearance of such people simply didn't go unnoticed.

'Maybe he was a foreigner,' the voice behind him continued. 'A Yank or a German over here for the Jubilee. It could be quite a while before the relatives back home start getting suspicious.'

Blackstone turned round to face Sergeant Patterson, and, as always, was mildly surprised by the pleasant—almost boyish—face of the hard-bitten officer who was his right-hand man.

'You really think a rich German or American visitor would go to all the trouble of disguising himself as an East Ender?' he asked. 'What would be the point of that?'

Patterson shrugged. 'Never can tell how foreigners will act,' he said. 'I mean, they're not like us, are they?'

'And what makes them so different?'

'Well, for a start, they're jealous of us.'

'Are they?' Blackstone asked.

''Course they are—because we belong to the greatest nation on earth and they don't.'

Blackstone grinned at his assistant's crude jingoism. But then, he reminded himself, Patterson was far from unique. At the centre of the great British Empire it was hard to find any man, from the lowest to the loftiest, who didn't think that his country soared high over every other in the world. He reflected, not for the first time, on the irony of the fact that though he did not share the British Imperial dream—though, indeed, it had robbed him of his father—he himself had done so much more to advance it than any of these people who seemed willing to sing 'Rule Britannia' at the drop of a hat.

'I don't think he *is* a foreigner,' the Inspector said, as much to himself as to Patterson.

The sergeant ran his right hand through his carrot-coloured hair. 'What makes you say that, sir?' he asked. 'Instinct?'

In a way, Blackstone supposed it was. But it was not the usual kind of instinct—the imaginative leap in the face of the facts. This time it was closer to home, a feeling that the man had to be English or his death would not have induced this feeling of personal danger the Inspector was experiencing now.

A loud knock on the door snapped Blackstone out of his reverie. 'Yes?' he said.

The door swung open, and he saw a uniformed sergeant standing there. 'Yer've got a visitor, sir,' the officer said.

Once more, Blackstone got a flash of walking the tightrope—or of avoiding the fallen granite. 'What kind of visitor?' he asked.

'A young lady. Says it's on a matter of the utmost importance.'

'Then you'd better show her up,' Blackstone said, as his gut turned over once more.

The lady with the urgent business was wearing a spotted silk dress with puff sleeves, and a wide-brimmed hat decorated with lace. Her hands were gloved, and she carried a stylish leather bag that would have cost Blackstone several weeks' pay. There could be absolutely no doubt that she came from the same class as the dead man.

She didn't seem comfortable with her surroundings. In fact, she looked around the room as if she was expecting a trap, and was ready, once she had spotted exactly where it lay, to flee like a frightened doe.

'Sit down, madam,' Blackstone said, indicating the chair in front of his desk.

The lady gathered her skirts and sat. She was scarcely more than a girl, Blackstone thought, taking the seat opposite hers. Twenty or twenty-one at the most. She had blonde hair that curled out from beneath her hat, a pale delicate skin, and blue eyes, which were probably extremely attractive when they were not filled with unease.

'I've...I've come about your advertisement in the newspaper.'

'Which advertisement would that be, madam?' Blackstone asked.

The girl opened her bag and took out a folded piece of newspaper.

'Anyone having information concerning a young man of genteel background whose body was discovered in the Thames on Monday last should contact Inspector Blackstone at New Scotland Yard,' she read aloud.

'And you think you might have such information?'

The woman glanced down at her lap. 'Yes. Yes I do,' she said in a voice so faint that the Inspector had to strain to hear it.

Blackstone reached for a pen and dipped it in the inkwell. 'I shall need your name,' he said.

The very idea seemed to come as a shock to the young lady. 'Is that really necessary?' she asked, her voice now much higher— and bordering on panic. 'Couldn't I just examine the body and see if it's anyone I know?'

It was possible that she might just be one of those people who take a ghoulish interest in murder but, looking at her sensitive features, Blackstone didn't think it was likely.

'If anyone should examine the body, then I think it should be a *male* acquaintance,' he said. 'But before we can get to that point, I really do need your name. Is there a reason why you're so unwilling to give it to me?'

The young lady bit her lower lip. 'My...my father doesn't know I'm here,' she confessed. 'He'd be very angry if he knew I'd come.'

'There's no reason he should ever find out,' Blackstone assured her. 'And I still need your name before we can go any further.'

The young lady hesitated. 'It's Emily Montcliffe,' she said finally. 'My...my father is Earl Montcliffe.'

So it was going to be every bit as bad as he'd suspected it might, Blackstone thought.

He cleared his throat. 'This young man...?' he began.

'I think he may be my brother Charles.'

'And why would you come to that conclusion?'

'Because Charles has been...missing...for the last three days.'

Blackstone scratched his large nose thoughtfully. 'So why have you waited so long to come forward?' he wondered aloud.

Though she should have been expecting it, the question seemed to confuse Lady Emily.

'Charles is often away for the evening,' she confessed.

'You mean he often *goes out* in the evening?'

Lady Emily shook her head. 'No, I mean there are nights when he doesn't come home at all. He's managed to hide it from the rest of the family, but—' she smiled nostalgically—'he's never been able to keep any secrets from me.'

'And do you have any idea where he goes when he stays out?'

Lady Emily shook her head, though without total conviction.

'You're sure?' the Inspector insisted.

'I've...I've been going through his pockets before his valet's had a chance to deal with them,' she admitted. 'Do you think that's a terrible thing to do?'

'Not if the motive is sisterly concern. What have you discovered through your searches?'

'Once there was a programme from a vulgar music hall, and on another occasion I found a map. Not a proper one, it was drawn in pencil on a brown paper bag. I can't remember what they're called.'

'A sketch map,' Patterson supplied.

'That's right,' Lady Emily agreed. 'A sketch map.'

'And what area did this sketch map cover?' Blackstone asked.

'I don't know.'

'You mean there were no names written on it?'

'There were names, yes. At least, I think they were names.'

Blackstone arched his thick brows. 'What exactly do you mean by that?'

'Something was scribbled along the sides of the streets. It could have been a kind of writing, but, then again, it could just have been squiggles.'

'You're not making sense,' the Inspector told her.

Lady Emily shrugged helplessly. 'I...the squiggles looked like they might be letters—one of them was an R written backwards—

but I've never seen anything like them before.'

Perhaps it was a code, Blackstone thought. Perhaps it was some exotic foreign language. Or maybe it *was* nothing more than squiggles.

'Do you have this sketch map now?' he asked.

Lady Emily shook her head. 'I didn't dare keep it, in case Charles wondered where it had gone. You see, I didn't want to make him angry.'

'Is he subject to fits of temper?'

Lady Emily looked shocked. 'Oh no, he's the sweetest, gentlest soul alive. But even so...'

Even so, none of us like to have our private lives investigated, Blackstone thought. Especially when we're involved in something we're ashamed of.

And that was the conclusion he was rapidly coming to—that the dead man, whoever he was, *did* have something to be ashamed of. Nothing else would square up to the facts and explain what a young man of quality had been doing getting himself killed in one of the poorer parts of London.

It certainly wouldn't be the first time a gentleman had gone into the slums in search of a bit of rough. The Ripper investigation had opened that particular can of worms, and uncovered scores of such men. Doctors and lawyers, pillars of respectable society, had been forced, in order to avoid having suspicion for the murders fall on them, to confess to visiting the commonest brothels. There'd even been the suggestion that one of the Royal Family—the Queen's grandson—had been seeking his pleasure in this disgusting manner.

Blackstone sighed inwardly. Would all the murders he investigated end up with sordid motives? he pondered. Would he ever be involved in a case in which the victim died for a noble purpose?

He turned his attention back to his visitor. 'For how long has your brother been in the habit of disappearing?'

Lady Emily pursed her brow thoughtfully. 'It must have started around the time I became engaged,' she said.

'Which would make it...?'

'About three weeks ago now.'

Blackstone wondered whether the timing was more than coincidence—whether, in fact, the young man felt more than brotherly love for Lady Emily, and her engagement had driven him into a desperate orgy of forbidden pleasure. But it was far too early for such suppositions, he rebuked himself.

'I see no point in worrying your family unduly about this matter, my lady,' he said, 'so I suggest you have one of your servants—perhaps your brother's valet—meet me at the morgue this afternoon.'

Lady Emily nodded her head gratefully. 'Yes, that would probably be for the best,' she agreed.

THREE

When there was the possibility of a good juicy inquest—the case of a man who'd thrown himself in front of a train, for example—the queue waiting outside Southwark Coroner's Court could stretch round the corner, but that afternoon there was no such excitement on offer, and Blackstone found himself waiting alone.

He turned to face the road. Buses, vans and cabs thundered past, some pulled by a single horse, others by a team of two or four. He'd read somewhere that the new horseless carriages—automobiles, was it?—would soon be taking over most of the work. But he couldn't see it happening—not in his lifetime.

The carriage that now appeared in the distance would have looked far more at home on one of London's more exclusive streets. Blackstone, who knew horses from his time in the Army, whistled appreciatively at the sight of the four jet-black animals pulling it. Beauties, they were—*real* beauties. And whoever owned them must have paid a pretty packet for the privilege.

As the carriage drew closer, the Inspector was able to take in more details. The woodwork was lacquered, and a coat of arms was exquisitely painted on the door. Nobility, then. Was there no end to the number of aristocrats who had a desire to slum it?

The carriage drew level with the Coroner's Court, and the coachman reined the magnificent horses in. Blackstone, still watching, expected the door to remain firmly closed until the coachman climbed down to turn the handle. Instead, it swung open immediately.

The Inspector was not quite sure whom he'd expected to climb out, but the man who did was certainly a surprise. For a start, at twenty-seven or twenty-eight, he seemed far too young to he travelling in such an august vehicle. Then there were his clothes. He was wearing a heavy cotton jacket, wide tie and a felt trilby. Presentable enough—smart, even—but again, scarcely appropriate to his majestic form of transport.

Blackstone quickly assessed the man. Broad brow, wide mouth, square jaw. An intelligent man, the Inspector decided. A decisive man.

The gentleman in question looked at him inquisitively. 'Are you, by any chance, Inspector Blackstone?'

Now that he thought he understood the situation, Blackstone almost laughed out loud. No wonder this man dressed well, but not like one of the rich. This wasn't one of the aristocracy at all. He himself had suggested to Lady Emily that she send her brother Charles' valet to view the body at the morgue—and that was exactly what she had done!

'Yes, I'm Blackstone,' he said. 'And you would be...?'

'Dalton,' the other man replied. 'Lord *William* Dalton.'

He had put the emphasis on the second word, but that did

not mean that he had intended Blackstone to miss the first. The Inspector bowed slightly. 'My Lord.'

'You may be surprised by my presence here,' Lord Dalton said. 'Well, I can clear that up for you right away. I'm here on behalf of my fiancée, Lady Emily Montcliffe.'

'We...er...we were expecting someone else...' Blackstone began.

'Of course you were,' Dalton agreed amiably. 'But now I am to be a part of the family, it seemed only fair to me that I should shoulder some of its responsibilities, as well as its privileges. Besides, my fiancée is eager, should this prove to be a false alarm, that...that...How shall I put this?'

'That her father does not find out she's been anywhere near Scotland Yard?' Blackstone suggested.

'Exactly,' Lord Dalton agreed. 'So with that in mind, I'd greatly appreciate it if you'd show me where the body is.'

'It isn't a pretty sight, my Lord,' Blackstone said.

The other man smiled. 'I don't imagine it can be,' he replied, 'but someone has to see it, and I would appear to be the most suitable person.'

Blackstone shrugged. 'Very well. If that's the way you want it, my Lord.'

Blackstone led his visitor down the maze of corridors to the mortuary. It was obvious that Lord Dalton was not used to the smell of formaldehyde—he probably wasn't used to *any* unpleasant smells—but glancing over his shoulder, Blackstone saw that the aristocrat was trying his hardest to make the best of it.

The morgue contained three bodies that day, the one that had been fished out of the Thames being closest to the door. 'Right, Sid, let's see it,' Blackstone said to the attendant. The constable pulled out the drawer, and lifted back the sheet.

Lord Dalton took a step forward. 'My God!' he exclaimed.

'I warned you it wouldn't be a pretty sight, sir,' Blackstone said.

Dalton leant against the wall to steady himself. 'It's not the wounds,' he gasped, 'though, God knows, they're bad enough.'

'Then what is it?' Blackstone asked gently.

'...I never expected it really *would* be him,' Dalton said. 'I mean, I knew in my mind that it was always a possibility it could be Charles, yet I never actually thought...'

'Then I take it that this *is* Charles Montcliffe?'

Dalton nodded. 'Yes, I'm afraid it is.'

'Would you like me to find you a chair, sir?' Blackstone asked, already reaching out for one.

'No, I wouldn't,' Lord Dalton said. 'What I'd like you to do, Inspector, is to take me to the nearest public house and let me buy us both a drink.'

*

Blackstone hesitated at the front door of the Chandler's Arms. True, it was the closest pub to the Coroner's Court—and Dalton looked as if he could really use a drink—but inside it was all spit and sawdust, and the Inspector was not sure how the lord would react to it.

'It will serve us perfectly well,' said Dalton, reading his mind.

Blackstone pushed open the door, and the two men entered the pub. The bar was furnished with cracked leather settles, rickety chairs and scarred tables. Dalton headed for the nearest table and sat down.

'A large whisky,' he called across to the landlord. 'The best you have.' He turned to Blackstone. 'And for you, Inspector?'

'A pint of the usual,' Blackstone told the landlord.

The drinks were brought, and Dalton swallowed half his whisky in one gulp. Then he took a deep breath, as if he were doing his very best to regain control of himself.

'I must apologize for my reaction in the mortuary, Inspector.' he said. 'It was weak of me, and I deplore weakness in any form.'

'If you'd like to go somewhere else now you're feeling a bit better, sir...' Blackstone suggested.

Dalton waved the offer aside, then looked straight into the Inspector's eyes. 'If we are going to be spending any time together, Mr Blackstone—and it looks as if, inevitably, we will have to— then it would he as well that you understand me from the start.'

'Understand you?' Blackstone repeated, mystified.

'My fiancée's family is very old stock,' Lord Dalton explained. 'There were Montcliffes with William the Conqueror at the Battle of Hastings. That means that they have been landed nobility for hundreds of years.'

'I see,' Blackstone said—although he didn't.

'My family, on the other hand, is not so well established,' the other man continued. 'My grandfather had a small business. He could, in fact, have been called a tradesman. My father worked hard to improve the situation he inherited, and became a very rich man. But he was not ennobled until three years before he died.'

'Why are you telling me all this, my Lord?' Blackstone asked.

'Because you will not understand my fiancée's family's world, and they will not understand yours,' Lord Dalton said. 'Whereas I, with a foot in both camps, could form an effective bridge between the two.'

Blackstone took a reflective swig of his pint. 'I'm not meaning to sound impertinent, my Lord, but what's in it for you?'

'I want the killer of that poor man who was to have been my brother-in-law brought to justice,' Dalton said firmly. 'And I am willing to do anything I can to help that process.'

He sounded sincere, but Blackstone felt he was holding something back. Still, it would be wise to tread warily when dealing with the aristocracy—even if it wasn't *real* aristocracy like the Montcliffes.

'Ask your question, Inspector,' Lord Dalton said.

'My question, my Lord?'

'I could see on your face that you weren't happy with my reason. Isn't that true?'

Easy, old son, Blackstone warned himself. Watch your step.

'People aren't normally as willing to become involved in police business as you seem to be, my Lord,' he said.

Dalton signalled for more drinks. 'All right, there is more to it than I might have said,' he admitted. 'Poor Charles is dead, and catching his killer won't alter that. But I am concerned to see that no more harm is done. I want to do all I can to protect the family.'

'Protect them from what, my Lord?' Blackstone asked obtusely.

'From the gutter press,' Dalton answered. 'From the heavy-handed part of the police inquiry. And, of course—' he lowered his voice—'from scandal.'

'What kind of scandal?'

A frank expression came to Dalton's face. 'If I knew that, I wouldn't need the resources of the police.'

Blackstone leant back in his chair. 'Indeed, my Lord,' he said.

'Indeed,' Dalton replied, without a trace of irony in his voice. 'If I knew, for example, that Charles had been gambling, I would simply pay off his debts. If there was a...er...woman involved, then I could pension her off to the South of France. But I have no idea what he was doing on those nights when, his sister now tells me, he disappeared. Nor do I have the means to find out. But you do.'

'Are you suggesting that I cover up a crime, my Lord?' Blackstone asked heavily.

'By no means,' Dalton assured him. 'As I told you, I want the criminal caught. But if it became necessary to...er...blur the motive behind the crime, and you were in a position to help me do that, I would find a way, at some time in the future, to show my appreciation.'

He isn't quite offering me a bribe, Blackstone thought—but he's coming damn close to it.

Yet he couldn't afford to dismiss the offer of help out of hand because—in many ways—Dalton was right. The noble lord *was* a bridge between two worlds that did not understand each other at all. And, treading on dangerous ground as he was in this case,

Blackstone couldn't help thinking that it wouldn't do him any harm to have friends in high places—always assuming he could make those friends without prejudicing his investigation.

'I can quite see your concern in this matter, my Lord,' he said, choosing his words carefully, 'and you can rest assured that if it's at all possible...'

'That's all I ask,' Dalton said. He stood up and placed a guinea on the table. 'And now, if you will excuse me, Inspector, I have some rather bad news to break to the family.'

Blackstone watched the other man until he reached the door, then turned round to examine the rest of the people in the bar. In one corner sat an itinerant chair mender, who after hours of knocking on doors was now nursing the half-pint of beer his labours had bought him. Standing at the bar counter were two leather workers, deadening the stink of the tannery that was trapped in their nostrils with glasses of best ale. An off-duty fireman sat at one of the tables; an old man who sold caged birds in the market at another.

These were his people, he thought. He had grown up among them and—had it not been for the Army—he could have been any one of them now. He understood them, perhaps even better than they understood themselves. But the society into which he was being thrust was an entirely different matter altogether. He didn't know how they thought, and he didn't know what rules they played by. He drained his pint, and permitted himself a short sigh. He was not looking forward to his first meeting with a family that had arrived in England with William the Conqueror.

FOUR

In all his time at the Yard, Blackstone had only seen Sir Edward Bradford, the Commissioner of Police, from a distance. Now, because of the murder of Charles Montcliffe, he was standing less than five feet from the great man, separated only by a mahogany desk.

Bradford was not alone. Sitting next to him was a thin, slightly older man wearing a frock coat, and it was obvious from the Commissioner's demeanour towards him that he was a Very Important Person indeed.

There was something familiar about the newcomer, Blackstone thought. He was sure they'd never met before, but perhaps... perhaps he had seen an engraving of the man's face in the newspapers.

The Commissioner cleared his throat. 'This is Inspector Blackstone, Home Secretary,' he said. 'He is the officer who will be conducting the investigation into Charles Montcliffe's death.'

Home Secretary? Blackstone repeated silently. *The* Home Secretary? Bloody hell fire!

The man in the frock coat nodded slightly in Blackstone's

direction. 'This is a very difficult situation we find ourselves in, Inspector,' he said.

'I appreciate that, sir,' Blackstone replied.

The Home Secretary raised his hands from the desk and clutched the lapels of his frock coat.

'I don't think you *do* quite appreciate it,' he said. 'How could you? You are one of the workers at the coalface, as it were, of this great city of ours. You can only see what is directly in front of you. Whereas I, from a more elevated position, can take a much broader view of the whole situation.'

He wasn't so much talking as making a speech, Blackstone thought, but maybe after so many years in politics, that was all he was capable of.

'In a few days' time, Inspector, we will be celebrating Her Majesty the Queen's Diamond Jubilee,' the Home Secretary continued. 'And those celebrations will not be centred on the small country in which she was crowned sixty years ago, but on the vast empire she rules over now.'

Why is he telling me this? Blackstone wondered. What could it possibly have to do with a murder in the East End?

'Her Majesty's hold over her overseas subjects is really quite remarkable,' the Home Secretary said. 'To them, she is the Great White Mother. The Malayan coolie and the African rubber gatherer, the Australian aborigine and the Canadian Indian, all of them—to a man—obey our colonial administrators not out of respect for them, but out of respect for the Queen. They are compliant because they know that is *her* wish. She is of as much value to government's imperial policy as half a dozen regiments of fighting men.'

He paused, almost as if he was expecting applause.

'She has made us the great nation we are,' Blackstone said, hoping there was enough conviction in his voice to keep the politician happy.

'Made us the great nation we are,' the Home Secretary repeated, savouring every word. 'Exactly! And that is why nothing must be allowed to distract attention from the celebrations. To put it simply, there must be no other news in the papers but the Diamond Jubilee.'

'Do you see where this is all leading?' the Commissioner asked.

Oh yes, Blackstone thought. I can see where it's leading, all right.

'What you're telling me is that this murder case might prove a distraction,' he said aloud.

'Just so!' the Home Secretary agreed enthusiastically. 'The brutal murder of a man who is a distant relative of Her Majesty would fill the front pages of even the most responsible newspapers.'

'It is for precisely that reason that there will be no announcement of the death of the Honourable Charles Montcliffe—at least for the time being,' the Commissioner said.

'You're going to try and keep it a secret?' Blackstone asked incredulously. 'You really think you can hide something like this?' He caught the look in his superior's eye, and pulled himself up short. 'I'm sorry, sir. I didn't mean to sound insubordinate. It's just that I don't see how it can possibly be done.'

'We cannot, of course, keep it *completely* secret,' the Home Secretary said. 'Charles Montcliffe's family will have to be informed, as is their right. Even as we speak, Lord William Dalton, who is almost a member of the family himself, will be carrying out that unpleasant function. And, naturally, Her Majesty will have to be told. But no one beyond that must know.'

What kind of make-believe world did this man inhabit? Blackstone wondered. Did he really think that the murder could be hushed up just because that was what was convenient?

'I see some doubts written on your face, Inspector,' the Commissioner said. 'Would you mind putting them into words?'

'It's too big a secret to keep, sir,' Blackstone said. 'For a start, there's the dead man's friends. They're bound to wonder—'

'From what I saw of Charles when I dined with his family, I would say he was a rather solitary young man,' the Home Secretary interrupted.

'And then there's the servants,' Blackstone continued. 'How can you ever hope to keep them completely in the dark?'

'The servants will be told a part of the truth—which is that Montcliffe has gone missing,' the Commissioner said. 'But they will also be told that there is no cause for concern.'

'They won't believe it,' Blackstone said firmly. 'First of all, they'll start speculating amongst themselves, then they'll pass it on to their family and friends. By tomorrow at the latest, at least a couple of hundred people will know that something strange has happened to Charles Montcliffe. And I guarantee that three or four of them will come up with the idea of selling the story to the papers.'

The Home Secretary smiled complacently. 'We have already considered that possibility and have resolved the dilemma,' he said. 'Would you care to hear the solution we have arrived at?'

'Very much so,' Blackstone said.

'Until the Jubilee celebrations are over, none of the servants will be allowed to leave the house.'

'There'll be tradesmen making deliveries all the time,' Blackstone pointed out. 'It only needs one of the servants to drop an indiscreet word and—'

'The butler—who is a very sound man indeed—will make certain that no tradesman has a conversation with any of the servants which goes beyond the transaction of business,' the Home Secretary countered.

A sudden look of irritation came to his face, as if he had just realized that he had been justifying himself to a mere inspector.

'At any rate, these details are none of your concern,' he continued. 'We have only told you as much as we have so that you will appreciate the amount of finesse that will he necessary as you conduct your inquiry.'

'So I'm to try and catch Charles Montcliffe's murderer without telling anybody he's dead, am I, sir?' Blackstone asked the Commissioner.

Sir Edward Bradford nodded gravely. 'Yes, Inspector,' he said. 'I'm afraid that's *exactly* what you've got to do.'

FIVE

The house on Park Lane had four storeys above ground level, and one below. It might have been built in what they called the Regency style, Blackstone thought, looking at it from across the street. Then again, it might not be Regency at all, because the self-improvement course he'd mapped out for himself when he'd left the Army had not included architecture. But whatever style it was in, he was sure of one thing—it could easily have accommodated the residents of his entire street in considerably more comfort than they knew now.

'Nice place,' said Sergeant Patterson, without even the slightest trace of irony in his voice.

'Very nice,' Blackstone agreed. 'I might have made Earl Montcliffe an offer for it if it hadn't been so far from the Yard.' He paused. 'Do you know what's bothering me about this case, Sergeant?'

Patterson shook his head. 'No, sir.'

'It's bothering me that Sherlock Blackstone and his faithful assistant, Dr Patterson, are still on it.'

The sergeant frowned. 'How d' you mean, sir?'

'When we were given this job, none of the top brass knew who the dead man was,' Blackstone explained. 'But now they do. They know he was the son of an earl—and that makes him important. So I say again, why are a couple of small fry like us still on the case?'

Patterson looked offended. 'We're good detectives, sir. Very good detectives.'

'We're good at solving the kinds of murders we normally come across,' Blackstone contradicted him. 'This is different. We're out of our depth here.'

'Most of the Force would be out of its depth.'

'But not all,' Blackstone pointed out. 'There are a couple of senior officers with aristocratic connections, and if they don't want to actually conduct the case themselves, they should at least be directing us. But that's not happening. I get a ten-minute chat with the Commissioner and the Home Secretary, in which I'm told to be discreet, then we're pretty much left to our own devices. Nobody else in the whole Yard seems to have any interest in this murder.'

'And why's that, sir?'

Blackstone sighed. 'I've no idea.'

But he had. The uneasy feeling he'd had from the start was deepening with every hour that passed. If the brass were keeping out of it, it was because they didn't want the case solved. Or—and this was even worse—they saw the dangers and pitfalls in such an investigation and were more than willing to put somebody else's neck in the noose, rather than risk their own.

Still, there was no point in worrying Patterson with thoughts like that. Better to let the lad live in blissful ignorance until everything came crashing down around them.

'Should we be making a move, sir?' Patterson asked.

Yes, they should. But in doing so, they would already be encountering their first problem, Blackstone thought. And that problem was which door they should use! Should they enter by the elegant teak one that stood at the top of three polished steps? Or the one that lay below the level of the iron railings? To knock on the former and be directed to the latter would be a humiliation. On the other hand, wasn't going directly to the servants' entrance an admission of his lowly status, even though he was in charge of a murder investigation?

'At what time do we have our appointment with the Earl, Sergeant?' the Inspector asked.

'Five o'clock, sir.'

Blackstone checked his pocket watch. They had a quarter of an hour to spare. Perhaps from that fact, he could pull out some face-saving device.

'Before we see him, let's have a word with the servants,' he said, turning towards the basement stairs.

The young woman who opened the door of the tradesmen's entrance was wearing a long black dress, white apron and maid's cap. It was plain from the cursory glance she gave the new arrivals that they did not impress her.

'Yes?' she said, standing squarely in the centre of the doorway, as if she thought the two men might make a sudden dash for the bowels of the house.

'We're from the police,' Blackstone told her. 'Could we come inside, please, miss?'

The girl hesitated. 'Well, I don't know, really. Yer see, I ain't 'ad no orders about no coppers.'

'Let us in, then go and fetch whoever's in charge of matters below stairs,' the Inspector said firmly.

The girl's hesitation lasted for another few seconds, then she said, 'I suppose that'll be all right.'

She led them down a succession of narrow corridors with the ease of one used to negotiating a maze. Finally, she stopped at a door indistinguishable from all the others they'd passed, and said, 'You can wait in there.'

Blackstone opened the door and found himself in a room that was dominated by a massive, scrubbed table.

'Servants' hall,' said Patterson, knowledgeably.

'Is it indeed?' Blackstone said, taking a seat that gave him a view of the door.

'Course, in an establishment this size, probably only the downstairs servants will eat here,' Patterson continued. 'The "upper" servants—the butler, valets and people like that—will have their own dining room.'

'For a humble detective sergeant, you seem to know a good deal about it,' Blackstone said.

Patterson grinned. 'My auntie was a lady's maid,' he explained. 'She was always telling me stories about life in the Big House. Said they used to have a right old time of it, them "upper" servants.

They dress up for dinner, just like the toffs—"demi-toilette" I think Auntie called it—and they get exactly the same to eat as the quality upstairs has.'

Blackstone shook his head in wonder. They were servants and he was a police inspector, yet he was willing to bet that most of them had a far better time of it than he did. Not for them the bubble and squeak his landlady served up at least once a week. They lived off the fat of the land—or rather, off the fat of the Montcliffes.

The door opened, and the maid who had shown them in appeared again.

'Mr Hoskins,' she announced, then stood aside to let a middle-aged man in tails sweep into the room.

The butler looked at the two detectives and frowned, as if he considered it an impertinence that they'd sat down. 'You're early,' he said.

'I thought I'd take the opportunity to talk to some of your staff,' Blackstone told him.

The butler's frown deepened. 'I have received no instructions from the master on that particular matter.'

'I don't need your master's permission to talk to them,' Blackstone said.

'I think you'll find that you do,' the butler replied.

To hear him, you'd never think he was addressing two detectives who carried the weight of the law behind them, Blackstone told himself. To hear *him*, you'd think I was some kind of tinker trying to sell ribbons and silvered teaspoons to his staff.

The butler consulted his watch. 'His lordship is expecting us in exactly three minutes. So if you will follow me, Inspector...'

Both Blackstone and Patterson rose to their feet, but the butler signalled Patterson to sit down again.

'His lordship has instructed me that he and the family are prepared to grant the Inspector an interview,' he said. 'No mention was made of an assistant also being present.'

'But I always—' Patterson began.

'You will wait here,' the butler interrupted.

Patterson glanced at his boss for guidance. Blackstone shook his head. There was no point in fighting a battle you couldn't win, the Inspector thought. But despite his best efforts to control his own emotions, he found that he was getting annoyed. Annoyed with aristocrats who saw him at *their* convenience, rather than at his. Annoyed at servants, so secure in the mantle of their master's power that they felt they could be as high-handed as they liked.

He half-hoped that one of the illustrious group waiting upstairs would turn out to he the murderer. Then he realized gloomily that if that did happen to be the case, the guilty party would probably he allowed to wriggle out of it.

Blackstone followed the butler up the broad staircase. Quite a contrast to the narrow steps that led up from the servants' hall, he thought.

The butler stopped in front of a polished oak door, and knocked twice. Then he turned the handle and stepped inside.

'Inspector Blackstone, my Lord,' he announced, moving to one side to allow Blackstone to enter the room.

The family was sitting in a semicircle around an inlaid rosewood coffee table. On the edge of the group sat Lady Emily, her face pinched and her eyes red from crying. Next to her was her fiancé, Lord Dalton. Dalton was holding Lady Emily's hand in his, as if he'd been doing his best to comfort her.

But it was the rest of the group that interested Blackstone. At the centre of the arc sat a tall, grey-haired man. He had a face like those that Blackstone had seen on his self-improvement visits to the National Portrait Gallery—the face of a man who is used to his orders being obeyed without question.

The woman sitting next to him—presumably the Countess—was handsome rather than beautiful. Like her daughter, she appeared to have been crying—though, in her case, face powder had been applied in an attempt to disguise the fact.

The last member of the group, at the far end of the arc, was a youngish man who, apart from his youth, was almost a carbon copy of the Earl.

Earl Montcliffe ran his eyes up and down the Inspector as if he were considering hiring him as a gamekeeper.

'You're Blackstone?' he asked.

'Yes, my Lord.'

The Earl nodded. 'Your superiors have a high opinion of you. If they did not, we would not now be having this meeting.'

'I'm grateful for any praise they might have given me,' Blackstone said, but he was thinking: This is like nothing so much as a bad play at the Tank Theatre, Islington.

'You've already met my daughter and Lord Dalton,' the Earl

continued.

Blackstone remembered how worried Lady Emily had been that her father would find out she'd visited Scotland Yard—and how he'd assured her that the Earl wouldn't.

'I...er...' he began.

'My daughter has already confessed to me that she has been in contact with you,' the Earl said. 'I am sure that she felt herself to he doing the proper thing at the time.' He inclined his head towards the two people sitting to his right. 'This is my wife, Lady Margaret, and my son, Viscount Montcliffe. My other two sons are serving Her Majesty in the colonies.'

My other two sons, Blackstone repeated silently to himself. The way the Earl had said it, it was almost as if he'd only ever had *two* other sons—almost as if, now Charles was dead, they could pretend he had never existed.

'As you may or may not be aware, Her Majesty has graciously instructed me to play a significant role in the Jubilee celebrations,' the Earl continued, 'and so, as you can imagine, my time is extremely limited. However,' he added generously, 'I suppose I can spare you ten minutes if it will help to clear this unpleasant matter up. What do you wish to know?'

Blackstone shifted his weight uncomfortably from one foot to the other. This was not going to be easy.

'I was wondering if any of you might know of a reason why someone might kill your son?' he said.

Earl Montcliffe looked briefly at all the others, who shook their heads.

'It came as a great shock to us,' he said. 'No one in this family has been murdered since the fourteenth century.'

'Perhaps it might help if I knew who he associated with,' Blackstone suggested. 'Who were his friends?'

The eldest son, Viscount Montcliffe, snorted. 'His friends?' he repeated. 'Charles didn't have any friends.'

'He didn't share the interests of most people in society,' Lady Emily explained, almost apologetically. 'His pursuits were more of an...er...private nature.'

'Readin'!' the Viscount said with disgust. 'Shuttin' himself up all day, when it was perfectly good huntin' weather outside.'

'He wasn't really robust enough for hunting,' the Countess said, in her dead son's defence. 'He was rather a delicate child and—'

'Delicate!' the Earl interrupted her. 'Balderdash. Sickly was what he was—the runt of the litter. Isn't that the truth, Margaret?'

Lady Margaret's hands were suddenly bunched into fists, and for a moment Blackstone thought she was about to attack her husband. Then the hands unfurled and the Countess bowed her head in what could only be interpreted as a gesture of submission.

'Isn't it the truth?' the Earl repeated.

'Yes, Roderick,' the Countess mumbled. 'That's the truth.'

It was almost as if they'd forgotten he was there, Blackstone thought. But given his lowly status that was only to be expected—servants were not noticed until they were needed.

The Inspector coughed discreetly. 'Surely your son must at least have had some close acquaintances,' he suggested.

'Charles did know some *journalists*,' Lady Emily said. 'He wanted to become one himself.'

'Journalists!' her brother repeated scornfully. 'Vermin is what I call 'em. They're forever stirrin' up trouble, talkin' about the rights of the common man, and goin' on about how the trades unions should be made stronger. Well, if they'd been to Australia—as I have—an' seen for themselves what damage strong trades unions can do, they'd soon drop that particular idea.'

'I can see how it might have embarrassed you to have your son associating with such people, my Lord,' Blackstone said to the Earl. 'Do you happen to know the names of any of these journalists?'

'Certainly not!' the Earl replied. 'Wouldn't clutter my brain with their names. Even if I did know, I'd never sully my lips by sayin' them out loud.'

'One of them is a man called Scott,' Lady Emily said. 'He runs a magazine called *The Radical*.'

'Government should have closed the damned thing down long ago,' the Viscount said.

The Earl took an elegant case from his jacket pocket and extracted a cigarette from it. Blackstone almost expected a footman in full livery to appear with a lighted taper, but, in fact, Montcliffe produced a humble box of matches, and lit the cigarette himself.

The Inspector ran his eyes quickly over the family again. There was no doubt that both Lady Emily and her mother had taken the death of Charles very much to heart. It was different with the men—while they were not exactly *glad* he was dead, there was at least some sense of relief that now he was gone he could no longer damage the family name.

'Lady Emily told me your son was in the habit of disappearing overnight,' the Inspector said.

Earl Montcliffe sucked on his cigarette, and blew smoke down his aristocratic nose.

'That would indeed appear to have been the case,' he agreed. 'Though his mother and I had no knowledge of it until after his murder,' he added, giving his daughter a censorious glance.

'And you have absolutely no idea where he might have been spending his time when he was missing?'

The Earl shook his head, regretfully. 'If the boy had had some spirit, I could have given you the names of some "establishments" he might have been usin'. But knowin' him as I did, I doubt very much whether he'd...whether he'd...'

Montcliffe realized he was perhaps saying too much in the presence of ladies and let the words trail off into nothingness.

'He was runnin' around with his *journalist* friends, I shouldn't wonder,' the Viscount chipped in.

Was he trying to cover up his father's gaffe? Blackstone wondered. Or was he so insensitive that he didn't even comprehend that a gaffe had been made, and wanted merely to take the opportunity to reiterate his contempt for his younger brother's activities?

Earl Montcliffe flicked the ash from the end of his cigarette on to the floor. 'Well, if that's all, Blackstone...' he said dismissively.

'There is one other thing, my Lord,' the Inspector said. 'I'd like your permission to question your servants.'

'The servants?' Montcliffe echoed incredulously. 'What possible good could it do to talk to the *servants*? You surely don't think that Charles, for all his faults, spent time gossipin' with them, do you?'

'No,' Blackstone admitted. 'But servants see more of what goes on than you sometimes might think. For instance, your son's valet must have been aware his master was missing, even when other members of his family were not.'

'But he kept his mouth shut about it,' said the Viscount. 'An' damn right, too. When servants start to forget who they owe their loyalty to, it'll be the end of civilization as we know it.'

Earl Montcliffe nodded his agreement. So the daughter was expected to tell the family what her brother was up to, Blackstone thought, but his valet was not. What a bizarre universe it was that these people seemed to inhabit.

'So if you could just give me your permission—' the Inspector said.

'Certainly not,' the Earl interrupted. 'Allow 'em to gossip to an outsider once, and they'll think they've got carte blanche to chat about family affairs to all an' sundry.'

'It might seriously impede the Inspector's inquiries if he's not allowed to talk to them,' said Lord Dalton, speaking for the first time.

'Can't help that,' the Earl replied. 'Any servant of mine who can't be discreet is out on the street before he knows what's happenin'. A firm hand. That's what the lower orders need. And—by God—I see they get it.'

'You are, of course, quite right,' Lord Dalton agreed. 'But don't you think that in this particular case, you should make an exception to your rule? We are, after all, talking about an investigation into the death of your youngest son.'

The hostile glance which the Earl bestowed on his future son-in-law was only there for a second, but Blackstone did not miss it. Nor had he missed the fact that behind Dalton's apparently mild words, there was the slightest, wispiest hint of a threat.

It was a very strange situation indeed, the Inspector thought. By rights, as a newcomer to the family, Dalton should be at the bottom of the pecking order, yet here he was, asserting his will as if he were the man in charge.

The Earl was examining the glowing end of his cigarette with an intensity it did not merit. His left eye had started to twitch, and his normally arrogant jaw had gone slack. The seconds ticked by agonizingly slowly, yet it seemed that no one in the room was prepared to break the silence.

Finally, the Earl spoke. 'It could set a very dangerous precedent,' he said weakly.

'Suppose I were to be present when the Inspector carried out his interviews?' Dalton suggested. 'I could make sure that the servants didn't go beyond the bounds of what you would consider proper.'

'Want to play the detective now, William?' chortled the Viscount. 'Joinin' the ranks of the workin' men? You're gettin' to be as bad as Charles was.'

Lord Dalton gave him a look cold enough to chill the blood, then turned his attention back to the Earl.

'Do you think that would be a satisfactory compromise?' he asked.

'Yes, I suppose so,' the Earl replied, without much conviction.

'And that would also be satisfactory to you, Inspector?' Dalton enquired.

No, of course it wouldn't be satisfactory, Blackstone thought. Having one of the aristocrats sitting in at the interviews would make his job harder—if not impossible. But he had heard enough in the last few minutes to realize it was the best deal he was going to get.

'That would be perfectly satisfactory, my Lord,' he said through gritted teeth.

'In that case, Blackstone, you may go now,' the Earl said dismissively.

The Inspector bowed, and took his leave.

Oh, I'd really like it to be the Earl, Blackstone thought as he followed the butler back down the corridor. I'd really like to be able to prove that he was responsible for culling one of the weaker members of his stock.

But the prospect of the silken rope ending up around the Earl's neck was as remote as the possibility that Blackstone would somehow end up inheriting his title.

SIX

The two young owners of the Empire Living Picture Company were carrying out a final check on their equipment when they heard an imperious rapping on their office door.

Their automatic reaction was to exchange the worried glances that had become almost second nature over the previous few months. Then the taller, skinnier of the two, whose name was Martin Wottle, grinned and said, 'Well, it can't be our creditors, because we don't owe anybody anything any more.'

'Don't owe anybody anything!' said Alfred Dobkins sourly. 'No, we don't owe our old creditors anything, but now that convict bastard from Australia owns us body and soul!'

'Not everybody from Australia is a convict,' Wottle said, in a placatory tone. 'Mr Seymour is a respectable businessman, and he's our partner, Alfred, not our *creditor.*'

There was more knocking, even louder this time.

'You'd better go and answer it,' Dobkins said.

Wottle crossed the room and opened the door to the street to reveal the visitor. It was a man dressed—very respectably—in a top hat and frock coat. Yet, though the clothes were of good quality and had been made by a bespoke tailor, they didn't look quite right on him. Nor did he seem particularly comfortable in *them*. In fact, he gave the impression that he'd be much happier wearing an open-necked shirt and a bushman's broad-rimmed hat.

'G'day, Mr Wottle,' said the visitor.

'Mr Seymour!' Wottle replied. 'We didn't expect to see you here at this time of night.'

'If there's one thing I learned back home, it's that when you've made an investment, it's a bloody good idea to keep an eye on it,' the other man told him. Wottle felt a small shiver run through him. Though he constantly reassured his partner that it had been a good idea to go into business with the Australian—and still believed that to be true himself—there was definitely something unsettling about Seymour.

'Well, are you goin' to invite me in or not?' the visitor asked.

'Y-yes...yes...of course,' Wottle stammered. 'You're always welcome at the office, Mr Seymour. You know that.'

The visitor stepped inside, and looked around him. The office in no way lived up to the grand title the company had given itself. Paint was peeling from the walls, and the faded linoleum was cracked. On the battered desk stood a Remington typewriting machine that looked at least twenty years old—and was probably more valuable as an antique than as a piece of working equipment. Two overstuffed armchairs faced each other across a cheap coffee table in the centre of the room. The only aspect of the whole place that was at all likely to generate any confidence was the workbench that ran along the back wall and held the two moving picture cameras.

Alfred Dobkins was still standing over the bench, with a screwdriver in his hand.

'It's Mr Seymour,' Wottle said unnecessarily. 'Come to check on his investments.'

Dobkins scowled. 'That's really not necessary, you know,' he said to Seymour. 'Your money's in good hands. Better than good. *We're* going to make *you* rich.'

Wottle raised his hand to his mouth and chewed nervously at one of his fingernails.

Why couldn't Alfred be pleasanter to Seymour? he asked himself. Didn't his partner sense the menace that lurked inside the Australian's bosom like a coiled serpent?

No, of course he didn't sense it! Dobkins had always been too bull-headed and self-absorbed to ever really notice what was going on with other people.

'I hope your partner's right,' Seymour said to Wottle. 'I do hope, for your sakes, that you *are* going to make me money.'

'The...the business can't fail,' Wottle said, realizing that he was starting to babble, yet not being able to do anything to prevent it. 'Living pictures are going to be the next big thing. Why, I must have told you that a couple of years ago, when the Lumière brothers showed their living pictures of a train entering a station—'

'You *did* tell me.'

'—when they showed the pictures of the train, some of the audience were so convinced it was a real train coming towards them that they ran out of the theatre in absolute terror.'

The visitor nodded curtly to indicate that he had heard enough, then turned his attention to Dobkins. 'What about the other side of the business?' he asked. 'Have you got all the necessary permits?'

'We've applied for them,' Dobkins said offhandedly.

The visitor frowned. 'That isn't what I asked you, now is it?'

For God's sake, be nice to him! Wottle prayed silently. For God's sake, tell him what he wants to hear!

'It's just a matter of time before the permits come through,' Dobkins said. 'The clerk who issues them assured me there'll be absolutely no problem.' An expression came into his eyes that indicated he probably considered what he was about to say cunning—though to the other two, it was merely obvious. 'Of course,' he continued, 'if we were to give that clerk in charge a gift, it might make him work just that little bit harder for us.'

'Work harder! You English don't know the *meaning* of hard work,' the visitor said. 'Back home in Australia, none of you would last five minutes in any kind of business.' But he reached for his wallet anyway. 'How much will it take to make this clerk do the job he's already been paid to do?'

'Five pounds would probably cover it,' Dobkins said. He licked his lips. 'Although, if you want to be certain, ten pounds would probably be better.'

The visitor handed over the money. 'I'll be pretty crook if the arrangements are not in place in time,' he said. 'And you wouldn't like that, you know. You really *wouldn't*.'

'We want things to work out just as much as you do, Mr Seymour,' said Wottle, babbling again. 'It's a really big chance for us. We could be famous. We could be—'

'You could be in a great deal of trouble—if you let me down!' the visitor cut in. He walked over to the door. 'By the way,' he said, as he reached for the handle, 'do you remember that journalist who was bothering you?'

'Smith?' Wottle asked. 'Charles Smith?'

'That's right,' Seymour agreed. 'Well, he won't be bothering you any more.'

Wottle felt his mouth go dry and his heart start to beat a little faster. 'What do you mean?' he asked.

'I mean what I say. That he won't be bothering you any more.'

'You don't mean to say you've...you haven't...'

The Australian laughed. It was not a pleasant sound. 'What an imagination you have, Mr Wottle. You think that something really terrible's happened to him, don't you?'

'Well I...I mean...the way you said it...' Wottle stammered.

'I've simply had a word with his Editor, and his Editor has had a word with him. It has been made perfectly plain to him that Empire Living Pictures are involved in an important undertaking, and have no time to answer pointless questions. But...' Seymour paused and raised a warning finger, '...but I would strongly advise you not to discuss this Charles Smith with anyone else. As far as both of you are concerned, it would be much better to forget that he ever existed. Have I made myself clear?'

Wottle looked down at the floor. 'Yes, Mr Seymour.'

'Mr Dobkins?' the Australian asked.

Alfred Dobkins banged his screwdriver exasperatedly down on the bench. 'Oh, all right, I suppose so,' he said. 'If that'll make you happy.'

'You shouldn't be concerned about what will make me happy,' the visitor said. 'It's what will make me unhappy which should bother you.' He tipped his hat. 'Well, g'day to the pair of youse.'

He stepped through the door and was gone.

Wottle placed his hand over his heart, and confirmed that it was galloping as fast as he'd suspected it was.

'When you think about it, Charles Smith didn't *really* bother us, did he?' he asked.

'He bothered me. I've got better things to do with my time than to waste it answering his damn-fool questions about political exiles,' Dobkins said curtly.

'So have I,' Wottle agreed. 'But it would have wasted a lot more of our time than Smith took up to have gone to his Editor to complain about him, wouldn't it? Yet that's what Seymour says he's done.'

'Nice to see that the Aussie bastard is finally starting to earn his share of the profits,' Dobkins said. 'It's about time he helped out.'

'But I don't think Seymour did it to help us,' said Wottle thoughtfully.

'Then what would have been the point of his going to see the Editor?'

'I think he did it because—in some way we don't understand— the person Smith was really bothering was *him*.'

SEVEN

The morning sun smiled down benevolently on Blackstone as he made his way towards Southwark Coroner's Court.

He would have preferred cloud, he thought. And possibly one of those bone-chilling winds that had blown down from the Hindu Kush during his Afghanistan days—because that kind of weather would have been much more in keeping with the gloomy mood he had woken up in—and was still not able to shrug off.

Four days! he told himself.

It had been *four days* since the Honourable Charles Montcliffe had been fished out of the Thames—and he knew no more now than he had when the River Police's Sergeant Roberts had first unrolled the body from its tarpaulin shroud.

He entered the court and took a seat towards the back of the room. The stink of chemicals—which was so powerful in the adjoining morgue—was no more than a hint of a smell in the courtroom itself. Yet even so, the feeling of death was everywhere. It was etched on the faces of the jurors, who had been compelled to examine all the bodies lying in the morgue before the inquests began. It was reflected in the wild, fascinated eyes of the spectators—a motley collection of men and women who licked their lips with anticipation when each case was announced. It was embodied in the grave bearing of the coroner, seated behind his raised desk and master of all he surveyed.

Blackstone scrutinized the jury. There were twenty-three of them—although only twelve would actually be called upon to produce a verdict—all ratepayers and voters, and all of them solid citizens. They must have heard at least half a dozen other cases before they finally arrived at the one he had come to listen to—and they were starting to look punch-drunk.

The clerk of the court stood up, and announced that the next case concerned an unidentified body of a man that had been fished out of the Thames.

The police surgeon, an elderly man with a shock of white hair, took the stand first, and testified that he had examined the corpse, and determined that life had been extinct for several hours.

What exactly was the cause of death? the coroner asked.

The man's throat had been slit, the doctor replied, and he had been stabbed more than a dozen times. In his professional opinion, the stab wounds had been inflicted when the victim was already dead.

The second and last witness was Sergeant Roberts of the Thames River Police. In carefully measured words he explained how he and his partner had retrieved the corpse from the river.

'Have you ever seen a murder of this nature before, Sergeant?' the coroner asked.

Roberts pondered over the question. 'Not *quite* like this,' he admitted finally. 'But I've seen some pretty nasty ones in my time.'

'And do you have any theories of your own about this particular case, Sergeant?'

Again, Roberts hesitated before speaking. 'It looks to me like it might 'ave been a cult murder, sir,' he said. 'What they call a ritual killin'.'

Could he be right? Blackstone wondered. Might Montcliffe, the would-be journalist, the perhaps-thrill-seeker, have got himself involved with one of the many cults that had been imported from all corners of the Empire? It was possible. But then, with this case, *anything* was possible.

The sergeant stepped down, and it took the jury less than five minutes to decide that the unidentified dead man had been murdered by person or persons unknown. The coroner thanked the jury for its work, and the business of the day was over.

The audience rose to their feet, and Blackstone, all speculative thoughts banished from his mind, looked keenly around the court. This was the moment he had been waiting for—the moment when, as in so many cases before this one, he might get his first real lead.

He recognized a number of the faces that passed him. Some of these people had been coming to inquests for years, and would continue to come until one day, perhaps, they would themselves be the star attractions. But there was one face among the sea of others that was not only new to him—but also seemed completely out of place!

The face in question belonged to a young man of about twenty-three. Though his features were clearly working class, his hair was neatly cut, he looked well-fed, and his eyes did not show any of the tiredness that comes with working fourteen-hour days in a lead works or a tannery. He had, Blackstone noted automatically, a small strawberry birthmark on his forehead.

The young man's clothes also marked him out from the rest of the spectators. They were obviously not new—but then who, in this area, ever wore anything other than second-hand?—yet they were certainly very good quality, and unlikely, therefore, to have been bought off a barrow down at the local market in the New Cut.

The young man noticed the attention he was getting from the Inspector, and the slightly mournful expression on his face was replaced by a look of pure panic. Then he was on the move— pushing and elbowing his way through the crowd, and heading for the door.

Blackstone was on his feet in a second, forcing his own way through the mob. For an instant he was so close to his man that he could almost have touched him. Then he hit a tight knot of people—already cursing at having been pushed aside once—and he was brought to a halt. Over the heads of the others he saw the young man reach the street and break into a run. By the time Blackstone managed to get out on to the pavement, there was no sign of his quarry.

You should have thought to post a couple of constables outside the door of the courtroom, the Inspector chided himself.

But he *hadn't* thought, and now it was too late. It might be days before he caught up with the young man—if he ever caught up with him at all. And the man was *important* to the case. Blackstone *knew* he was. He could feel it deep in his gut.

The Inspector stamped his foot in frustration.

'Damn and blast!' he said, so loudly that people some distance away turned around to see who was causing the disturbance.

*

Blackstone ambled slowly along Southwark Bridge Road, stopping occasionally to observe a small segment of its life. An orderly boy was dodging in and out of the heavy traffic—risking his life in order to scoop up horse dung—and the Inspector remembered that in the Montcliffe household there were servants whose job it was to wait on servants. He nodded to an old woman selling camphor from a tray slung around her neck, and wondered if her idea of heaven even came close to the life the Montcliffes took for granted. He flung a coin at the feet of a blind clog dancer—and might have speculated about him, too, had it not been for the cry of the newspaper vendor who was standing on the corner of Lant Street.

''Orrible murder near the docks,' the man was shouting. 'Is the Ripper on the loose again? Read all abhart it!'

The Ripper! Just the sound of the name made Blackstone shiver. He'd only been a young copper at the time Jack had struck, and therefore no more than on the fringe of that investigation, but he'd never forget the fear that had settled like a thick, choking fog over the whole of the East End. Yet despite their fear—despite knowing the risk they were running—there had still been women willing to work the streets, driven there either by grinding poverty or the desperate need for a drink.

'Sensational murder!' the vendor chanted. ''As Jack returned?'

Blackstone bought a paper and turned hurriedly to the article. A prostitute, identified by other prostitutes as Mary Atkins, aged 37, had been found buried under a pile of rubbish on Burr Street. Her throat had been cut, and the police surgeon estimated that she had been dead for at least four days. A spokesman for Scotland Yard was doing his best to play down the Ripper connection by pointing out that the prostitute had not been killed in Jack's old hunting ground, that she had not been strangled before being slashed, and that there had been no disembowelling after death.

Yes, it all sounded very logical when put like that, Blackstone thought, but it would do little to quell the sense of alarm that must already have been growing in the poorer parts of the city.

He had reached the river when an idea—which was too vague yet to be even called a theory—hit him with the force of a sledgehammer.

'She could have seen him!' he said aloud. 'She could have seen Charles Montcliffe!'

Because, given the tides on the night Montcliffe was thrown into the river, it was perfectly conceivable that his point of entry into the water had been Aldermans Stairs. And those stairs were conveniently close to Burr Street.

So was it possible that Mary Atkins' death was purely the result of her being in the wrong place at the wrong time? Had she been killed not for something she'd done, but simply because of what she'd accidentally witnessed? And if that were the case, would it lead him anywhere?

*

Blackstone gazed down at the body of Mary Atkins. Her skin had the sallow, veined look of a woman who ate unhealthily and drank too much. The paper had said that she was thirty-seven, but she could easily have passed for sixty. Not that that would have mattered to most of her customers—she had the right equipment between her legs, and that was all they required for their brief, joyless encounters in some back alley. There were even some men who got an extra thrill out of the fact that the whore they were with was so raddled.

Blackstone reached down and picked up the prostitute's right hand. The skin was rough, which suggested that before she'd taken to the streets she'd been involved in hard domestic work—perhaps as a servant or a washerwoman. The nails were either broken or chewed down. The whole hand was covered with a layer of dirt that could only have built up over years.

''Ave to 'ave been a really dark night before I'd pay 'er for 'er services,' said the coroner's officer, who was standing on the other side of the slab.

Blackstone nodded absently. 'Any idea who's investigating this case?' he asked.

'Inspector Todd,' the other man replied. ''E was in 'ere earlier, givin' 'er the once-over.'

But not a very *careful* once-over, Blackstone thought, noticing the tiny thread of material caught under one of the dirty nails.

Taking a match out of the box he carried in his pocket, he inserted the stick under the nail, and carefully extracted the piece of evidence.

'What d' you reckon this is, George?' he asked.

The coroner's assistant took the sliver of material from the Inspector, gazed at it for a second, then brushed it gently against his cheek.

'I fort it was wool at first sight,' he said. 'But it ain't. If yer asked me ter give a definite opinion, I'd 'ave to say it was fur.'

So would I, Blackstone thought. But it wasn't the cheap rabbit fur that lined the collars of coats worn by women in the East End. There was a silkiness about it that said it had come from a much more expensive source.

An aristocratic connection again?

It was possible. Assuming, of course, that Mary Atkins' murder really did have something to do with the death of the Honourable Charles Montcliffe.

Blackstone put the piece of fur in an envelope, and slid it into his pocket. He examined the dead woman's other hand, and found nothing. He studied the rest of her body—the slack breasts, the wrinkled stomach, the veined legs—without coming across any additional clues. He turned the corpse over, but to no avail. So the fur was the only lead he had. Still, he supposed, that was better than nothing.

EIGHT

The moment he entered his office, Blackstone noticed the smile on his sergeant's face. It spread almost from ear to ear, and proclaimed to the whole world that Patterson was very pleased with himself.

'Who did it then?' the Inspector asked, as he made his way over to his own desk.

Patterson gave the big man with the arched eyebrows a puzzled look. 'I beg your pardon, sir?'

Blackstone sighed. 'You're grinning like the cat who's got the cream, from which I infer that at the very least you can tell me who killed Charles Montcliffe and why.'

Patterson's smile acquired a slightly sheepish edge. 'Well, no, I can't quite do that, sir,' he admitted, 'but I have come up with some interesting stuff on the people you asked me to make inquiries about.'

Blackstone lowered himself into his chair, and swung his feet up on to the desk—thinking as he did so that it was a great thing to *have* a desk to put your feet on.

'Let's hear all about it, then,' he said.

The sergeant consulted his carefully written notes. 'The Montcliffes have a large estate somewhere up in Staffordshire,' he said. 'It's been in the family for I don't know how long.'

'Probably since 1066—ever since one of the Earl's ancestors helped William the Conqueror to steal the country from the people who were already living here,' Blackstone said gruffly. 'Sorry, I interrupted you. Go on, son.'

'Anyway, I know this bloke in the Staffordshire police, so I rang him up.' The sergeant smiled again. 'Just like that. Picked up a telephone and there I was talking to him. Isn't it a wonderful invention?'

'Wonderful,' agreed Blackstone, who never ceased to be amazed by his assistant's fascination with the latest gadgets. If they ever got flying machines to work, he thought dryly, Sergeant Patterson would be one of the first reckless people to go up in the air.

'So you rang this bloke on the wonderful telephone,' he continued. 'And did he have anything interesting to tell you?'

'Quite a lot,' Patterson replied. 'Like I said, it's a large estate they've got up there—but it isn't nearly as big as it used to be.'

'And why is that?' Blackstone asked, feeling a slight prick of interest.

'A few years ago, the Earl began selling off some of his land. Nobody thought much about it at the time, but when he kept *on* selling it, well, then people started to sit up and take notice— especially when he went and sold the part that the river ran through.'

'Why should that be significant?'

Patterson shook his head, almost pityingly.

'It means he lost his fishing rights,' he explained. 'And fishing's very important to your aristocrats. Now when he goes out with his rod, it's to fish on somebody else's land—and he has to have permission from the owner.'

Yes, that must gall him, Blackstone thought. And there could only be one reason why Earl Montcliffe would have put himself in that position—he didn't have any choice.

'Got any pals in Australia?' he asked.

'I have, as a matter of fact,' Patterson said. 'A bloke I joined the Force with went out to work for the New South Wales police three or four years ago. Why exactly are you interested, sir?'

'When I was talking to the family, Viscount Montcliffe let it slip out that he'd been to Australia.'

'I'm afraid I still don't see the point.'

'A lot of fortunes have been made in Australia. And a lot of fortunes have been lost there, as well. Maybe that's where some of the family money went—down the shaft of a gold mine that didn't actually have any gold in it.' Blackstone paused for a second. 'How long would it take your Aussie pal to find out just what young Montcliffe was up to in the colonies?'

Patterson shrugged. 'Not long. If I send him the telegram today, he can be on the case tomorrow. And from what I've heard about Australia, it's like a village—everybody knows everybody else's business.'

'What about your inquiries into Lord William Dalton's background? Did you manage to dig up anything interesting on him?'

'I did. And it's a completely different story there. I talked to a couple of blokes I know in the City about him, and—'

'Is there anywhere in the whole bloody Empire where you don't know "a bloke"?' Blackstone interrupted.

He'd meant it as a joke, but Patterson gave the matter serious thought before saying, 'No, I don't think so. Not really.'

Blackstone shook his head in wonder. Patterson was a good detective in his own right, but it was his contacts that made him truly invaluable.

'So what did your City friends have to say about Lord Dalton?' the Inspector asked.

'Nothing bad. I think they rather admire him, if the truth be told.'

'And why's that?'

'Because however much money most businessmen have made, a lot of the aristocracy still look down on them. Lord Dalton's not like that. In fact, he's a businessman himself.'

'Yes, I think he mentioned something about that. What particular business is he in?'

'All sorts. He owns part of a shipyard on Tyneside for a start. Then he's got a couple of cotton mills in Lancashire, an iron works in Shropshire, three or four coal mines in South Wales, shares in railways and banks—'

'So he's rich, is he?'

'Very.'

Dalton was rich, and for all its arrogance, the Montcliffe family was not. That would certainly explain the influence Lord Dalton seemed to have over Earl Montcliffe—even though it was plain that the latter obviously disliked the former. And it also explained Dalton's willingness to play such an active part in the case of the unfortunate young man who would have been his brother-in-law. In marrying Emily, he was also marrying the family—and because he had the money, he was assuming the role of the head of that family, and protecting it as best he could.

For a moment, Blackstone almost felt sorry for Earl Montcliffe. The man had been brought up to believe that he answered only to God, and now, in late middle age, he had been forced to accept that was no longer true.

How he must hate having to swallow the bitter pill, the Inspector thought. And how he must loathe the man who was administering it. If it had been Dalton who'd been found floating in the Thames, Blackstone didn't think he would have had to look far to find the murderer.

A noise that had sounded like distant thunder only seconds earlier grew louder and louder until it broke into Blackstone's consciousness and destroyed his thought process completely.

Horses! Dozens of them by the sound of it. And all of them moving at the same pace.

With a sigh, the Inspector got up from his desk and walked over to the window. A troop of Indian cavalry, their heads turbaned, their leather webbing shining in the sunlight, were making their way along the Embankment.

A rehearsal for the Jubilee, no doubt. Watching them, Blackstone felt a pang of nostalgia. Life had been so simple when he'd been in the Army. Of course, there had been dangerous moments, but even then—even when your heart had been pounding in your chest and your mouth was suddenly dry—you at least had the advantage of knowing who your enemy was.

Not like now! Now he was groping in the dark, never sure when he was going to put a foot wrong. He was glad that he had Lord William Dalton on his side. But how long would *that* situation continue? Suppose the investigation *did* implicate one of the Montcliffes. Whom did he think Lord Dalton would choose to sacrifice—a member of his new family or a humble detective inspector?

Blackstone took out his pocket watch. It was half past twelve. In three hours, after the Montcliffe family had finished their luncheon and would no doubt be taking a well-earned afternoon nap, he was to be allowed his one and only opportunity to question all the staff who worked in Earl Montcliffe's London home. He wondered whether the interviews would yield anything—and, if they didn't, where he would look next.

Perhaps he should take a more relaxed attitude to this case, he thought. After all, no one else seemed particularly eager to have it cleared up, and the safest course might simply be to let it drift until it was nothing more than a memory. But even as these ideas passed through his mind, he knew he would eventually dismiss them—because he simply wasn't that kind of copper.

NINE

The seats around the large scrubbed table in the servants' hall were all filled. Blackstone ran his eyes from the top to the bottom. At the head of the table, furthest away from him, sat the butler and the housekeeper. Flanking them were footmen. Next came the ladies' maids and valets. Then the coachmen and ordinary maids. Finally there were the tweenies and boot boys, who were so close to him that he had only to reach out to touch them.

He turned his attention back to the butler. Mr Hoskins was around forty-five. He had pale grey eyes that looked as if they would miss nothing, a tight mouth and a square jaw. This man would know some secrets about the house, the Inspector thought—but wild horses wouldn't drag them out of him.

Blackstone leant slightly forward. 'Are *all* the servants here?' he asked the butler.

'All the ones who could be spared from essential duties,' Mr Hoskins replied coldly.

Ah yes, essential duties had to go on whatever else was happening, Blackstone thought. After all, if Earl Montcliffe were suddenly to develop an itchy arse, it was only right that there should be some minion hovering around to scratch it for him.

'As you're probably aware, the Honourable Charles Montcliffe has disappeared,' Lord Dalton said. 'There is absolutely no cause for alarm, but naturally your master and mistress are eager to find him as soon as possible, and so have called in the police. This is Inspector Blackstone. I want you to answer his questions as truthfully as you can.' He turned to Blackstone. 'Inspector?'

'I would be interested to learn if any of you, especially those who work above stairs, have noticed anything unusual in Charles Montcliffe's behaviour recently,' Blackstone said. 'For instance—'

'The staff are trained to do their jobs, and to notice nothing beyond the scope of those tasks,' Mr Hoskins interrupted.

'That might be theoretically true—' Blackstone said.

'In this house, it is not theoretical in the slightest,' the other man countered. 'We may be *in* the room at the same time as the Family, but we are certainly not *of* the room.'

'I appear to have left my cigarette case in the grand parlour, Hoskins,' Lord Dalton said to the butler. 'Could you go and get it for me, please?'

The butler gave a slight bow. 'I will send one of the maids to retrieve it immediately, my Lord.'

'No, you will not,' Dalton told him. 'It is an expensive case, and I would prefer it to be handled only by a man of taste who knows how to look after valuable things. A man such as you, Hoskins.'

'But, my Lord—' the butler protested.

'Thank you, Hoskins,' Lord Dalton said firmly.

The butler stood up. 'As you wish, my Lord,' he said.

'And Hoskins...'

'Yes, my Lord.'

'Please do not return to this room until you've found the case. Do you understand?'

'Yes, my Lord,' Hoskins said, giving Dalton a full bow and heading towards the exit.

As the butler closed the door behind him, Lord Dalton unconsciously tapped his jacket pocket where—Blackstone was almost sure—the cigarette case had been all along.

'Mr Hoskins is a fine, upstanding man whose only desire is to protect the Family,' Dalton told the remaining staff. 'You could all take a lesson from him on the nature of duty. However—' his voice softened and became somehow more persuasive—'I feel that on this one occasion he has failed to grasp the point, which is that the Family does not need—indeed does not *want*—to be protected. On the contrary, they would be very grateful for any information you could provide. And let me assure you of this: no one who speaks now will be punished, but anyone who reports what has been said to Mr Hoskins in his absence will be instantly dismissed.'

To speak like that, Dalton must be the one who was paying their wages, Blackstone realized—and if he could work that out, then the servants probably could too.

One of the maids raised a timorous hand.

'Yes?' Dalton said encouragingly.

'One day when I was dustin' the staircase, Mr Charles come up to me an' asked me where he might buy some second-hand clothes.'

'When was this?'

'Must 'ave been about three weeks ago now.'

'And did he say why he wanted them?'

'No, my Lord.'

'Not even a hint?'

The maid shrugged. 'No, 'e just asked me where 'e could buy them, an' I said down at the market.'

Charles Montcliffe must have felt as out of place in my world as I do in his, Blackstone thought. Imagine having lived such a privileged existence that you'd have no idea where to buy second-hand clothes.

Yet he had obtained them—and had been wearing them when he met his death.

'Does anyone else have anything to add?' Lord Dalton asked.

Blackstone quickly scanned the table. Most of the servants were either looking at him or at each other, but one of the footmen seemed to be fascinated with the scrubbed tabletop.

'You!' the Inspector said, pointing.

Reluctantly, the man looked up. 'Me?'

Blackstone nodded. 'Why don't you tell us what's on your mind?'

The footman looked appealingly at Dalton. 'It's a family matter, my Lord,' he said.

Lord Dalton shook his head. 'I've already explained that you should tell the Inspector anything which might help him to find Mr Charles, and that no one will be punished for doing so. However, if I learn that any of you have been holding useful information back...'

He left the rest of the threat unstated, but the footman did not miss the implication.

'A...a few days ago I was standing on the first-floor main corridor waiting for Lady Margaret and...and...' he stuttered.

'Well, come on, man—spit it out!' Lord Dalton said exasperatedly.

'I heard the sound of raised voices. It was coming from the Viscount's sitting room.'

'You heard an *argument*, you mean?'

'That's...that's what it sounded like to me,' the footman admitted reluctantly.

'And do you happen to know who was involved in this argument?'

'The Viscount and Mr Charles.'

'How can you be so sure of that?'

'Because while I was still standing there, the door opened and Mr Charles came out.'

'What was this argument about?' Blackstone interjected.

'I don't know,' the footman told him. 'The doors are too solid for you to hear what's actually being said.' A look of panic flashed across his face. 'Not that I'd have listened, anyway,' he added hastily.

He was still holding something back—Blackstone was willing to swear to it. And he had a pretty good idea of what that *something* was. He pictured the corpse of Charles Montcliffe lying at the top of Battle Bridge Stairs. His throat had been cut and he had received multiple stab wounds only a few hours earlier. But there was another injury that had been inflicted much earlier than that!

'How did Mr Charles seem when he came out of his brother's sitting room?' Blackstone asked the footman. 'Seem?' the other man stalled.

'What was his state of mind?'

'He...he looked a bit shaken.'

'And, of course, he had a black eye, didn't he?'

The footman jumped as if he'd just been given a totally unexpected electric shock.

'There...there was a slight swelling under the eye,' he admitted. 'He must have seen me looking at it, because he said he'd walked into a door.'

Blackstone hardly heard the last few words. Long ago—in Afghanistan—he had developed an instinct for when he was being watched or overheard, and he felt that instinct tingling now.

The Inspector rose quickly to his feet, knocking his chair over in his haste. He flung open the door of the servants' hall and stepped out into the corridor just in time to see a broad back retreating down it.

Blackstone closed the door, cutting himself off from the servants' world, and said—in a loud voice—'Can I help you, my Lord?'

Viscount Montcliffe stopped, and slowly turned around. 'Just wanted to know how much longer you'd be wastin' the servants' time, Blackstone,' he said defensively.

'And you came yourself, instead of putting any of your lackeys to the trouble,' Blackstone retorted. 'How thoughtful.'

'Most of my lackeys—as you call 'em—are already fully occupied in takin' lessons in insolence from you,' the Viscount said.

A good recovery under the circumstances, Blackstone thought—but not quite good enough.

'I expect you know your way to the servants' hall because you visit every Christmas Day to share in their Yuletide cheer,' he said.

The Viscount relaxed a little. 'That's right,' he agreed. 'Not that it's any of your damn business.'

Blackstone looked down at the other man's right hand.

'But what I don't understand is why you should bring a glass tumbler with you,' he said. 'Unless, of course, you were using it to listen at the door.'

'I think you're forgettin' your place, Blackstone,' the Viscount said, his shoulders tensing again. 'Don't see why I should tolerate from you what I wouldn't tolerate from a second gardener or an assistant groom. Expect to be hearin' from your superiors.'

And with that parting shot, the Viscount turned again, and strode furiously towards the servants' stairs.

Blackstone returned to the servants' hall. Lord Dalton gave him a quizzical look, and the Inspector returned one that said he would explain it all later.

Righting his chair, Blackstone sat down again. 'Does anyone have anything to add to what's already been said?'

Some of the servants shook their heads slightly—others merely gazed blankly at him.

'None of you?' Blackstone persisted.

No one spoke.

'Not even Mr Charles' valet?'

Suddenly, all the servants were looking uncomfortable—and several pairs of eyes had turned on a pretty blonde parlour maid.

'The valet isn't here, is he?' Blackstone guessed.

The parlour maid coughed nervously. 'No sir, he...he isn't.'

'Why not? He can't be attending to his essential duties, because as long as his master is missing, he doesn't have any.'

'Thomas is missin' himself,' the maid admitted.

'Since when?'

'Four days ago. He went out on an errand for Mr Charles, an' never came back.'

'And does the Family know about this?'

The parlour maid glanced imploringly at Lord Dalton.

'Well? Do they?' Dalton demanded.

'No. Mr Hoskins said there was no need to bother them with matters like that—leastways, not until Mr Charles turns up again.'

Then it would be a long time indeed before the Family learned of Thomas's absence, Blackstone thought.

'What's your name?' he asked the parlour maid.

'Molly, sir.'

Blackstone filed the name in his mind for later use. 'And what you're saying is that Thomas disappeared at the same time as his master?'

'Yes, sir.'

'Could you describe him to me?'

The girl shrugged helplessly. 'He's just ordinary.'

'How old is he?'

'Twenty-four next birthday.'

'Average height?'

'I suppose so.'

'Black hair?'

'Yes. Almost like coal.'

'No distinguishing marks?'

'I beg your pardon, sir.'

'Any scars?'

'Well, not a scar exactly—but he does have a strawberry birthmark on his forehead.'

Of course he had, Blackstone thought. Unlike the rest of the servants, Thomas must have guessed that his master had been murdered, and had gone into hiding. But however scared he was, he just hadn't been able to stay away from Charles Montcliffe's inquest.

TEN

The man sitting on the opposite side of the desk to Blackstone was perhaps forty-seven or forty-eight. His hair was thinning and his jaw was starting to sag, but any suggestion that he might be losing his enthusiasm for his trade was soon dispelled by his eyes, which burned with intelligence and enthusiasm.

This man—Archibald Scott, the founder of *The Radical*— was the sworn enemy of unearned privilege in any form. Earl Montcliffe hated him with a passion, Blackstone reminded himself. Well, you couldn't get a better recommendation for a person than that!

'My secretary tells me you have some questions you want to ask me about Charles Montcliffe,' the journalist said, with an edge of suspicion in both his voice and his eyes. 'What sort of questions, Mr...?'

'Robertson,' Blackstone supplied. 'Josiah Robertson.'

He despised this, he told himself—despised having to pretend to be something he wasn't. Yet what choice did he have? If he'd announced himself as a policeman and then started asking questions about Charles Montcliffe, Scott's journalistic instincts would have immediately told him there was a story in it.

'What sort of questions, Mr *Robertson*?' Scott asked, the wariness still there in his tone.

'I'd just like some background information.'

'"Background information" can cover a multitude of sins. You're not, by any chance, working for the police, are you? Because if you are, you can get out of here right now.'

Blackstone laughed. 'Do I *look* like a policeman?'

No, Scott thought, you look more like an evangelist. But aloud, all he said was, 'Policemen come in all shapes and sizes, and whatever their appearance they're all searching for any excuse to close this place down.'

'The fact of the matter is, I work for a firm of solicitors, who, in turn, work for a client whose name I am not at liberty to reveal,' Blackstone said.

Scott nodded gravely. 'Go on.'

'Charles Montcliffe has asked to look at some confidential papers that our client holds. He claims it would help him with the story he's working on. The client himself has no objection to showing the papers to a serious journalist, but he must first assure himself that Montcliffe *is* serious. That's where I think you might be able to help me—by providing such an assurance.'

Scott let his eyes wander around the room as he considered what response to make.

'I first met Charles a few months ago,' he said finally. 'He turned up on the doorstep and said he wanted to learn how to be a journalist.'

'And you agreed? Just like that?'

'I was a little suspicious at first. We don't get many people with plummy accents who want to roll around in the gutter with the likes of us. But since he didn't expect to be paid for his work, I said I'd take him on.'

'What kind of work did...does he do?'

'At first, he was nothing but a glorified office boy. I thought he'd soon get tired of it and give up. To be honest, I have to say I *hoped* he would.' The journalist grinned. 'I don't like having my prejudices overturned as a rule, but I have to admit that whatever else he is, Charlie's not one of the *idle* rich. He really puts his back into a job, however tedious its nature.'

'You said he *started out* as an office boy,' Blackstone reminded Scott. 'But he's not an office boy now, is he?'

'No. After a few weeks I started to give him bits of writing to do—just the odd paragraph here and there. He made a good job of that too, and I could see he would soon be ready to take the next step. Well, he's a lad with spirit, isn't he? Reminds me of myself at his age.'

'So you gave him a proper story to cover?'

'No, he came to *me* with the idea. He wanted to do an exposé on a child pornography ring.'

'Dangerous work,' Blackstone said.

And he was thinking: Dangerous enough to get him killed!

'Yes, I warned him there might be danger, but he said that the truth was a shining beacon, and the only thing in life which really mattered. And, as a matter of fact, I agree with him entirely.'

'When are you expecting him to hand in his article?'

'Oh, he handed it in weeks ago. And a very fine piece of work it was. In fact, it was *so* good it even convinced the police to get off their big fat backsides and do something.'

'They arrested the pornographers?' Blackstone asked, feeling another lead in his investigation start to melt away.

'Every single one of them,' Scott said with satisfaction.

'What else has he worked on?'

'Nothing we've actually published, but he's very excited about his current story. He says it will rock the world. But, of course he's young, and when you're young you think *every* story you produce will rock the world.'

'What's the story about?'

'He was very scant with the detail, but...' Scott's eyes suddenly narrowed and the suspicion was back in them again. 'I don't know the name of your client, or the nature of the papers which young Charlie has requested access to,' he continued, 'but surely, since *you* do, you should be perfectly capable of working out the nature of the story yourself.'

Damn it to hell! Blackstone thought. How am I expected to conduct an inquiry under these conditions?

'I expressed myself badly,' he said. 'Of course I know through the client what story Charles Montcliffe is working on. I was just wondering if he was perhaps working on another at the same time.'

'You can rest assured he would never do that. He's far too single-minded to chase two birds with one net.'

Blackstone sighed. He could push the conversation no further without revealing the depths of his own ignorance—and once he had done that the journalist would clam up like a ha'penny oyster.

The Inspector rose to his feet and held out his hand. 'It was very good of you to spare me your time, Mr Scott,' he said. They shook hands.

'Would you mind answering one question for me, in return for the ones I've answered for you?' the journalist asked.

'Of course not.'

'I'm curious about who this client of yours might be.'

Blackstone held up his hands. 'I'm afraid that under the circumstances I couldn't possibly...' he began.

'I know you can't give me his name,' Scott said hastily, 'but—tell me—is he, by any chance, a Russian?'

Blackstone faked a rueful grin. 'Clever of you to work it out, Mr Scott,' he said.

*

Anyone seeing the tall man standing on the Embankment and gazing across the river might have guessed that he was deep in thought. And they would have been right. Blackstone had so much on his mind—so many questions buzzing around in there—that it was giving him a headache.

Was his mythical client a Russian? the journalist had wanted to know.

Now why had he asked that? There could only be one reason— because the story Charles Montcliffe had been working on when he met his death had involved a Russian in some way.

Blackstone reached into his pocket and took out the match-box containing the piece of fur he'd found in the hand of Mary Atkins, the murdered prostitute. He'd thought at the time it was from an expensive pelt, and now he was willing to bet that it was sable.

And there was more—if more were needed.

There was the sketch map that Emily Montcliffe had found in her brother's room—a sketch map that was covered with what, to her, were meaningless squiggles, but could just as easily have been Russian writing.

Even more significant was the fact that Charles Montcliffe had probably been killed on or near Aldermans Stairs. And what lay to the north of those stairs? A triangle of London that was bordered by Whitechapel Road and Commercial Road—and was known throughout the East End as 'Little Russia'!

PART TWO

LITTLE RUSSIA

ELEVEN

It really was like stepping into another world, Blackstone thought, as he made his way along Commercial Road the next morning. It was not just that the shops had strange writing above them—squiggles and backward 'R's, probably like the ones Lady Emily had seen on the sketch map. It was not even that the smells which wafted through the doorways were sometimes exotic and sometimes repulsive. It was the *people* that really surprised him.

There was nothing remotely English about the features of the folk he passed—yet within their difference there was a great variety. He saw tall, sharp-featured men with long hair and beards; and brutish-featured men with squat bodies and wary, suspicious expressions. He saw women who walked as if they were well aware they were fashionably dressed—though the fashion was not of London—and women wearing the coarse skirts and headscarves of peasants. But however they looked or were dressed, they all moved with the assurance of people on their own territory. They had never really left Russia, Blackstone realized—they had brought Russia to London with them.

He came to a halt in front of one of the shop-fronts. The

writing over the doorway was meaningless to him, but through the window he could see a counter, on top of which sat a steaming samovar. A café restaurant of some sort, then. That seemed as good a place as any to start his investigation. He opened the door and stepped inside.

There were several scrubbed tables in the room, with a group of people sitting around each one. Some were eating food Blackstone could only begin to guess the origin of. Others were playing cards. There were almost as many women as men, Blackstone estimated. Most of the men were smoking cigars or pipes, as might have been expected, but it came as something of a surprise to see that several of the women were smoking cigarettes.

The Inspector walked over to the bar counter. The man standing behind it was around thirty-five. He had greying hair and the wiry figure of a man who knows when to fight and when to run.

'I don't suppose you sell beer, do you?' Blackstone asked.

The man gave him a blank stare. 'Don' unerstan'.'

'Beer?' Blackstone said, miming the pulling of a pint. 'Bitter?'

'*Bitte?*' the barman repeated.

From the corner of his eye, Blackstone saw a woman rise from one of the tables.

'Dimitri speaks Russian, Uzbecki, Turkaman, some Yiddish and a little German,' she said to him. 'That is perhaps three and a half more languages than most Englishmen speak.'

Blackstone turned to look at her. She was around twenty-seven years old and five feet four in height. She had black eyes and black curly hair. Her nose was a little hooked, and the slight smile on her full lips suggested that she did not lack a sense of humour.

'Perhaps you can help me,' he said. 'I wanted a pint of bitter.'

'Then try one of the public houses on Leman Street,' the woman suggested. 'Here, you will only obtain Crimean wine, Russian tea and seventeen kinds of Russian vodka.'

'Which kind of Russian vodka would you recommend I try?'

The woman's smile broadened, and she said something to the man behind the bar that Blackstone found incomprehensible.

'This will be as good an introduction as any,' she said, when Dimitri had poured large shots of a colourless liquid into two glasses.

Blackstone reached into his pocket. 'How much will that be?'

'Forget it,' the woman told him, sliding a few small coins across the bar. 'They only take roubles here, and I doubt if you have any of those.' She looked across the room, and saw that a group of people had just vacated a table. 'Shall we sit down?'

'Why not?'

They walked over to the table, and sat down facing each other. 'You're being very kind,' Blackstone said. 'Is that just part of your nature—or is there some ulterior motive behind it?'

'I am *naturally* a helpful person,' the woman said, 'but I am also eager to find out what an English policeman is doing in a Russian café.'

Blackstone grinned, despite himself. 'Is it that obvious I'm a copper?' he asked.

'When you have lived in Russia, you learn to recognize policemen however well they try to disguise themselves. And you are making no attempt at disguise at all. So what brings you here?'

'I'm looking for a man,' Blackstone confessed.

The woman nodded seriously. 'Does this man have a name?'

'Yes,' Blackstone said. 'But I'm not sure that he would have been using it here.'

'Describe him to me,' the woman said—and it was more like an order than a request.

'Twenty-three or twenty-four. Slight build. Blond hair. Sensitive features—perhaps almost aristocratic.'

'Charles Smith,' the woman said decisively.

'His first name *may* be Charles,' Blackstone admitted.

'He is a journalist.'

'I take it then that you know him.'

'I know him.'

'And why might that he?'

The woman smiled again. 'Because this is Little Russia, and when an English journalist—or an English policeman, for that matter—comes into this area, he needs the help of someone like me.'

'Because you know the territory?'

'Because I speak the languages.' The woman brushed one of the black curls out of her eyes. 'I told you how many languages Dimitri speaks. But even he cannot communicate with half the people who live within a stone's throw of this café.' She laughed. 'You English are so amusing. You think that because you can get from one end of your country to the other in a couple of days the whole world must be like that. But let me tell you, it isn't. Russia is a vast country, and living within its boundaries are many different peoples—more than your narrow English brains can even begin to imagine.'

Blackstone wasn't quite sure why it should sting him to be classified with every other Englishman the woman had ever met—but it did.

'I may have seen more than you think,' he said, noting how defensive he was sounding. 'I served in the British Army in India—and I took part in the long march to Kandahar back in '79.'

Rather than these words being taken as a rebuke, they only seemed to add to the woman's amusement. 'So you are a mighty empire builder, are you?' she asked. 'A believer in Britain's imperial dream.'

Blackstone shook his head. 'My father was a soldier. He married my mother, got her in the pudding club—'

'The pudding club?'

'Got her pregnant,' Blackstone explained. 'And then sailed off to India. The year,' he added heavily, 'was 1857.'

'The year of the Indian Mutiny?'

'That's right. By the time I was born, he was already dead—killed by rebel Indian soldiers in Cawnpore. There's nothing like growing up in poverty to teach you that the imperial dream is nothing but a hollow sham.'

'And yet you joined the Army yourself.'

'Yes, I did. My mother died when I was eight. It was the work that killed her. She was slaving from morning to night to get what little food she could for our table. After she'd gone, they put me in Dr Barnardo's home for orphans. It was the warden there who suggested I joined up as soon as I was old enough. And I agreed with him, because it seemed the only way to escape from the poverty—my one chance to try and build a better life for myself.'

He paused. He had already told this complete stranger more about his life than he'd told most people who knew him well. Worse yet, he was starting to take himself far too seriously.

He forced another grin to his face. 'To escape from the poverty,' he repeated. 'And it worked. Look at me now. I have not one, but *two* pairs of boots—a pair for weekdays and a pair for Sundays. But I've talked enough about me. Tell me about yourself. You're Jewish, aren't you?'

The woman smiled again, slightly wistfully this time. 'If only it were as simple as that.'

'Surely you're either Jewish or you're not?'

'I am Khazari. At one time, my people controlled a vast Empire in what is now Southern Russia. We are a Turkic people, but in about AD 740—according to your calendar, that is—our supreme ruler, who was known as the *khagan*, adopted Judaism as his faith. Most of the ruling class converted soon after. So I am a Khazari, a Russian and a Jew.'

'And an exile?'

The woman sighed. 'Yes, that too.'

'And why should that be?'

'Most Russian Jews live in the *Cherta Osedlosti*—the Pale of Settlement,' the woman said. 'It is not a matter of choice for them.

It is the law—a way of ensuring that St Petersburg, Moscow and the central part of Mother Russia are left uncontaminated by the Jewish presence. You would think that would make us bitter, wouldn't you?'

'I think I'd feel pretty bitter if I was forced to live in North Wales,' Blackstone said.

The woman laughed. 'We *should* have been bitter. But we weren't. Instead, we were amazingly—almost blindly—hopeful. We believed that His Majesty the Tsar was a good man, and that once we had cast off some of our Jewishness and proved we could be model citizens, he would emancipate us—give us the same rights as other Russians.'

'So what went wrong?'

'The Tsar was assassinated in '81. The rumour swept Russia that the murder had been a Jewish conspiracy. It led to the first of the pogroms.'

'Pogroms?' Blackstone repeated.

'That is the Russian word for it. I suppose an English translation would be something between "devastation" and "riot". What it meant in practical terms was that in over two hundred towns and cities around the Pale, Jews were attacked—and sometimes killed—and their properties were looted.'

'How long did this go on for?'

'It has never stopped. Even today it only needs one drunkard railing against the Jews to make the mob go on the rampage. Why shouldn't they? There are rich pickings to be had from Jewish houses—and the rioters know that the authorities will do nothing to punish them.'

Blackstone took a cautious sip of his vodka. But not cautious enough! The fiery liquid seemed to be burning a hole in the back of his throat.

'When did you leave Russia?' he asked, when he'd finished coughing.

The woman raised her glass and knocked back the entire contents in one easy gulp.

'When I was sixteen, my father decided that things were never going to get any better for us,' she said. 'We sold all we had—at a tenth of its real value—and moved to London.'

'And what do you do now?'

'What *can* I do? I have education, but no training. Perhaps if I *had* to work, I would find some form of employment, but we still have enough money left to live modestly. And so I amuse myself by reading, thinking—and talking to people like you and Charles Smith.'

Mention of the journalist brought Blackstone up with a jolt and he realized that for the past several minutes he had forgotten about the case altogether and instead had been enthralled by the woman's story.

'What's your name?' he asked.

The woman smiled again. 'My given name is Hannah. To pronounce my family name correctly, you would probably have to stuff a rag in your mouth.'

'I'm Blackstone,' the Inspector told her. 'Sam Blackstone. What can you tell me about Charles Smith?'

Another smile. 'What would you like to know?'

'What was his interest in Little Russia?'

The corners of the smile turned downwards, forming a lightly puzzled frown. 'He told me that he wanted to write a newspaper article about the lives of the Russian exiles.'

'But you didn't believe him, did you?' Blackstone guessed. 'Now why was that?'

'Perhaps because I am an exile myself, and he did not seem very interested in my life. Besides...'

'Besides what?'

'Though he claimed he had never been in this part of London before, I got the distinct impression that he already knew something about some of the people who live here.'

'Could you give me an example?'

'He said he had read something about Count Turgenev, but the Count is the kind of man who goes out of his way to make sure his name does *not* appear in the newspapers.'

Blackstone leant forward slightly. 'Tell me more.'

'About Charles?'

'About Count Turgenev.'

'He first appeared in the area a few months ago. He is typical of a certain kind of Russian aristocrat.'

'Which means?'

'That he drinks too much—even for a Russian. That he likes money, but is rarely prepared to do anything to earn it. That he is a compulsive gambler, but feels no compulsion to pay his debts.'

'And what's he doing in London?'

Hannah shrugged. 'Back in Russia, he probably got himself into scalding water...'

'Hot water,' Blackstone corrected her.

'Thank you. He probably got himself into hot water, and came here to give the scandal time to die down.'

'And Charles Smith seemed interested in him?'

'That's right.'

'I'd like to meet him if I could. Or at least get a look at him.'

'I think that can be arranged,' Hannah told him. 'Come back here at seven o'clock this evening, and I will take you to one of his haunts.'

'Will we be escorted?'

'You mean *chaperoned*? Of course not.'

'You seem to have a lot of freedom for a young woman,' Blackstone said. 'Does that come from being Jewish—or from being Russian?'

'It comes from being *me*,' Hannah said.

TWELVE

Blackstone had walked past the club on Pall Mall many times, but it had never once occurred to him that he might one day pass through its impressive portal. Even now, as he followed one of the club servants down an avenue of black marble pillars, he could hardly bring himself to believe that he was actually inside.

The place reeked of money, he thought—not just of the prosperity that he'd had a sniff of on some of his other cases, but of genuine, unmistakable wealth. The men who sat reading their newspapers in quiet alcoves had never had to worry about where their next meal was coming from, as so many Londoners did daily. They need not concern themselves about what would happen to them when they no longer had the strength to tackle hard physical labour. Blackstone could almost see the aura of certainty and complacency that hovered over their heads, and felt an urge to walk over to one of these fine gentlemen and give him the shaking of his life.

Lord Dalton was waiting for him in the dining room. He smiled when the Inspector entered and gestured him to sit down.

'I hope you don't mind having our meeting over luncheon,' he said, with a slightly apologetic air, 'but it was the only time I had free during an extremely busy day.'

'I quite understand, my Lord,' Blackstone told him.

Dalton opened the menu. 'There are those who believe that luncheon should be light, and restricted to no more than three or four courses,' he said easily, 'but I have always regarded it as my main meal of the day.' He handed the menu over to the Inspector. 'Would you care to choose?'

Blackstone glanced down at the card. The whole thing was written in some foreign language—probably French—and unlike in the ABC restaurant where he normally ate, there were no prices.

For a moment, he wondered whether Dalton had invited him to the club with the sole intention of humiliating him. Then he dismissed the idea. For surely, if the noble lord had wanted to make him look a fool, he would have chosen an easier, less time-consuming way of doing it.

The Inspector handed the menu back to Dalton. 'I'll be guided by you, my Lord,' he said.

Lord Dalton nodded and ran his eyes over the bill of fare. 'I think we'll start with Hors d'oeuvres Russes,' he said. 'We'll follow that with Pot-au-feu, Sole Waleska, Noisette d'agneau Lavallière, Parfait de foie-gras and Cailles en cocotte. Anything else we may desire can be ordered later. Are you happy with that, Inspector?'

Blackstone gave a nod that he hoped carried with it the suggestion that he considered Dalton had chosen well. And at the same time as his head was doing the nodding, his brain was wondering just what it was that he was about to eat.

For the first half of the gargantuan meal, Dalton did most of the talking, and restricted himself to subjects of general interest— the weather, the government and the preparations for the Jubilee. It was only when the lamb arrived that he took a sip from his wine glass and said, 'How is your investigation proceeding, Inspector?'

Blackstone shifted positions, and tried to estimate just how close his stomach was to exploding.

'It's early days yet, my Lord,' he said.

'But you must have discovered *something*?' Dalton persisted.

'I think Charles Montcliffe was working on a story which he hoped to eventually have published in *The Radical*,' the Inspector conceded.

Dalton grinned. 'That would certainly have enraged his father. What kind of story was it?'

'I'm not sure yet, but I think it might involve Little Russia.'

Dalton shook his wonderingly. 'Whatever made him waste his time on such trivial matters when he could have held a responsible position in one of my companies?'

'You offered him a job, did you?'

'Oh yes. Several times. And not just because I was about to marry into the family. He was an intelligent young man. He would have been an asset to the company.'

'Unlike his brother, the Viscount,' Blackstone said, just to see how far he could push things.

'Exactly,' Lord Dalton said, refusing to rise to the bait— pretending, in fact, that there was no bait to take at all. 'I doubt if Hugo Montcliffe would ever consent to he associated with "trade", but even if he would, he'd be of no use to me.' He took another sip of his wine. 'By the way, I've been responsible for doing what I believe is commonly known as "saving your bacon".'

'You have?'

'Indeed. After that little incident outside the servants' hall yesterday, Hugo was all for contacting the Home Secretary and demanding you be roasted over a slow spit. I talked him out of it.'

'Thank you, my Lord,' Blackstone said. 'Why do *you* think he was listening at the door?'

It's an interesting question. Perhaps he merely wanted to make sure that you weren't giving the servants ideas above their station.'

'I thought that's why *you* were there,' Blackstone said, pushing his luck once more.

'True,' Dalton agreed. 'That is partly why I was there. But a fool like Hugo never fully recognizes quite how foolish he is. Nor does he often recognize a wiser man when he sees one. It is perfectly possible that my future brother-in-law feared I would make a hash of the whole thing, and wanted to hear for himself what was going on.'

'Your engagement to Lady Emily Montcliffe seems to have brought any number of headaches,' said Blackstone, emboldened by the bottle and a half of wine he'd drunk.

'It has,' Dalton admitted. 'But it is worth it. I have never really loved anyone in my life like I love her. I would do anything for her.'

A sudden cloud of embarrassment descended over the two men, as both realized that their conversation had suddenly become far too intimate.

Blackstone coughed. 'I apologize, my Lord,' he told Dalton. 'I had no right to say that.'

Dalton shrugged. 'If you invite a man out to luncheon, I suppose you must expect him to start thinking that he can address you on equal terms. I like you, Blackstone. I think that in different circumstances we could have become friends.'

But the circumstances weren't different, Blackstone reminded himself, and it was time to get the conversation back on a proper footing.

'It might further my investigation if I had an opportunity to talk to Charles Montcliffe's valet,' he said, adopting an official tone.

'You really think that Thomas Grey might be somehow involved in this ghastly affair?'

'He's disappeared.'

'Servants disappear all the time.'

'Do they now?' Blackstone asked—appreciating, once again, how little he knew of the life of grand houses.

'*All* the time,' Dalton said. 'Maids find themselves in "a certain condition" as a result of liaisons with soldiers in the park, and leave the house before it becomes obvious. Others join the household purely because they are involved with some gang which plans to burgle it, and as soon as the robbery has taken place, they vanish without trace.'

'Has the Montcliffe house been burgled?'

'No,' Lord Dalton admitted. 'But you do understand the point that I'm making?'

'Yes.'

'When male servants disappear, you will normally find that gambling is at the bottom of it—either the turf or the ring. They start by making modest bets, but they all eventually overreach themselves. To cover their debts, they steal something from the house—plate or silver spoons. If that goes unnoticed, they steal more. They tell themselves they are only doing it in order to raise the cash to win their money back. Eventually, when they have stolen so much that discovery becomes inevitable, they flee.'

'You talk as if you've had some personal experience in these matters, my Lord.'

Dalton laughed airily. 'No, not me. I pride myself on being a better judge of men and women than to allow such a person under my roof. But it is possible that Charles' Thomas is just such a one as I've described.'

'And his disappearing at the time of Charles Montcliffe's death was no more than a coincidence?'

'Exactly.'

But remembering the pale-faced young man with the strawberry birthmark at the inquest, Blackstone didn't think that was likely—because if the valet had only been interested in his master for what he could get out of him, why would Charles have continued to be of any interest after his death?

'I need to ask another favour of you, my Lord,' Blackstone said.

'What kind of favour?'

'I would like to see Charles Montcliffe's private papers. It's unlikely that his father would give them to me, but if you were to ask...'

He left the rest of the statement unsaid.

Dalton thought for a moment, then nodded his head slowly. 'I can promise nothing,' he said, 'but if you think they will be of value to your investigation, I'll see what I can do.'

'That's all I ask,' Blackstone told him.

THIRTEEN

It was late afternoon, and from his seat behind his desk, Blackstone could see the sun casting its golden glow over the normally murky Thames. He belched, and turned his attention back to his sergeant.

'I tell you, Patterson, I've never had a meal like that in my life,' he said. 'Nothing *near* like it. We finished on brandies, you know. I saw the bottle. It was over sixty years old.'

'And how did it taste?' Patterson asked.

'Like drinking liquid silk.'

A sudden, unexpected wave of guilt swept over the Inspector as he realized that when he'd walked into Lord Dalton's club he'd wanted to shake the complacent members until their teeth rattled, yet only a few minutes later he, himself, had been revelling in a feast.

How easy it was to become corrupted!

'Did you learn anything useful while you were stuffing yourself, sir?' Patterson asked.

Yes, Blackstone thought—I learned not to become over-familiar with members of the aristocracy.

But aloud, he said, 'Not really, Sergeant—except that Lord Dalton doesn't seem to think that there's any real point in searching for Thomas, Charles Montcliffe's valet.'

'And do you agree with him?'

'No. Even if Dalton's right, and the valet's just done a runner to keep himself out of trouble, he still might be able to tell us something useful about his master.'

'So assuming this valet has gone into hiding, how do we go about finding him?'

'I've been thinking about that. Lord Dalton said that a lot of servants get into trouble with their gambling habits, and maybe he was right about Thomas on that point at least. Now if he *had* been nicking the family silverware to cover his debts, what do you think he'd have done with it?'

'Pawned it?'

'Or taken it to a fence. So tomorrow morning, I want you hoofing it round all the pawnbrokers *and* all the known fences. Make it perfectly plain to them right from the start that we're not interested in running anybody in—we only want to know if they've seen Thomas Grey.'

'Big job,' Patterson muttered. 'There must be hundreds of pawnbrokers in London.'

'Six hundred and ninety-two within ten miles of the Royal Exchange, according to the last issue of the Pawnbrokers' *Gazette*,' Blackstone said cheerfully. 'But you're not interested in all of them. The ones where most of the customers are women who pawn the family linen on Monday or Tuesday and redeem it again on Saturday—after their husbands have been paid—won't give us what we want. You'll be looking at the ones that handle better quality goods as well—because if Thomas has been stealing the Montcliffes' silver, he'll have expected more than a few bob for it.'

'It's still a big job for one man to do,' Patterson said doubtfully. 'A bloody big job.'

'Then it's just as well you're an eager young copper hell-bent on making it all the way to commissioner, isn't it?' Blackstone responded. 'And count yourself lucky, lad. Your job may be boring at times, but at least it's nice and safe. When I was your age, I was surrounded by tribesmen who would have cut my throat as soon as think about it.'

'Afghanistan?' Patterson asked.

'Afghanistan,' Blackstone agreed.

'I've never quite understood what we were doing there in the first place,' Patterson told him. 'I mean, it's not rich like India, is it?'

'No,' Blackstone agreed. 'It's one of the poorest, most desolate places on earth.'

'Well then?'

'We weren't there so much for what it *had* as for where it *was*,' Blackstone explained. 'We didn't want it ourselves, but we didn't want *the Russians* to have it either.'

'And why should the Russians have wanted it?'

Blackstone sighed. 'I don't know what they teach you in board school these days. What can you tell me about Russia, Sergeant?'

'Big place?' Patterson said hopefully.

'Very big place,' Blackstone agreed, 'and for a good half of the year the only way out of it is overland.'

'I'm not following you, sir.'

Blackstone sighed again. 'It doesn't have a warm-weather port, so it doesn't matter how big the Russian navy is, because during the winter it either stays in port or is cut off from the mother country entirely.'

'I see,' Patterson said.

'Well, maybe you're starting to,' Blackstone admitted. 'Now the Russians call a warm-weather port "the keys to our house" and—'

'Don't they own the Crimea?' Patterson interrupted.

'Indeed they do.'

'And aren't there warm-weather ports there?'

'Yes, there are,' Blackstone agreed. 'The problem is that the only way from the Black Sea to the Mediterranean is through a narrow strait called the Dardanelles, which is controlled by the Ottoman Empire. So, in effect, it's the Turks who have the keys to Russia's house in their pocket.'

'Why don't they just invade Turkey, then?' Patterson asked.

'They'd love to,' Blackstone told him. 'And the Ottoman Empire is so weak and so corrupt that they could do it easily. The only problem is, the other European powers won't let them. That's what the Crimean War was about. Which is why the Russians started thinking of other alternatives.'

'India!' Patterson exclaimed.

'Exactly. If they could have overrun India, they'd have had their warm seaport, not to mention all the wealth the country's got to offer. The only problem was, an independent Afghanistan stood right in the way. And we were determined to make sure it *stayed* like that.'

Blackstone was suddenly wistful—a state he often found himself in whenever he thought of the country that had managed to both attract and repel him.

'But that's all past history now,' he continued. 'Let's get back to the case. Why do you think Viscount Montcliffe was eavesdropping on my little chat with the servants?'

'So he could find out what was being said?'

'Thank you, Sergeant. That was really helpful. But why do you think he *wanted* to know what was being said?'

'Maybe because he killed his own brother?'

'Motive?'

'To prevent him writing any more stories for *The Radical*? To stop Charles from—as the Viscount probably saw it—dragging the family name even further through the mud?'

Blackstone nodded. 'There's a lot of sense in what you argue. But if he was going to kill his own brother, why go all the way to Aldermans Stairs to do it?'

'Because it's less likely to draw suspicion on him than if he did so closer to home?' Patterson suggested. 'Anyway, sir, I'm not necessarily saying he killed Charles himself. He could have hired some ruffians to do it.'

'True enough,' Blackstone said. 'And he's certainly got *something* to hide. Any news from Australia yet?'

Patterson shook his head. 'My pal out there is still working on it. He's found out that the Viscount did visit the place four or five years ago, but he still doesn't know why.'

'Maybe we should be searching closer to home, anyway,' Blackstone mused. 'I'll tell you what, Sergeant—when you've finished with the pawnbrokers and the fences, get on to some more of your pals and see if they can come up with any new dirt on the Viscount.'

'Would you like me to clean out the stables while I'm at it?' Patterson mumbled.

'What was that, Sergeant?' Blackstone asked.

'Nothing, sir.'

'And in the meantime, I'll concentrate my attention on this Count Turgenev bloke.'

'How do you think he fits into the case, sir?'

'I don't know,' Blackstone admitted. 'But if Charles Montcliffe was interested in him, then so am I.'

FOURTEEN

Hannah was waiting for Blackstone, as she'd promised she would be, on the corner of Pennington Street and Old Gravel Lane. She was wearing a blue dress with a pleated frill and—though at that moment it was pinned back—there was a veil attached to her broad-brimmed hat.

'Why the netting?' Blackstone asked, pointing to the veil. 'Because we are going to a place where even *I* like to be a little discreet,' the Russian woman said.

'That sounds mysterious.'

Hannah chuckled. 'It was meant to be. Shall we go?'

They walked side by side down Old Gravel Lane. To their right was the Western Dock, to their left the viaduct which carried the East London Railway. The Russian woman seemed disinclined to talk, and Blackstone—though he was bursting to know just what kind of place would make even a free spirit like her decide to don a veil—kept his questions to himself.

At the corner of Cinnamon Street they turned left and headed towards the viaduct.

'We're almost there,' Hannah said, pulling down her veil.

She led him to a boarded-up railway arch, outside of which were standing two large men who looked like ex-boxers gone to seed.

''Ere again, are we, darlin'?' asked one of them.

'That's right,' Hannah agreed, and Blackstone noticed that her voice had suddenly developed a slight cockney twang.

'Should be a good one tonight,' the doorman said. 'The Basingstoke Bull's on the bill.'

Hannah reached into her purse and fished out some coins. 'Bob each, same as usual?' she asked.

'Bob each,' the man agreed, taking the money and opening a small door for them.

The cavern they stepped into was illuminated by a single gas jet, which hung from the ceiling and shot out flame like an angry blowlamp. In the centre of the room was an open square, but the rest of the space was taken with tiered wooden benches that were already half-filled with eager spectators.

'We must choose our seats carefully,' Hannah said.

'Why?'

'So that you can get a good look at the Count, of course.' She led him up the rickety steps to a bench midway between the ring and the top tier.

'Are you sure the Count will turn up?' Blackstone asked, as they took their seats.

'Nothing in this world is ever certain. But I would be surprised if he missed the opportunity to see the Basingstoke Bull fight.'

Blackstone took a look around the room. He saw men who

probably worked as costermongers and dockers, as horse grooms, factory workers, road sweepers and undertakers' mutes. But he did not see a single woman.

'Why do you come here?' he asked Hannah. 'Do you really enjoy seeing fights?'

The Russian woman shook her head. 'If I were a true *aficionada* of boxing, I would go to the Whitechapel Wonderland, where there is at least some art to what the fighters do. Here, it is just a case of two men pounding at each other until one of them falls over.'

'You haven't answered my question,' Blackstone pointed out.

'The first time I came, it was to see the audience,' Hannah said seriously. 'I needed to understand the reason that men for whom life is already a brutal thing will hand over their hard-earned money to see even more brutality.'

'And what *is* the reason?'

'I think there are two answers to that. They seem at first to contradict each other, but in fact they don't. One reason they come is because they like to see another man get badly beaten, then they can tell themselves that however miserable their own lives are, there is probably someone who is feeling even worse than they do.'

'And what's the other?'

'As well as the man who loses, there is also a man who wins. And when they see the referee raise the victor's hand, they can tell themselves that there is hope for themselves, too. But, of course, there isn't—at least, not as long as things go on the way they are.'

'So if you've got all that figured out already, why do you keep on coming back?'

'I need to be reminded occasionally of the horror of their existence. It gives me the strength to carry on.'

Half the time he wasn't even sure he knew what she was talking about, Blackstone thought. Yet there was no doubt that she was the most fascinating woman he'd ever met, and he could only look forward with regret to the day when the case was over and he would never see her again.

The archway had been filling up, and now only three seats remained empty. These seats were in the centre of the front row, which, from the appearance of the spectators who already occupied it, had been reserved for the establishment's better class of customer.

Three new men entered the room and took the vacant seats. One was a tall man wearing a cloak. The other two, who flanked him, were shorter, but had the tight, hard bodies of men who know how to handle themselves. All three of them were wearing fur hats.

Hannah touched Blackstone's arm. She only did it lightly, but it sent a tingle down his spine.

'That's him,' she whispered. 'That's Count Turgenev.'

The Inspector took a closer look at the man he'd come to observe. Turgenev was around forty-five or forty-six. He was at least six feet four inches tall, had a broad forehead, a large nose and black eyes. A scar ran down his right cheek. But what impressed Blackstone was not his physical appearance but the aura of malevolence that seemed to emanate from him even from a distance—an aura that hung over him like a huge dark cloud.

The master of ceremonies entered the ring.

'My lords, ladies and gentlemen...' he bawled, 'the first bout of the evenin' is between Jackie "Iron Fist" Baker an' Ted Tulley, better known to you all as the Basingstoke Bull.'

The two contestants had stripped down to their fighting tights, and now stood up facing each other. They were both muscular, but their faces had the pinched look that comes from the experience of childhood poverty, and their bodies bore the scars of a hundred bloody fights.

Blackstone turned his attention back to the Russian. Turgenev was scrutinizing the fighters with all the cold professionalism of a butcher examining meat. His inspection apparently over, he reached into his pocket and took out a wad of banknotes, peeled off several, and handed them to people sitting close to him.

'Does he always bet so heavily?' Blackstone asked Hannah in a whisper.

The woman shrugged. 'I have not made a study of Count Turgenev,' she told him, 'but I have heard that he will gamble on anything and everything.'

The fight began. As Hannah had predicted, there was very little art to it—Blackstone had seen more skilful displays of fisticuffs in brawls behind the barracks—but the audience went wild. Except for the Count. He watched the whole thing with an impassivity that gave absolutely nothing away.

Blackstone felt a sudden tingling sensation—not like the one he'd experienced when Hannah had touched him, but the one that told him he was being watched. He swept the room with his eyes. He'd been right! Someone *had* been watching him, and though the man had realized he was about to be spotted and turned his head away, he did it just a second too late.

The watcher was in his late thirties, and of about medium height. He had a broad, flat face, which didn't look in the least English, and though he was dressed like most of the other men in the audience were, Blackstone suspected that the clothes were no more than a disguise.

A roar went up as the Basingstoke Bull landed a powerful punch, and Iron-fist Baker keeled over. The referee stepped forwards, one hand held out to keep the Bull at bay, the other raised in the air to assist his counting.

'Er...one,' he began. 'Er...two, er...three...er...four...'

Iron-fist made an attempt to struggle to his knees, but the effort was too much for him and he slumped back on to the floor.

'Er...eight, er...nine, er...ten!'

The crowd cheered. The winning boxer, who now hardly seemed aware of where he was, submitted meekly as the referee held his right arm in the air.

Turgenev had picked the right man to bet on. His money was already being passed back to him, supplemented by the money of the men who had put their faith in Iron-fist. The Count had made a great deal in a few minutes, yet as he checked his winnings his face remained as impassive as it had been throughout the whole fight.

Two new fighters were entering the ring, but the thought of witnessing another bout of savagery sickened Blackstone.

'I've seen enough,' he told Hannah. 'I'll wait for you outside.'

'I think I've seen enough, too,' the Russian woman said, with an edge of distaste in her voice. 'You may walk me back to my home.'

Night had fallen while they'd been in the archway, and the mists that had risen from the river snaked their way through the narrow streets, giving the whole area north of the river an eerie, slightly unreal, appearance.

But it was not the darkness or the mist that was disturbing Blackstone. He was thinking about the man who'd been watching him during the fight—the flat-faced man who didn't look entirely comfortable in English clothes. Where had he come from? And why should he be interested in a police inspector? Blackstone had been the hunter for a long time—he didn't like the idea that now he might be the hunted.

They had reached the edge of Little Russia when Hannah said, 'If you want a pint of bitter rather than a glass of Russian vodka, we had better stop soon.'

An English woman would never have phrased it like that, Blackstone thought. She would never have assumed that they would be stopping for a drink at all. And she would have waited, even if a drink was what she wanted herself, until her escort suggested it.

They were drawing level with a pub. Hannah stopped, looked up at the sign that was hanging over the door, and laughed.

'What's so funny?' Blackstone asked.

It's called the Trafalgar,' Hannah replied.

'Something wrong with that?'

'No. I just find it amusing the way you English always feel it so necessary to keep on celebrating your long-gone glorious victories.'

'The trouble with victories is that for most people they're just something they've read about in the papers,' Blackstone said. 'If they'd actually been there themselves, they wouldn't use the word "glorious" quite so freely.'

'I apologize,' Hannah said.

'Why?' Blackstone asked, puzzled. 'What have you done?'

'That is the second time I have lumped you in with all the other Englishmen I have met. But you're not like them, are you?' Hannah touched him lightly on the arm again. 'I'm ready for a drink now.'

They entered the lounge, which was sandwiched between the public bar and the off-licence. Most of the customers were either middle-aged women or courting couples. Blackstone wondered whether some of the drinkers would mistake the two of *them* for a courting couple, and decided that any who did must also believe in leprechauns and fairies at the bottom of the garden.

The pub did not serve vodka, but Hannah said that gin was an adequate substitute, and—based on what he'd seen of her previous drinking capacity—Blackstone ordered her a large one.

They took their drinks over to a table in the corner. 'You'll forgive me for asking you,' Blackstone said, 'but I can't see what you're getting out of all this.'

'Out of all what?'

'Out of helping me like you have been doing.'

Hannah shrugged. 'I would have gone to see the fight whether you were there with me or not. Besides—' her voice dropped— 'though I don't know Charles Smith well, I am quite fond of him. And if he is in trouble, I am certainly willing to do all I can to help him out.'

'I never said he was in trouble.'

Hannah laughed. 'A policeman turns up in Little Russia asking questions about Charles, and he is *not* in trouble? You must think I'm a very stupid person indeed.'

'No,' Blackstone said. 'That's one thing I wouldn't accuse you of. But you'll excuse me if I'm a little suspicious of finding a guardian angel in my first few minutes in alien territory.'

Hannah laughed again. 'I am far from a guardian angel. At best, I am a guide. And a very imperfect one.'

'Imperfect?'

'Yes. For instance, you asked me about Count Turgenev, and all I could tell you was common gossip.'

'Nevertheless—' Blackstone persisted.

'If you are to understand me at all, you must accept that most of the things I do are for my own amusement,' Hannah interrupted. 'You do amuse me, Inspector Samuel Blackstone, and so I am prepared to spend some of my not-so-precious time with you.'

'I appreciate it.'

Hannah gave him a beautiful, enigmatic smile. 'And perhaps

later I will ask for some token of that appreciation,' she said, knocking back enough gin to make most men go cross-eyed. 'But for the moment it is enough that you walk me back to my home.'

It was as Blackstone rose from his seat that he saw the man standing at the public bar.

'Do you know him?' he asked Hannah.

'Know who?' the Russian woman asked.

But where the man had been positioned, there was now nothing more than an empty space.

It was almost as if the man hadn't been there at all, Blackstone thought. But he was convinced he had—holding his pint of ale in the same unfamiliar, uncomfortable way as he had been pretending to enjoy the fight under the archway.

FIFTEEN

The pubs were closed and the streets all but deserted as Blackstone made his way back to his lodgings. If someone had been following him he would have known about it—and no one was. Yet he still could not shake off the feeling that even if the flat-faced foreigner was not watching him now, it was merely a respite.

The gas light in his landlady's front parlour was still flickering when he reached the house. Blackstone unlocked the front door with his latchkey and stepped into the hallway. He hesitated for a moment, then knocked lightly on the parlour door.

'Come in, Mr Blackstone,' said a voice from the other side of it.

He opened the door and popped his head inside. His landlady, Mrs Huggett, was sitting on a low stool in the centre of the room. In front of her was a hollow cardboard cylinder that she had just glued together, and while she held it firmly with one hand, she sewed a bottom on to it with the other. To her left was a stack of cardboard from which she would make more of the cylinders, and to her right were several teetering towers of completed hat boxes.

'Still at it, I see,' Blackstone said.

His landlady smiled.

'Gawd, Mr Blackstone, yer so sharp yer should be a detective. Yes, I'm still at it. Got ter be. Yer don't get rich makin' hat boxes at two an' a tanner a gross.'

'I shouldn't imagine you would.'

Mrs Huggett reached for another sheet of cardboard, and as she did, the expression on her face changed to one of mild disapproval.

'Yer missed yer supper again,' she said accusingly. 'It's a sin to waste good food, yer know.'

She sounded just like his dead mother, he thought. In so many ways she *was* just like his mother.

'A policeman can't always choose the hours he works, you know,' he told her.

'Well, it's no skin off my nose,' the landlady said, though she still sounded offended. 'Yer pay for yer meals whether yer eat 'em or not.'

'True enough,' Blackstone agreed. 'Well, I'll wish you good night Mrs H.'

'Good night, sleep tight, an' make sure the bugs don't bite,' the landlady chanted automatically.

Blackstone stepped back out into the corridor. From the kitchen at the back of the house came the unmistakable odour of boiled beef and cabbage, and he found himself thinking back to the sumptuous meal he'd eaten earlier in the day at the expense of Lord Dalton.

He climbed the creaking, protesting stairs, and opened the first door to the left at the top of them. This was where he lived—or rather, this was where he *slept*. A room just big enough for a narrow single bed, a wardrobe, a washbasin stand, a bookcase and a rickety writing table.

He could move, he thought. On an inspector's salary he could afford much better than this.

But then Mrs Huggett would have to go to all the trouble of finding another suitable tenant. Besides, he had better—much more worthy—uses for the money he saved by lodging where he did.

Blackstone walked over to the bookcase, selected *On Liberty* by John Stuart Mill, then slipped the volume back on to the shelf. He was too tired to pick his way through Mill's complex arguments on what constituted the greatest good for the greatest number that night.

He started to undress. The other lodger, Mr Dimmock, who was a traveller in patent tooth powder, was often away for days at a time. But tonight he was home, and Blackstone could hear him snoring loudly through the thin wall.

Blackstone hung his suit and shirt, and climbed into bed. For a while, he just lay there, his mind full of the visions of another way of life he had caught a glimpse of in the previous days—Earl Montcliffe's town house, Lord Dalton's club—and then he drifted into sleep.

*

The air, which enveloped him like a tightly fitting overcoat, was hot and dry. The smells that filled his nose were exotic and totally alien to the streets of London. Blackstone had absolutely no idea where he was—but he strongly suspected that he should.

He looked around him. The walls of the room in which he found himself had expensive silk carpets hung from them. The floor beneath his feet was tiled with an elaborate swirling pattern. And through the window came a noise that sounded like the roar of an angry, wounded animal.

Blackstone moved over to the window—his body felt so light that it was almost as if he were floating rather than walking—and looked out. In the courtyard below him he could see the turbaned heads of perhaps a couple of dozen Indian soldiers. They were holding a line, and had their bayonets at the ready. Beyond them, on the other side of the compound wall, stood a howling mob of two or three thousand men. The men were variously armed with spears, swords, daggers and muskets. Some were even carrying the lances they used when on horseback. They were dirty, unkempt creatures, but from the odd scraps of uniform that some of them were wearing, it was possible to work out that they were what—in Afghanistan—passed for soldiers.

So now he knew where he was. He was in Afghanistan. In the British Residency in Kabul. He even knew the date—the 4th of September 1879— and what was about to happen.

This is impossible, he told himself. I can't be here. I'm not due to arrive until it's all over. I'm with Roberts, not Cavagnari.

Yet, he could not dispute the evidence of his own eyes. He was there—feeling the heat, smelling the smells, listening to the howling of the mob.

The door opened, and a tall, upright man strode into the room. Blackstone recognized the new arrival at once. He was Major Pierre Louis Napoleon

Cavagnari, the half-French half-Irish adventurer who was already a legend on the Northwest Frontier.

Cavagnari looked him straight in the eye. 'This is a bad business, Sergeant Blackstone,' he said. 'A very bad business. Those Afghan soldiers out there haven't been paid for months, and they blame us for it.'

Blackstone nodded—how did he dare merely to nod *to an officer? he wondered—and then turned his attention back to the scene outside. He saw tall, fierce Pathans, shorter but no less frightening Tajikis, Uzbeckis and Hazari—tribes that spent much of their time fighting each other, but now were united in the hatred of a common foe.*

He found his eyes drawn to one particular man. He was standing close to the edge of the mob yet seemed, in some subtle way, to he controlling it. He was an imposing figure—well over six feet tall, which was large even for a Pathan—and was draped in a black cloak. Immense malevolent power seemed to emanate from him, and though the lower half qf his face was covered with a cloth, he looked vaguely familiar.

Blackstone turned back to his chief.

'How can the Amir allow this?' he demanded, again surprised at his own effrontery. 'We're supposed to be under his protection, aren't we?'

Cavagnari did not take offence. Instead, he merely gave a hollow laugh.

'I'd rather be under the protection of my washerwoman than under the protection of that clown Yakub Khan,' he said. 'I've sent messages to him asking for help, and do you know how he responded?'

'How could I?'

'He said his horoscope was not favourable to doing anything himself. He sent his son to try to disperse the mob. The boy is only eight years old—and so, of course, the rabble would not listen to him.'

There was fresh activity down below. Under the urgings of the tall man at the edge of the crowd, a number of Afghani soldiers were advancing cautiously towards the gate with bunches of kindling in their hands.

'They're going to try and burn us out!' Blackstone said.

Cavagnari nodded his head gravely. 'I'm not surprised. But they're in for a surprise if they think we'll be easy game for them. They may kill us all, but not before we've accounted for at least ten times our own number.'

Blackstone shook his head. Was it worth dying, just so that in a few years' time there'd be a pub called the 'Cavagnari Arms'? he wondered.

There was a smell of wood smoke in the air now, and clouds of black smoke were beginning to rise over the wall.

'The Russians are behind this,' the major said. 'They've never forgiven us for forcing the Amir to expel their mission, and they have agents provocateurs all over Afghanistan preaching hatred against the British.'

And a lot of good it does me to know that, Blackstone thought.

The archway over the gate crumbled, the gate itself fell with a loud crash, and the howling mob rushed forward, leaping through the flames.

The Indian troops in the courtyard went down on their knees, and fired their rifles. The first wave of Afghanis did a crazy, demented dance as the bullets hit them, then fell to the ground only to be trampled by the horde immediately behind them. Some of the Indian soldiers managed to fire a second volley, but it was a fairly ragged response, and now the demonstrators were setting about them with knives, spears and clubs.

'Dulce et decorum est pro patria mori,' Cavagnari said, and then, for the benefit of his uneducated sergeant, he added, 'Sweet and honourable it is to die for your country.'

And Blackstone, as he checked the bolt on his rifle, hoped that, while he had no wish to die for his country, he could at least die like a man.

*

Blackstone found himself sitting upright, the top edge of his bed sheet clasped tightly in his hands. The entire mission to Kabul had been slaughtered swiftly and without mercy, he remembered. But he had not died because—as he'd told himself when he'd first realized where he was—he wasn't *really* there at all.

No, he'd been in India at the time of the massacre, and it was not until months later—when he'd been one small part of the five battalions of infantry that General Roberts had march with much pomp and circumstance into Kabul—that he'd even seen the residency.

Its floors had been stained black with dried blood, he recalled. Its grounds had been strewn with the bleached bones of the defenders—which was all that was left of them when the vultures had finished their work. It had been, all General Roberts' soldiers agreed—a vision of hell.

Blackstone's heart was beating at double rate. He wondered why, after eighteen long years, he should suddenly have had such a dream. And why, if he was to dream about Afghanistan at all, it should be of an event he'd never witnessed?

Why not, instead, remember the march from Kabul to Kandahar? What a memorable event that had been! Three hundred and thirty-three miles across some of the toughest terrain in the world. They had frozen at night, yet in the day the mer-ciless sun had peeled strips of skin off their unprotected hands and faces. They had had to contend with dust storms and mountain passes, and when they had reached Kandahar, exhausted and sick, they had still had to fight a battle with a rebel army.

So why not dream of *that*? He did not think of himself as a particularly imaginative man. Why weave himself into something he had only heard about second-hand?

There had to be some purpose to it, Blackstone decided. He ran through the dream again in his mind. Realizing he was in Kabul. Hearing the mob. Talking to Major Cavagnari as if they were equals.

None of that was it! None of that pointed him in the direction in which he wished to travel!

Even though his bedroom was in total darkness, he squeezed his eyes tightly shut in the hope that would aid his concentration.

And suddenly he had it! The dream was not about himself! Or about the Indian troops! It was not even about Cavagnari! No, it was about the tall dark-cloaked man with a rag over his face, the man who had been standing at the edge of the mob and urging it on.

Though Blackstone knew he would never be able to prove it, he was convinced that that man had not been an Afghani at all. He had not even been an Asian. No, he was European—and his name was Count Turgenev.

SIXTEEN

It was the third pawnbroker's shop that Sergeant Patterson had visited that morning. Like the previous two, its main entrance was—for the sake of discretion—down a side street, and the only sign of the nature of the business conducted inside was the three brass balls, or 'swinging dumplings' as they were popularly known.

Inside, too, it resembled the previous establishments he had called at. A single counter ran the length of the room, but on the customers' side it had been divided into booths, so that those with something to pawn could have a modicum of privacy.

Not that there were many customers at that time of day. A chimney sweep—as was obvious from his sooty clothes—stood in one booth, trying to persuade the counter clerk to increase his offer for the brushes he held out in his blackened hand. Three booths down from him, a woman of genteel appearance was whispering earnestly as she held out a silver photograph frame. But other than that the place was deserted.

A middle-aged man emerged from a door at the other end of the room. He ran his eyes professionally over Patterson's face and good second-hand suit, then said, 'I'm Mr Dawkins, the general manager of this establishment. What are you? The police?'

Patterson grinned ruefully. 'How can you tell?'

'It's part of my business to spot things like that,' the other man replied. 'What can I do for you, officer?'

'I'd like to speak to someone who handles more expensive items than your normal customers bring in,' Patterson said.

'How *much* more expensive? Are you talking about stately coronets or humble silver service?'

'Did you say *coronets*?' Patterson asked, astounded. 'You're not telling me you do business with the royal family, are you?'

The pawnbroker laughed. 'Not with *our* royal family, no. They'd never stoop to anything like that. But some of the continental royals aren't always so particular. Do you know,' he continued, lowering his voice, 'we got a pledge from a certain Austrian nobleman of his coronet. And can you guess how much we advanced him on the strength of it?'

'I've no idea,' Patterson admitted.

'Fifteen thousand pounds!'

Patterson whistled softly, did his best to try to comprehend such a huge amount of money, then remembered why he was there.

'I think I'm more interested in quality cutlery, silver plate, and watches,' he said.

'In that case, you'd better speak to our Mr Tompkins,' the pawnbroker said. He gave Patterson a knowing look. 'He's our resident expert on the kinds of things that servants steal.'

*

Patterson sat in one of the private offices that were reserved for clients who demanded extra discretion, and looked across the table at the man who was an expert in the kinds of things servants steal.

Thaddeus Tompkins was a small man of around thirty. He had thinnish black hair that was swept back from a widow's peak, crafty brown eyes and a sharp nose. He didn't seem the kind of man who allowed himself to he fooled by his customers very often. But then, neither did he look entirely comfortable in the presence of a policeman.

'Tell me, do you often get offered stolen property, Mr Tompkins?' the sergeant asked.

The other man shrugged. It was probably meant to be a casual gesture, Patterson guessed—but it didn't *quite* come off.

'Not too often,' the pawnbroker's clerk said.

'What exactly do you mean by that?'

'Once a week, at most. Some weeks we don't get any at all.'

'And how do you *know* it's stolen?' Patterson demanded.

'I...er...look through the Police List.'

'And if it's not on the list, then you automatically accept it as a pledge, do you?'

The pawnbroker's clerk shook his head—a little too vigorously. 'No, of course I don't,' he protested.

'Why? What's stopping you?'

'The Police List isn't comprehensive.' Tompkins held up his

hands as if he were afraid Patterson might take it as a personal criticism. 'It's not your fault, but it isn't. Some the articles I'm offered aren't on the list because the owners don't even realize they've gone missing.'

'So what leads you to suspect that the articles are, in fact, stolen?'

Tompkins shifted uncomfortably in his chair.

'You can tell by the way some of these people are dressed that they couldn't afford the things they're trying to pawn. And then there's the way they act. Their hands won't keep still...'

And neither will yours, the sergeant thought.

'...and they're forever looking over their shoulders,' the pawnbroker's clerk continued.

'So what do you do when you've decided the pledge they're offering is stolen?' Patterson asked. 'Call the police?'

Tompkins hesitated. 'I used to.'

'But not now?'

'No.'

'Why not?'

The pawnbroker's clerk shrugged again.

'I used to ask them to wait while I attended to something else, but most of the thieves are as frightened as rabbits, and if there's any delay in handing over the money, they do a runner. So by the time the constables arrive, there's nobody for them to arrest. That's why I don't bother them anymore—because it's nothing but a waste of police time.'

'You could detain your suspects until the police arrived,' Patterson pointed out.

'You mean *physically*?'

'If that was what was necessary.'

'I tried that once,' Tompkins said, 'and got knocked to the floor for my pains. Look, I'm a law-abiding man, Sergeant, but I don't really see why I should get hurt just to defend somebody else's property.'

It was a fair point, Patterson thought—if, that was, the pawnbroker's clerk was telling the truth.

The sergeant reached in his jacket pocket, pulled out the photograph of Thomas, Charles Montcliffe's valet, and slid it across the table. 'Have you seen this man?'

Tompkins studied the picture carefully. 'Yes,' he said.

'You're sure?'

'I'm sure. I've got a good memory for faces.'

'Tell me about your meeting with him.'

'He came in a few days ago. He offered me a hunting whip with a sterling silver handle. He wanted two pounds. I'd have offered more for it—but not to him, because he clearly wasn't the owner.'

'How did he react when you told him you wouldn't accept the pledge?'

'He was almost in despair. I think he needed money quickly—probably to pay off a gambling debt.'

'Is there anything else you can tell me?'

'Only that I don't think he would have tried to sell it somewhere else after he'd failed here.'

'And why's that?'

'Because he'd summoned up all the nerve he had to come and

see me. Once I'd turned him down, he wouldn't have had the courage to take the whip to anyone else.'

'So what do you think has happened to him?'

'I have no idea.'

'Take a guess,' Patterson said.

'He...he may have gone back to the village he came from—many of these servants are country boys originally. Or perhaps he's already paid the price for defaulting on his debt. Maybe in a few days, or a few weeks, you'll find him floating in the Thames with his throat cut. He could even be posing as a pauper, and hiding in one of the workhouses. But I doubt that.'

'Why?'

'He looked far too well-fed to pass himself off as a vagabond.'

Patterson stood up. 'Thank you for your help.'

'That's all?' Tompkins asked, the relief evident in his voice.

'For the moment,' Patterson said heavily. 'But I may want to talk to you again.'

*

Thaddeus Tompkins stood at the window, watching the policeman walk down the street until he passed out of his range of vision. Even now, some minutes after the encounter, the clerk was sweating.

He wondered, almost hysterically, whether Patterson had noticed how worried he'd been, and, if he had, what conclusions the policeman had drawn from it. He could only pray that if Patterson *had* been suspicious, that suspicion had centred on him being a dealer in stolen property. Because then he only ran the risk of going to gaol—and he could survive imprisonment. On the other hand, if Sergeant Patterson had guessed the truth...

With trembling hands, Tompkins picked up the telephone. When the operator asked him what number he wanted, he couldn't control the shake in his voice.

The wait while he was being connected couldn't have been more than a few seconds, yet it seemed interminable. Then a voice said, 'G'day?'

'They've been, Mr Seymour,' the clerk said. 'Or at least, one of them has.'

'What was his name?'

'Sergeant Patterson.'

There was a pause, then the other man said, 'Yes, I know all about him. He wanted to know if you'd seen Thomas, did he?'

'Yes.'

'And what did you tell him?'

'Exactly what you instructed me to—that he'd tried to pawn a riding whip with a silver handle, but that I wouldn't accept it.'

'Good.'

Tompkins wished his heart would slow down a little—wished he could draw some small comfort from the other man's last word.

'I will be all right, won't I?' he asked.

'All right?'

'Now that I've done what you wanted me to, I'll be looked after?'

'Oh, don't worry on that score,' the other man said reassuringly. 'You'll certainly be taken care of.'

SEVENTEEN

Fresh bunting continued to appear all over London—thousands, perhaps hundreds of thousands, of Union Jacks fluttered in the breeze—but as far as Little Russia was concerned, the Jubilee might not even be happening.

And why should these people get excited about the sixty years of Victoria's reign? Blackstone asked himself as he walked down Church Lane, looking at the women in their bright peasant headscarves and the men with their long white beards. Why should they glory in the fact that she ruled a quarter of the world's surface and nearly a quarter of the world's people? They felt no emotional attachment to the British Crown. Their loyalties lay with a vast, wild land that was thousands of miles away.

He caught sight of Hannah, who was standing in front of the cigar shop just ahead of him, and was *almost* surprised to discover that his heart had started to beat a little faster. It was absurd that someone at least fifteen years younger than he was should produce this effect on him, he told himself—but there was no doubt in his mind that she did.

She smiled at him, and he felt the heartbeats crank up a little more. 'It was good of you to spare me your time,' he said.

'It's no trouble at all,' Hannah replied. 'As I've explained before, men like you are something of a hobby of mine.' The smile turned into a rueful grin. 'There I go again—there are no men *quite* like you, are there? At least, not in England.'

He tried not to bask too much in the glow of her approval. She made him feel almost boyish—and that was not a state he felt entirely comfortable with.

'Where will our investigations be taking us today?' he asked, injecting a semi-official note in his voice.

'We're already there,' Hannah told him.

She took a step to the side and pointed to a wooden door. Several notices were pinned to it, written in those squiggles that made perfect sense to the inhabitants of Little Russia, but were meaningless to Blackstone.

Yet there was one notice, written entirely in English, that he did understand.

Free Russian Library
Open from 11 a.m. to 10 p.m.

Blackstone looked questioningly at Hannah. 'A library? What's the point of going to a library?'

The woman laughed. 'It is not *just* a library. It is a place where Russians come to meet their friends and catch up on all the news from home. I brought Mr Smith here, and I thought you might want to talk to some of the people who talked to him.'

'That might be useful,' Blackstone agreed.

'But you must not expect them to be like your English witnesses,'

Hannah cautioned. 'They are Russians, and so they are suspicious of all officials. Even if they want to help, they will pick their words very carefully.'

'I'll remember that,' Blackstone said.

She was almost running his case for him, he thought, and was surprised—this woman always seemed to be surprising him—to discover that there was at least a part of him that didn't really mind.

Hannah took his hand and led him through the door and up a flight of stairs. Was holding his hand really necessary? he wondered. And did he really care whether it was or not?

The library was housed in a single room. Every inch of wall space had bookshelves fixed to it. Two wooden tables ran down the centre of the library, and there were a couple of desks at the far end. It really wasn't much of a place to speak of, yet already, only half an hour after it had opened, it was filled with men who—judging by their dress—came from all walks of society.

Hannah led him over to one of the desks, at which a grey-haired woman was sitting.

'This is Olga,' she said. 'She is the librarian. Olga, this is Mr Blackstone. He is a very important English policeman—but do not worry, he is really as gentle as a lamb. He has some questions he wants to ask you.'

The librarian gave Blackstone a guarded smile. 'How can I help you?' she asked.

'I'd like to know everything you can tell me about a man who Hannah brought here,' he said.

'Mr Smith,' Hannah prompted. 'You remember him, don't you?'

The librarian nodded. 'Yes, I talked to him.'

'If you will excuse me, I would like to look at the latest papers which have come in from Russia,' Hannah said tactfully, before turning and walking towards the other end of the room.

Blackstone pulled up a chair and sat down opposite the librarian. 'What did you and this Mr Smith talk *about?*' he asked. 'Could it perhaps have been Count Turgenev?'

Olga's eyes filled with unease. 'He...he did ask me about the Count,' she admitted, 'but there was nothing I could tell him.'

'But you have heard things about Turgenev?'

'My business is with books. I was not in a position to tell Mr Smith what he wanted to know.'

'And what exactly *did* he want to know?'

'He asked what the Count had done before he came to London. I told him that if Count Turgenev is like most of the *dvorianstvo*—'

'The dv-what?'

'The aristocracy. If he behaved like most of them, he will have spent a great deal of his time eating, drinking and hunting. But do not put too much importance on his questions about the Count,' the librarian continued, with a pleading note creeping into her voice. 'It was only the second time he came to see me that Mr Smith wanted to know about him.'

'And what did he want to know the first time?'

'He asked me if I had seen an Englishman.'

'An Englishman?' Blackstone repeated.

'Yes. He said the man he was interested in was under thirty

years old and probably dressed very smartly. He wanted to know if such a man had ever visited the Russian library.'

'And had he?'

'I do not think so. I do not see what interest such a man could have in coming here.'

'Smith didn't say why he was interested in this man?'

'He claimed that the man was a relative of his, but I do not think he was telling the truth.'

'Why?'

The librarian shrugged. 'I just do not think he was being honest with me. Do you not ever get that feeling?'

All the time, Blackstone thought—but already his mind was changing gear as he felt the familiar prickle at the back of his neck.

He swung round suddenly. The flat-faced man, whom he had seen at the archway boxing match and in the pub, was standing at the top of the stairs. Their eyes locked. The other man showed neither surprise nor fear. If anything, the eyes said that after so much pussyfooting around, they welcomed such direct contact.

'You see that man standing in the doorway?' Blackstone asked the librarian out of the corner of his mouth.

'Yes, I see him.'

But even as the librarian spoke, the man was calmly turning his back on them and beginning to descend the stairs. Blackstone was on the point of following—of demanding to know what the hell his game was—when something inside him counselled caution. It was possible, he argued, that following him was exactly what the man had intended him to do. It was *possible* that the foreigner was nothing more than a decoy, leading him into a trap.

The Inspector turned his attention back to the librarian. 'What can you tell me about him? Do you know who he is or where he lives?'

The librarian shook her head. 'No.'

But there was something in that single word that was far too evasive to allow Blackstone to willingly to drop the subject.

'You might not know his name, but he's not a complete stranger to you, is he?' he demanded.

'I've never spoken to him.'

'That isn't what I asked.'

'He has been here two or three times in the last few days,' Olga admitted reluctantly.

'For what purpose? To read a book? To glance through the Russian newspapers?'

The woman shook her head again. 'He just stands near the door for a while, and then leaves. I think perhaps he is lonely. They are often lonely when they first get off the boat.'

'You mean, he's only recently arrived in England?'

'That is right.'

'How d'you know that, when you don't know his name and have never even spoken to him?' Blackstone asked suspiciously.

The librarian laughed with what sounded like genuine amusement, and for the first time since the start of the interview, she seemed relaxed.

'Many of the new arrivals come from small backward towns

on the Steppe,' she said. 'For them, London is nothing like they could ever have imagined. Even for those who are used to the sophisticated life of Petersburg and Moscow, this city is a confusing, and often frightening, place. And they show it.'

'How?'

'By the puzzled expression which never leaves their faces. By the uncertain way they move.'

'But this is Little Russia,' Blackstone pointed out. 'It must be just like being at home for them.'

The librarian laughed again. 'To those of us who have lived here for some time, it begins to feel like Russia. But for those who have just left the real thing, it is a strange, alien place.'

Maybe she was right, Blackstone thought. Perhaps the man whose path had crossed his three times in less than twenty-four hours *was* a new arrival. But even if that were true—even if he found himself disorientated by London—he also seemed to have a sense of purpose about him. He was, the policeman decided, nothing less than a man with a mission.

Blackstone thanked the librarian for her time, and made his way over to the other end of the room, where Hannah was leafing through a Russian newspaper.

She looked up at him. 'You've finished?'

'I've finished,' Blackstone agreed.

'Good. Then you can buy me luncheon.'

'I'm afraid not.'

'Why not? You don't think I've earned it?'

'Oh, you've earned it, right enough. It's just that I have to get back to the Yard for a while.'

Hannah pouted. 'A paltry excuse,' she said. 'Is that the right word—"paltry"?'

Blackstone laughed. 'I suppose so. Look, I'll make it up to you. If you can spare me some more of your time this afternoon...'

'But of course.'

'Then when it's over, I'll take you out for supper.'

'I would like that,' Hannah said, the sly smile creeping across her face. 'Suppers are so much more intimate than luncheons, don't you think?'

'So they say.'

'And what do I have to do to earn my supper? Where would you like me to take you this afternoon?'

'Anywhere you took Charles Smith, though preferably somewhere he acted as if he might have learned something useful.'

Hannah gave the matter some thought. 'I think I'll take you to the Ghetto Bank,' she said finally.

EIGHTEEN

Blackstone walked along the Embankment, looking up at New Scotland Yard and wondering what a stranger who knew nothing about the building would make of it. With its four huge gables and a circular tower on each corner, would the stranger perhaps mistake it for the home of a minor royal? Or was there something stiff and imposing about the place that would always identify it as a source of control and authority?

You've got to stop educating yourself, Sam, he told himself. It's doing your head no good at all.

He had reached the big double gates that led into the courtyard. There were two uniformed constables on duty as always—and they seemed unusually relieved to see him.

'You've got a visitor, sir,' said the senior constable. His voice dropped to almost a whisper. 'He's a lord!'

'Lord Dalton?' Blackstone asked.

The constable nodded. 'He's been *waiting* in your office for you. For over *twenty* minutes.'

'And a lord's time—any old lord's time—is, of course, much more valuable than that of a Scotland Yard police inspector working on an important case, isn't it?' Blackstone said.

'That's right, sir,' the constable agreed. Then he caught the dangerous look in Blackstone's eye and realized he'd made a mistake. 'I mean...' he mumbled. 'What I was tryin' to say was...'

'Forget it,' Blackstone ordered him. 'Did Lord Dalton say why he'd come to see me?'

'I didn't think it was my place to ask,' the constable said weakly.

Blackstone sighed. 'But you are sure it's really him? You did ask for some kind of identification?'

'No, Inspector.'

'Why not?'

'Well...he...he acted like he was a lord.'

Blackstone shook his head in amazement. A few years earlier, he recalled, the Fenians had managed to plant a bomb in the offices of the Irish Special Branch, and since then, security had been tightened up. But that security was obviously still balefully inadequate if all it took to get through the gates was to act like a lord!

He wondered what—other than habit—made ordinary people so deferential to those who were considered their betters. He himself went through the correct form when addressing Lord Dalton, but though he liked—and perhaps even admired—the man, he still considered Dalton, on a fundamental level, to be no more than his equal. Perhaps he was slowly turning from a mild sceptic into a fully-fledged republican, he thought worriedly.

'I'm expecting the Pope to drop round this afternoon,' he told the two constables. 'He won't be in his robes—he likes to travel incognito—but when he arrives, send him straight up.'

The constables laughed nervously. Blackstone turned on his heel, and strode rapidly towards his office.

The Inspector found Lord Dalton sitting in the same chair Emily Montcliffe had used only a few days earlier, when she'd revealed her worries about her brother. Dalton was reading a copy of the *Times*, and smoking an expensive cigar. He did not stand up when Blackstone entered the room.

'I'm sorry to have kept you waiting, my Lord,' the Inspector said.

'It's entirely my own fault,' Dalton replied easily. 'I could have avoided the wait by simply having one of my people ring the Yard and tell you when I expected to find you here. But—' he shrugged—'I happened to be in the area, and I thought there was a good chance you might be in your office.' He gave Blackstone a smile that might almost have been called a grin. 'You don't set me particularly easy tasks, do you, Inspector?'

'Which task are we talking about, my Lord? Getting your hands on Charles Montcliffe's private papers?'

'Exactly.'

'But you *do* have them?'

'Yes, I have them.' Lord Dalton indicated a leather attaché case that was resting next to his chair. 'But the Earl was only prepared to release them under the most stringent conditions.'

'And what might those conditions be?'

'That you are to be allowed to read them, but not retain them. That you are to make no notes. That I myself never lose sight of the papers.'

'What's his game?'

'His game?' Dalton repeated, and there was just the slightest hint of rebuke in his voice.

Blackstone sighed. 'Why do you think the Earl has imposed so many restrictions?'

'His son's death will have to become public knowledge at some point. Probably, in fact, in the next few days. And when it does become generally known, he is most anxious that there should be no scandal.'

'So he's more concerned about protecting the family name than he is about seeing his son's murderer brought to justice, is he?'

Dalton frowned, perhaps issuing a second warning that Blackstone might be going a little too far.

'Of course he wants his son's murderer arrested,' the noble lord said, 'but,' he conceded, softening his tone slightly, 'if it came to a choice between justice and the family name, I rather think that the weight of all his ancestors would compel him to put the family name first.'

'You've just pretty much confirmed what I've been thinking myself,' Blackstone said. 'Thank you for being so honest with me, my Lord.'

'My family does not yet have enough history behind it to have acquired the Montcliffes' style of honour,' Dalton said, 'but I like to think that I can at least honour the truth.'

He paused, as if he'd realized that he'd once again allowed their conversation to slip beyond what was the strictly acceptable.

'Would you care to examine the documents now, Inspector?' he continued.

'Very much so.'

'Well, there they are.'

Blackstone bent down and picked up the attaché case. Then, having undone the buckles and extracted perhaps a dozen sheets of closely written notes, he placed the case back where he had found it.

It would be difficult to examine the papers when he was standing, he thought, but was it the done thing to sit down in the presence of a lord without first being invited to do so?

Bugger it—it *was* his office, wasn't it? he told himself, as he walked round his desk and sat down in his usual chair.

Blackstone quickly scanned the first of the sheets. It was headed, 'Reasons exiles have had to leave their homeland.' Below the heading was a numbered list, which included 'political opposition' and 'religious persecution'. The second sheet listed the occupations the exiles followed—bamboo workers and slipper makers in the Commercial Road area; shipwrights and engineers in the East India dock, cabinetmakers, tailors and bootmakers in Whitechapel; and skin-dressers, seamstresses and bow makers all over the East End.

By the time he had reached the bottom of the second sheet, he was starting to feel a little uneasy. All the material he had read so far was worthy enough, but it didn't quite square with the image of a man who had had the courage and the imagination both to have infiltrated a ring of child pornographers and to write an explosive exposure of their filthy trade.

Well, perhaps this was no more than essential background to the story Montcliffe had been working on, Blackstone thought, and the real meat would come on the pages which followed.

Real meat *didn't* follow! There were more meticulously collected facts, and a few character sketches. Blackstone certainly knew more about the people of Little Russia when he'd finished reading, but his understanding of what made Charles Montcliffe tick had not been advanced a jot. And yet, while acknowledging that the papers were practically useless in terms of his investigation, he felt a sudden, irrational reluctance to hand them back to Lord Dalton.

He brushed the feeling aside. There had to be something more, he decided—other notes which spelled out the real story Charles Montcliffe had been working on when he died.

He looked up from his desk. Lord Dalton was engrossed in his copy of the *Times*.

'Where did these papers come from, my Lord?' Blackstone asked.

Lord Dalton lowered his newspaper. 'They came from the writing desk in Charles' room.'

'Can you he sure of that?'

'Absolutely certain.'

'Perhaps the servant who brought them to you—'

'There was no servant involved. Once I had Earl Montcliffe's permission, I went and collected them myself.'

'There were no other papers there—papers which you perhaps

decided were not worth bringing to me?'

And he was thinking: Or papers which you left behind because they might show the Montcliffes in a bad light.

Lord Dalton looked him squarely in the eyes. 'There were no other papers of any description,' he said firmly.

If he ruled out the possibility that such notes ever existed, then what other possibilities was he left with? Blackstone asked himself.

The first was that Earl Montcliffe, or some other member of his household, had already destroyed them. The second—and Blackstone felt his heart miss a beat when this idea occurred to him—was that Charles Montcliffe had chosen to hide his more sensational material away.

'Desks sometimes have secret drawers,' he pointed out.

'The same thought occurred to me,' Lord Dalton replied. 'I made sure that wasn't the case with Charles' desk.'

'How?'

'I took the senior cabinetmaker from one of my factories to look at it. He's been in the trade for over thirty years, and he swears that if there had been a hidden drawer, he'd have found it.'

Blackstone felt a momentary stab of disappointment, but it was soon overtaken by the realization that there was one line of approach—possibly a very useful one—that they hadn't even tried yet.

'The servants are still confined to the house on the order of the Home Secretary, aren't they?' he asked.

'That is correct,' Dalton replied. 'They are to stay there until after the Jubilee celebrations are over.'

'But Earl Montcliffe has great political influence,' Blackstone said. 'If he wanted that order overruled, he'd probably get his way. And *you* have enough influence over *him* to persuade him that's just what he should do.'

'Have you lost your mind, Blackstone?' Lord Dalton demanded, clearly astounded by the suggestion. 'Let the servants leave the house? That would be tantamount to announcing to the newspapers that Charles is missing. It's an insane idea.'

'It would be insane to let *all* the servants out,' Blackstone agreed. 'But it makes very sound sense indeed to let just *one* of them go.'

It took ten minutes of persuasive argument to convince Lord Dalton that the plan was a good one, and even then Blackstone was not sure that Dalton was enthusiastic enough about it to play his part with the necessary conviction. Still, he had done all that it was humanly possible to do.

As he stood up, with Charles Montcliffe's notes in his hand, he experienced a second sharp attack of the feeling that had overcome him earlier. It was true that the notes had told him nothing, and he couldn't see how they would ever be of value—but he simply did not want to give them back!

Yet what choice did he have? he thought as he walked around the side of the desk. If he refused to hand the papers over, then Lord Dalton—however much he might be on Blackstone's side—would be compelled to report the matter to Earl Montcliffe. And the Earl, for his part, would immediately telephone the Commissioner. Then the fat would really he in the fire—and

Blackstone could say goodbye to his job and his pension.

The Inspector was halfway between his desk and Lord Dalton when he suddenly missed his footing. He lurched forward, and it was only by an effort that he stopped himself falling flat on his face. But in saving himself, he had lost his grip on the papers and they scattered all over the floor.

Dalton quickly rose to his feet to assist the detective, but the other man waved him away.

'I'll be perfectly all right,' Blackstone said. 'It was a stupid thing to do—losing my balance like that. I don't know what came over me. Haven't even had a drink today.'

'These things happen,' Dalton said understandingly. Blackstone knelt down and began to collect the papers. He straightened up and handed them over to Dalton.

'I'm sorry about the mess I've got them into,' he said. 'They're probably all out of order.'

'That doesn't matter,' Dalton told him. 'I don't expect the Earl will look at them. It is not so much that he wants them himself as that he doesn't want anyone else to have them.' He checked his pocket watch. 'I must be going.'

Since Dalton was obviously not enough of a democrat to offer to shake hands, and Blackstone not yet quite enough of a republican to ignore the alternative, the policeman bowed slightly and the lord took his leave.

Blackstone listened to Lord Dalton's footsteps retreating down the stairs, then reached into his jacket pocket and brushed his fingers against the ball of paper that was sitting there. He still wasn't sure why he'd bothered to steal one sheet of Charles Montcliffe's notes—but he was glad that he had.

NINETEEN

It was some fifteen minutes to luncheon, and the Montcliffe family had gathered, as was their custom, in the parlour. Earl Montcliffe stood at the window, gloomily looking down on Park Lane.

The London that he had loved as a boy had changed beyond recognition, he thought. And not just the capital—the whole country. Servants left their employment whenever they felt like it, instead of serving loyally for as long as they were physically able. Radicals, like that bounder Scott, were allowed to publish almost anything they wished to. Even some members of parliament were now being drawn from the ranks of the lower middle classes. No one seemed to know his place any more.

In the good old days, there would have been no problem similar to the one they were now experiencing with Charles' valet. And why? Because the valet would have known he was expected to keep quiet, at whatever cost to himself. And even if he hadn't held his tongue—even if he had revealed all—who would have listened to him? Who, in their right mind, would have taken his word against the word of one of the Quality?

Earl Montcliffe took a sip of the dry sherry he had specially imported from an exclusive vineyard in Jerez. Hoskins had deferentially informed him, only that morning, that there were just three barrels left in the cellar. And when that had gone? Well, he would have no alternative but to ask little Billy Dalton, the grandson of a common tradesman, to order him some more.

There was the sound of the door opening, then Hoskins announced, 'Lord Dalton, my Lord.'

Montcliffe forced a smile to his lips, and turned around.

'William!' he said feigning delight. 'We don't often see you at this time of day.'

'No, I'm usually kept rather busy during City hours,' Lord Dalton agreed. He walked over and kissed his fiancée's hand. 'The only reason I'm here now is to convey a request from Inspector Blackstone.'

'A request!' Viscount Hugo Montcliffe snorted. 'Become Blackstone's messenger boy now, have you, William?'

'Why don't you tell Father what the request *is*, William?' Lady Emily said hastily, before Dalton had time to respond to her brother's comment.

Dalton shot the Viscount a look of pure contempt, then turned to the Earl. 'Blackstone thinks that Charles' valet may provide one of the keys to the investigation,' he said.

Damn and blast the bloody policeman! the Earl thought. And damn and blast William Dalton for going along with him!

'Blackstone thinks *Thomas* is important!' Hugo Montcliffe said. 'Can't see how he'd be any help at all. Fellow's almost a mental defective, as far as I can tell.'

'If he were an idiot, he'd never have been able to fill his post as he did,' Lord Dalton countered.

'Balderdash!' the Viscount said. 'Nothin' much to valettin'.'

'There's far more to being a good valet than you seem to appreciate, Hugo,' Dalton said. 'I doubt very much whether you would be able to cope with the demands of the job.'

'Wasn't brought up to be a valet,' Hugo said, missing the point.

But it was plain that Hugo's sister Emily hadn't missed it, the Earl thought, as he saw the slight smile play on her lips. Damn and blast her, too! She could afford to smile—because she didn't know what *he* knew.

'Anyway, even if the man's a total brainbox, still won't do you any good,' Hugo Montcliffe continued. 'Last time I spoke to Hoskins, he said he had no idea where Thomas was—an' if the butler don't know, you can bet your last guinea that nobody does.'

If only we had a last guinea *to* bet, the Earl thought. But they didn't. Now, all the money seemed to be in the hands of people like Dalton—men without a drop of decent blood flowing through their veins.

'Blackstone thinks there might be a way to find Thomas,' Lord Dalton said.

'Thinks far too much, if you ask me,' Hugo Montcliffe retorted.

'You see, when he was questioning the servants, he thought he noticed that one of the parlour maids—a girl called Molly—seemed unnaturally upset by Thomas's disappearance,' Dalton continued, ignoring the interruption. 'I have just spoken to

Hoskins, and he confirms the fact that—while as butler he did not encourage it in any way—they appear to have fallen in love.'

'Fallen in love!' Hugo sneered. 'They're nothin' but servants, for God's sake!'

'Blackstone believes that Molly might know where Thomas has gone to ground. His plan is to have the housekeeper assign Molly an errand which would give her an excuse to be out of the house for quite some time. If he's right about her, then instead of performing that task she'll run straight to where Thomas is hiding.'

'So instead of losin' one servant, we'll lose two,' Hugo Montcliffe said.

'Blackstone intends to have two of his best men posted outside the house when she leaves. She'll never notice them following her.'

'Waste of time,' Hugo told him. 'Don't even *want* Thomas back in the house. Never liked the man. Shifty eyes.'

'You're forgetting that the reason Inspector Blackstone is looking for him is because he might know who killed Charles,' Lord Dalton reminded him.

'Don't believe it,' Hugo replied. 'Said earlier, don't think the man knows anything.'

Hugo was doing his best to block the plan, the Earl thought. But his son was still floundering and perhaps it was time to step in himself.

'Bit of a pointless discussion, this,' he said. 'The Home Secretary has asked me to allow none of the servants to leave the house.

Doesn't want news of Charles' death gettin' out until after the Jubilee. So you see, the matter's completely out of my hands.'

'We both know that the Home Secretary will do exactly what the Prime Minister tells him to do,' Dalton responded, 'and we also know that the Prime Minister would be very unlikely to refuse a personal request from you.'

'Perhaps it might be best to let sleepin' dogs lie,' the Earl suggested.

'You're worried that Thomas might have knowledge of something scandalous,' Dalton said. 'I can understand that. But you must see that as long as we don't know where he is, he's like a ticking bomb which might explode at any time. Whereas, once we've caught him, we can go about defusing him.'

'But it won't be us who'll be talkin' to him,' the Earl objected. 'It'll be that fellow Blackstone.'

'He has agreed that I may be present at the interrogation, and that nothing which might harm the family will be allowed to go beyond that room. And once Thomas has told the police what they need to know, I will immediately dispatch him to Italy with a generous pension. After that, you'll never hear from him again.'

Blackstone isn't the problem, the Earl thought. The problem is that once *you*—Lord William Dalton—have heard what Thomas has got to say, you'll drop any idea of marryin' into this family like a hot potato.

'I'm afraid I can't allow my influence with the Prime Minister to be used in a private matter,' he said.

'Charles and I had become close friends,' Dalton replied. 'And as a close friend, I consider it my duty to do all I can to find those responsible for his death. I would consider it a personal favour if you would speak to the Prime Minister on my behalf.'

He made it sound as if he were making a request, the Earl thought. But he wasn't. How could it be a request, when a very clear message lay behind it? And that message was, 'Do what I say or I'll cut the money off.' But he'd probably cut the money off anyway, when he'd listened to Thomas. There *had* to be another way round the problem.

'Very well, I will speak to Lord Salisbury after luncheon,' the Earl said, hoping that in the intervening period he would come up with a solution to the dilemma.

'Perhaps it might be better to do it before luncheon,' Dalton suggested firmly.

There was no way he could refuse, the Earl decided. 'Yes, it might be better to call him now,' he agreed.

He made his way reluctantly over to the telephone—but not before he had exchanged a worried glance with his eldest son.

TWENTY

The Ghetto Bank of Whitechapel stood at the corner of Osborn Street, next to a branch of the Post Office. The post office had signs in both English and Russian, but the bank, in addition to those two languages, also had posters stuck to its frontage in what Blackstone had come to recognize as Hebrew.

'What do they all mean?' the Inspector asked the Russian woman.

'That one says that the bank will transfer money back to your relations in Russia for you,' Hannah explained. 'The one next to it says that the bank's agents in Russia, Poland and Germany will help those same relations to emigrate to England. The third offers to change coins and paper money into any European currency.'

'Seems to do a good trade,' Blackstone said, watching the constant stream of customers passing through the bank's door.

'Of course it does,' Hannah said. 'There is no other bank in England which provides the services this one does.'

She laughed.

'What's so funny?' Blackstone asked.

'It is funny that the Russians—by which I mean the *pure*

Russians—so despised us Jews when they were in their homeland, but now that they are abroad they would be lost without us.'

'That's the first time I've ever really heard you sound bitter,' Blackstone told her.

Hannah shrugged. 'I shouldn't be, I suppose. It is not their fault. They are raised from birth to look down on the Jewish people. They will not change until society itself has changed.' Her voice had been growing wistful—almost visionary—but now her body tensed slightly and when she spoke again it was with a crispness that proclaimed that she remembered her job was to guide a policeman around Little Russia. 'Shall we go into the bank?' she suggested.

'Why not?' Blackstone agreed.

Hannah pushed open the door and Blackstone followed her into the bank. Running the length of the room was a heavy wooden counter, behind which stood clerks in suits and ties. At either end of the counter were metal grilles, sealing the cashiers off from the outside world. It was, in so many ways, like every other bank the inspector had ever visited, but never before had Blackstone heard so many conversations in languages he didn't understand.

There was a long queue in front of every position, but Hannah marched to the head of the nearest line.

'Do you speak English?' she asked the clerk.

The man shook his head.

'*Gabaresh pa-ruski?*' Hannah demanded.

'*Da.*'

Hannah said something more to the man. He shook his head.

She spoke again, and there was a new urgency in her voice. The clerk responded with an even more vehement shake of his head, and Blackstone thought he could detect disdain in the man's tone.

Obviously having had enough of the preliminary sparring, Hannah slammed her hand down on the counter, and spoke in a cold, hissing way that almost chilled Blackstone's blood. The effect on the clerk was instantaneous. He nodded for a third time—but now defeatedly—and, ignoring his waiting customers, disappeared into the hack room.

'What was that all about?' Blackstone asked.

'I said we needed to see the manager immediately on a matter of great urgency, and he told me that was completely impossible because Mr Bialik was far too busy. I told him you were a very important policeman from New Scotland Yard, and he said that would make no difference—you would still have to make an appointment.'

'That's when you slammed your hand down on the counter,' Blackstone guessed.

'Yes.'

'And what did you say next?'

'I told him that the police had been watching him for some weeks, building up an extensive dossier on him, and that if he didn't make it possible for us to see the manager, action would have to be taken against him.'

'What kind of action?' Blackstone asked. 'What's he done?'

'Probably nothing,' Hannah said indifferently, 'but Russians are born with a strong sense of guilt, and it only needs someone to tell them they have done wrong for them to start imagining that they actually have.'

Blackstone shook his head, and wondered if this fascinating young woman would *ever* stop surprising him.

*

Blackstone sat in the Ghetto Bank's manager's office. Mr Bialik was around forty. He had a hooked nose, olive skin and jet black hair that was swept severely back. His expression was both watchful and calculating, and Blackstone decided that even seeing him on the street, it would have been impossible to take him for anything but a Jewish banker.

'My clerk tells me you have some qvestions you vish to ask me, Inspector,' he said.

'That's right, sir,' Blackstone agreed pleasantly. 'I wonder if you remember talking to a journalist called Smith.'

The banker nodded gravely. 'He came to see me under false pretences.'

'Would you care to explain that?'

'Ven he asked for an appointment, he said it vas because he vanted to learn how the bank works.'

'And didn't he?'

'Not in the general vay that he pretended to be interested.'

'Go on,' Blackstone said encouragingly.

'We have our fingers in many pies here—as you English say— but our biggest piece of business is to transfer money to the

East. Some of our customers only send a little to their families in Russia each time, perhaps no more than five or ten roubles—'

'Excuse my ignorance, sir, but what's a rouble worth?' Blackstone interrupted.

'There are roughly ten roubles to the pound sterling.'

Blackstone nodded. 'I see. Carry on, sir.'

'All those small transfers add up. Last year, ve sent over a million roubles back to Russia.'

Blackstone whistled softly. 'That is a lot of money, sir,' he admitted. 'But I'm not quite sure I see how that particular piece of knowledge fits in with your suspicions about Mr Smith.'

'I am no journalist,' the bank manager replied, 'but if I vas, I think I vould write my story about that one million roubles—and Mr Smith showed no interest in it at all.'

'So what *was* he interested in?'

'He vas interested in money travelling the other vay.'

'The other way?'

'From Russia to here.'

'But surely that can only be a trifling amount?' Blackstone suggested. 'Barely a trickle?'

The bank manager looked away. 'There can be very few Russians who have either the means or the desire to send their money to England,' he said evasively. 'It is true that the rich keep some money in the South of France, because that is vere they spend their vinters, but who would vant to spend a vinter in London? And as for inwestment—if they vish to inwest, there are far better returns to be had in our own country.'

'You haven't really answered my question, have you, sir?' Blackstone asked, a little sternly.

'I don't understand.'

'Oh, with respect, sir, I think that you do. I said that the money which came from Russia couldn't be more than a trickle, and you didn't agree with me. Now why was that?'

The banker looked down at his hands. 'Until recently, vat you said was true. But in the last few veeks...'

'A lot of money has been coming in?'

'A substantial amount.'

'How much?'

'That I cannot tell you.'

'Can't? Or won't?'

The banker spread his hands helplessly in front of him. 'I see no difference betveen the two.'

'It is not a good idea, in this country, to do or say anything which might make the police want to take an interest in you,' Blackstone said, remembering Hannah's comment on Russians earlier.

But the bank manager was made of sterner stuff than his clerk had been. 'It is not a good idea in my own country, either, but however much you threaten me, I vill not betray the confidence of my clients.'

'Perhaps you can help me a little more without actually betraying that confidence,' Blackstone suggested. 'Will you try?'

'All right.'

'This "substantial" amount of money which you say has been

coming into the bank? Is it still here?'

The bank manager hesitated for quite a while. 'No, it has been vithdrawn,' he said finally.

'All of it?'

'All of it.'

'I see,' Blackstone mused. 'So from that I take it that it all belonged to the same man.'

'I do not see how you could possibly reach such a conclusion,' the manager said.

'That's easy,' Blackstone told him. 'Let's suppose that the substantial amount you talk of were made up of ten sums for each of ten men. The chances of all of them withdrawing their money over such a short time are very slim indeed. Five or six might withdraw it, perhaps even seven or eight. But there would always be one or two who didn't need their money quite yet, so why shouldn't they leave it in a nice safe bank, where it would be earning interest? Yet you say *all* the money has been withdrawn. Therefore, it's likely it was sent to only one man. Am I right?'

The bank manager hesitated again. 'I cannot say,' he told the policeman. 'It vould not be right.'

Blackstone nodded sympathetically. 'I understand your dilemma,' he said. 'And I must apologize if I seemed to be threatening you a few moments ago. I assure you that was never my intention.'

The bank manager visibly relaxed. 'I am pleased to accept your assurances,' he said.

Blackstone stood up and held out his arm. 'Thank you for sparing me some of your valuable time, Mr Bialik.'

'Not at all,' the bank manager said, shaking his hand. 'I am always villing to help the police.'

Blackstone turned and ambled lazily over to the door. It was not until his hand was on the brass handle that his body tensed and he swung round on his heel.

'It was Count Turgenev, wasn't it?' he demanded.

'Vat!'

'The man who transferred those large sums of money? It was Count Turgenev.'

'I could not possibly tell you that!' the manager protested.

But the expression on his face already had.

TWENTY-ONE

Blackstone had been right to decide not to come on this particular operation, Sergeant Patterson told himself as he looked through the window of the hansom cab at Montcliffe House. It would have been an unnecessary risk for the Inspector—whom Molly had seen at close quarters in the servants' hall—to have involved himself in tailing her. Yet Patterson could not help but wish that his boss were sitting by his side at that moment. And however much he tried to persuade himself it was a simple, straightforward job, he could do nothing to quell the uneasy rumbling in his stomach.

It was a quarter past four when the girl emerged from the servants' entrance. She was wearing a dress of finely striped cotton. On her head, she had an extravagant hat with a lacquered feather trim—a hat that would be easily spotted in a crowd. But even that stroke of luck did little for Patterson's feeling of foreboding.

Once she had reached the pavement, Molly stopped to look into her handbag. Patterson had been told that she had instructions to visit a dressmaker's on Wigmore Street, and if she turned right that was probably exactly what she intended to do.

'Turn left!' the sergeant urged her silently. 'Turn left!' The maid turned left—and Patterson realized that for the previous few seconds he had been holding his breath.

'So far, so good,' said the man sitting next to him.

Patterson turned to face Sergeant Dickens, a slightly overweight forty-year-old, who looked more like a greengrocer than a detective.

'There's many a slip twixt the cup and the lip,' he said. Yet why should there be a slip this time? Why shouldn't Molly lead them straight to her lover? And once she had done that, why shouldn't Thomas Grey tell them who killed his master, and why?

The girl was already some distance down the road, and Patterson, whose gut still refused to be pacified, banged on the roof of the hansom to tell the cabbie to pull away from the kerb.

There was something wrong with the way the parlour maid was walking, Patterson decided, but he couldn't quite put his finger on what it was.

And then he had it!

What was wrong was there was *nothing* wrong! Molly was sauntering along as if she were merely out for an afternoon stroll.

And she shouldn't have been! A girl like her—a girl who was fleeing from her employers and into the arms of a lover who was wanted by the police—should have been almost running, and checking over her shoulder every few seconds for signs of pursuit. So why wasn't she? Because she knew they were on to her? Knew—and didn't care?

Molly reached a bus stop and came to a halt. She opened her handbag, and took out a powder puff.

Wrong again! Patterson thought. She should have been far too nervous to even think about making herself look pretty.

A double-decker omnibus, pulled by two black horses, came to a halt in front of the stop. The girl stepped on to the platform, and disappeared inside the bus.

It would have been better for them if she'd chosen to go up the outside spiral staircase to the open top deck, Patterson thought, because from there she would have been clearly visible. But perhaps he was worrying unnecessarily. She was on the bus, and she could not get off without them seeing her do it—so why did it matter where she sat?

The bus pulled off, and the cab fell in behind it. Patterson lit a cigarette and tried to persuade himself that everything was still going according to plan.

The sergeant was smoking his fifth cigarette as the bus, with the cab keeping a discreet distance behind it, crossed Southwark Bridge. It was a good sign that the girl had not got off the bus yet. It was good that she was going to Southwark, because the anonymous, teeming backstreets of the borough were *just* the sort of place that a man on the run—as Thomas seemed to be—would choose to hide.

The bus stopped at the corner of Quilp Street, and the girl in the cotton dress and feather hat got off. Patterson banged on the roof of the cab, and had opened the door and climbed out even before it came to a full stop.

The girl was heading up Quilp Street, walking faster than she had been when she'd left the Montcliffe mansion. Why the change of pace? Patterson wondered. What had happened to her on the omnibus to make her suddenly want to hurry?

But whatever the reason for her change of speed, it didn't really matter, did it? Even if she failed to lead them to Thomas, she had no excuse for being in Southwark. That fact, in itself, was enough to pull her in for questioning. And even hardened criminals found it difficult to keep their secrets locked in their breasts once they were inside the confines of Scotland Yard.

The girl crossed Marshalsea Road, paying scant attention to the traffic, and continued on along Quilp Street. As Patterson and Dickens crossed the road themselves, she turned right up Dorrit Street.

They had lost sight of her, and that was not good, Patterson thought, as he dodged between the buses, cabs and carts. But she was not *so* far ahead of them that it should cause real concern.

It came as a shock, when he turned the corner of Dorrit Street himself, to discover that there was no sign of Molly.

'Where the bloody hell could she have gone?' asked Dickens, who was just behind him.

A good question, Patterson thought, as he felt the sweat break out on his brow.

Though what he really wanted to do was to roar with frustration, he forced himself to calm down and consider the possibilities. There were only two as far as he could see. The first was that Molly had disappeared into one of the houses on Dorrit Street.

The second—almost too awful to contemplate—was that once she'd turned off Quilp Street she'd put on an extra spurt of speed, and was now somewhere on Peter Street.

Even as these thoughts flashed through his mind, he had broken into a sprint. He stopped, gasping for breath, when he reached the corner, but when he looked hopefully up and down Peter Street, he could see no woman in a striped dress.

Behind him, he heard Sergeant Dickens come to a puffing halt. 'What do we do now?' Dickens asked.

'Now we go knocking a few doors to see if anybody knows what's happened to her,' Patterson said grimly.

It did not take long to establish that the servant girl had chosen to run rather than hide. Two dirty urchins sitting on a doorstep said they had seen her dashing down the street. A costermonger pushing a barrow load of vegetables swore that, in her haste, she had almost crashed into him. A door-to-door brush-seller was positive she'd taken a left turn on Peter Street.

'Your boss isn't going to be very happy about this, is he?' Dickens said unhelpfully.

Not very happy? Patterson repeated silently. Yes, that was one way of putting it! He could almost hear the words Blackstone would fire off at him later—'I gave you a simple job, and you made a complete pig's arse of it. You let yourself be outwitted by a simple parlour maid. And you call yourself a detective!'

'So what do we do now?' Dickens said.

'We keep on looking,' Patterson told him. 'There's still a chance that even if she's reached Thomas Grey's bolt-hole by now, we'll catch her when she's leaving it again.'

But he did not sound very convincing—even to himself.

They trudged dispiritedly up Disney Street and crossed George Yard. They questioned the workers who were just leaving the jam factory and fur warehouse on Marshalsea Road. When they had no luck there, they expanded their search, checking out Harrow Street and Vine Yard. With every step he took, Patterson felt a little more of his remaining hope drain away, and by the time they had reached the pub next to the cart and wheel works on Lant Street, he had just about given up.

'Fancy a drink?' Dickens suggested, looking thirstily at the pub door.

Patterson sighed. 'Bearing in mind what Sam Blackstone's going to put me through later, I think I'll *need* one,' he said.

He pushed the main door open, and was about to head for the public bar. Then he saw something in the parlour that stopped him in his tracks. Sitting at one of the tables was a woman wearing a striped cotton dress and an extravagant hat of lacquered bird feathers. She might have been pretty quick on her feet earlier, but now her head was slumped forward, and there was an empty gin glass in front of her.

Patterson offered up a silent prayer to whatever guardian angel had saved him from Blackstone's wrath, and strode over to the table.

'Well, you've led us a merry dance, Molly,' he said, 'but now it's all over, and I'd advise you to come quietly.'

The woman looked up. 'Don't know what yer talkin' about,' she said, slurring her words slightly.

She was older than Patterson had expected her to be—perhaps as much as thirty. She was wearing more make-up than most servant girls did, even when they had escaped the watchful, ever disapproving, eye of the housekeeper. And now he was close to her he could see that the dress and hat—while very similar—were not *exactly* the same as the ones he remembered Molly wearing when she left the Montcliffe house.

'I said I don't know what yer talkin' about,' the woman repeated.

And suddenly—while his stomach was doing a sickening somersault—Patterson realized what must have happened.

*

It had been a stupid idea to go to the inquest, the valet told himself as he paced the nearly empty room. Very stupid. And yet he had felt that he'd owed it to his kind and generous master— had felt that Charles Montcliffe was entitled to have at least one person there who knew him and cared about him.

He stopped pacing, and looked around him. In one corner of the room was the heap of rags on which he slept, in the other the bucket that he used as his lavatory. A small paraffin stove stood in the centre of the room, on which, if he wished, he could have cooked a simple meal. But he hadn't felt like eating much at all for days, because his stomach was filled with a terror that seemed to grow with each passing hour.

He wondered when exactly things had started to go wrong—

when Charles Montcliffe's great adventure had turned into his darkest nightmare. Was it when Charles had first begun to follow the Russian aristocrat? Or when he had learned about the Empire Living Pictures Company, and understood for the first time the true nature of the diabolical plot that was afoot?

Thomas shivered, then hugged himself tightly. It was pointless to try and pick out one incident, he thought. Though neither he nor his master had known it at the time, it had been a nightmare from the very beginning.

His heart jumped as he heard an urgent knocking on the front door.

The police?

Or *them*—come to silence him as they'd silenced Charles Montcliffe?

The front window was boarded up, but there was a small gap between the boards, and by twisting his head at an awkward angle, he could just see the woman in the striped cotton dress on the doorstep.

Molly! Standing out there on the street—as bold as brass—for any bugger to see.

The parlour maid knocked again—even louder and more insistently this time. Thomas rushed into the hallway, flung open the door and pulled her inside.

'What the bloody hell are you doin' 'ere?' the valet demanded angrily.

'Let go of me arm, can't you?' Molly protested. 'You're really 'urtin' me, Thomas.'

The valet looked down at his hand, as if he were surprised it belonged to him, then released his grip on the girl.

'You shouldn't have come,' he moaned. 'It was insane to come.'

Molly looked hurt and disappointed. 'I'd thought you'd be pleased to see me,' she said. She stepped around him, entered the parlour, and sniffed. 'Crikey, it pongs a bit in 'ere, don't it?'

'It's the bucket,' Thomas explained. 'I don't dare empty it in the daytime. I only go out when it's dark. Do you understand what I'm sayin'? It's too dangerous for me to go out when it's light—an' it was too dangerous for you to come an' see me in the light.'

'It was as safe as anyfink,' Molly said complacently.

Thomas ran his hands through his hair in desperation. 'How do you know the police weren't followin' you?' he demanded.

'They were,' Molly told him. 'But I lost them.'

'You lost them!' Thomas repeated in a voice that was verging on a scream. 'How do you know you lost them? You've not been trained like they have.'

'So what?' Molly said. 'I had help.'

'Help? What kind of help?'

Molly slowly shook her head, as if she were amazed he'd taken so long to catch on. 'You've got more friends than you know about, Thomas Grey,' she said. 'Friends who'll—'

'Shut up!' Thomas said hysterically.

'What's the matter?'

'I think there's somebody at the back door.'

Molly laughed. 'You're imaginin' things,' she said.

And then she heard the unmistakable sound of splintering wood.

TWENTY-TWO

Being brought to Scotland Yard had been enough to make the woman in the cotton striped dress suspect she was in serious trouble, and the expressions on the faces of the two men facing her across the desk turned that suspicion into a certainty. 'What's your name?' Blackstone demanded.

'Nellie.'

'Nellie what?'

'Nellie Weeks, sir,' the woman muttered.

She had sobered up somewhat since Patterson arrested her, so she was no longer slurring her words—but it was obvious from the lines on her face that she was a habitual heavy drinker. 'What do you do for a living, Nellie?' Blackstone asked.

'A bit o' this, a bit o' that.'

'In other words,' Blackstone said, 'you're a prostitute.'

'No, I ain't!' the woman protested.

The Inspector sighed. 'Come on, Nellie. If you've ever been nicked—and I'm pretty sure you have—we'll have a record of it. So why don't you stop wasting my time and just admit to the truth?'

The woman shrugged. 'Well, you know 'ow it is, sir—a girl 'as to eat.'

'And a girl has to drink! How was it you happened to be on that particular bus?'

'I've already told yer sergeant the answer to that.'

'Well now you can tell me.'

'I was takin' a walk...'

'You were out looking for customers.'

'I was takin' a walk,' the woman said firmly, 'an' this gentleman come up to me an' asked me if I'd like to earn some money.'

'How much?'

'A guinea.'

'And what do you usually charge?'

'A guinea.'

Blackstone shook his head, almost despairingly. 'If anybody normally offered you more than a shilling, you'd think Christmas had come early this year,' he said. 'So what did this gentleman say you had to do to earn his guinea?'

''E 'ad a brown paper parcel in one 'and an' 'n 'at box in the other. He said there was a dress in the parcel, an' I was to put it on.'

'And then?'

'I was ter travel up west an' get on a certain bus at a certain stop at a certain time. Anuvver woman would get on at the next stop. She'd be dressed just like me—well, near enough, anyway—but I was to ignore 'er. I was ter stay on the bus till it got ter Quilp Street, then I was ter get off.'

'And make a run for it,' Patterson said ruefully.

'The gen'leman said 'e was playin' a joke on one of 'is friends,' Nellie Weeks said. ''E told me this friend would probably be follerin' me, but I wasn't to worry 'cos there was no 'arm in 'im.'

'And you believed him, did you? It didn't bother you that there'd be a man on your tail?'

'When yer've been out lookin' for business on a dark night in Whitechapel, yer fink nuffink about bein' follered by a bloke in broad daylight.'

'What else did he tell you?'

'That I shouldn't let 'is friend catch up wiv me for at least ten minutes.' Despite her situation, she grinned at Patterson. 'Took you a lot longer than that to catch me, didn't it? An' if I'd 'ave been able to stay away from the drink, yer'd probably *never* 'ave caught me.'

Thanks a bunch, Patterson thought. That little comment will certainly make my life a *lot* easier.

'What did this man who gave you the clothes and the money look like?' Blackstone asked.

''E wasn't what yer might call a big bloke, but 'e looked like a very 'ard case.'

'And did he have a foreign accent?'

'Yes, 'e did,' Nellie said. ''Owever did yer know that?'

Because the description perfectly matched the two men Blackstone had seen acting as bodyguards to Count Turgenev at the archway boxing match.

'Did he give you half the money then, and promise you the rest later?' the Inspector asked.

'No. 'E gave me all the money right then, an' said I could keep the dress an' 'at as well.'

Of course he did, Blackstone thought. These were careful men. Meeting Nellie again—with the possibility of falling into a police ambush—was not a chance they'd be willing to run.

'What I don't understand,' he said, 'is why you went along with the ruse after you'd been paid.'

'I beg yer pardon?'

'You'd got the money—why bother to take the omnibus ride?'

'Because I'm an honest woman, I am,' Nellie said, without much conviction. 'Besides...'

'Besides what?'

''E said that 'im an' 'is mates would be watchin' me.'

'And you believed him?'

Nellie gave an involuntary shudder. 'Oh yes, I believed 'im all right. 'E was a pleasant enough bloke on the surface, but then there was 'is eyes.'

'What about them?'

'They said that 'e'd kill yer soon as fink about it.'

*

Lord Dalton, sitting opposite Blackstone, took his time lighting one of his expensive cigars and then said, 'I'm not at all happy with the way things have worked out, Inspector.'

'Neither am I,' Blackstone admitted.

'I had to use considerable influence in order to get the Earl to persuade the Home Secretary to let Molly leave the house. It will be a long time before I can ask for another favour. And what was the result of all my efforts? Within an hour, your men had lost her.'

'They didn't lose her,' Blackstone said.

'No?'

'No! They didn't lose her—she was stolen from them.'

'I think you'd better explain yourself,' Dalton said.

'She could never have escaped on her own. She had help from someone inside the house.'

'One of the servants?'

'Possibly,' Blackstone said, noncommittally.

'Or are you suggesting it was one of the family?'

'That's possible, too.'

Dalton laughed. 'You're not seriously putting forward the theory that the Earl bought a dress like Molly's and then hired a prostitute to wear it?'

'Of course not,' Blackstone agreed. 'That part of the operation was handled by a man called Count Turgenev.'

'Count Turgenev!' Dalton repeated.

'You know him?'

Dalton shook his head. 'No. But I assume from the name that he belongs to the Russian aristocracy?'

'That's right.'

'What business would a Russian aristocrat have with an English parlour maid?'

'What business would have an *English* aristocrat have which could get him brutally murdered in the East End of London?' Blackstone countered. 'But that's not really the point, is it? What matters is that Turgenev could not have set up his operation without knowing when Molly would be leaving the house, what general direction she would be going in, and what she would be wearing.'

'I see your point,' Lord Dalton conceded.

'Was there anyone else there when you discussed the matter with the Earl?' Blackstone asked.

'Yes. The Countess, Hugo and Emily were also in the room.'

I hate all this pussyfooting around! Blackstone thought. I hate having other people doing the work I should be doing myself.

'You didn't think it might have been wiser to have a word with the Earl in private?' he asked.

'It didn't occur to me that any of the family might be suspects,' Lord Dalton said. 'As far as I am concerned, they are *still* all above suspicion.'

Blackstone shook his head. He felt, he thought, like a man who was conducting major surgery in the dark, without even knowing the nature of the instrument he was holding in his hand.

'Which of the servants knew what was going on?' he asked.

'The butler had to know, of course. Ever since the servants have been confined to the house, he's been acting more as a warder than anything else. And Mrs Whitely...'

'Mrs Whitely?'

'That's the housekeeper. She had to be told because she was the one whose job it was to send Molly out on her fictitious errand.'

'So they both knew she'd be followed by the police?'

'No, that's not the case at all. I just told them that they should invent a reason for Molly leaving the house.'

'And they didn't wonder why?'

Lord Dalton laughed again. 'It is not a servant's place to wonder why, *especially* in the Montcliffe household.'

'But they could have worked it out, couldn't they?'

'Hoskins probably could have. He's an intelligent man—he wouldn't be much good as a butler if he wasn't—and he keeps his finger on the pulse of the house. Yes, I think it's perfectly possibly that he could easily have worked out what we were doing.'

'I shall need to talk to him,' Blackstone said.

'I will try to persuade the Earl to give his perm—' Lord Dalton began.

'Try to persuade the Earl!' Blackstone exploded. 'Good God, man, don't you realize I'm investigating a murder—probably more than one by now. I don't need Montcliffe's permission for *anything*.'

'I think you'll find that you do,' Lord Dalton said, and his voice was so cold that Blackstone felt as if he'd had a bucket of icy water thrown over him.

This was no good—no good at all—the Inspector thought. He needed Lord Dalton's co-operation, and if swallowing his own pride was the only way of obtaining it, then he'd better get on with it.

'I'm sorry, my Lord,' he said.

'I have given you a great deal of leeway because I think you are a good policeman who only wants to do his job,' Dalton said. 'But there have to be limits set somewhere. There has to come a point at which your insolent disregard for the social order must be called to a halt.'

'I accept that,' Blackstone said. 'I was overwrought. If Thomas and Molly have been killed because of what I arranged today, then at least some of their blood is on my hands.'

'And because I helped you, it is on my hands too,' Dalton said, his tone considerably softened. 'But we cannot do the impossible, Inspector. We must both work within the rules of society as we find them.'

*

The Commissioner glared across his desk at Blackstone. 'You are skating on very thin ice, Inspector,' he said.

Just how much shit was he going to have to eat in one day? Blackstone wondered.

But aloud, all he said was, 'I'm only trying to do the job that I'm paid to do, sir.'

'And does that include harassing members of one of the highest families in the land?'

'Has any of them complained about me?'

'No. At least, not directly. But I have been hearing whispers. Grumblings. And they *will* grow into complaints—make no mistake about that. So why don't you drop that side of your investigation while you still have the chance?'

'I'm afraid I can't do that, sir,' Blackstone said.

'Why not?'

'Because there are clear indications that at least a part of the solution to the murder lies in Montcliffe House.'

'Perhaps you're completely wrong about that,' the Commissioner countered. 'Isn't it possible that there's a much simpler solution? Couldn't Charles Montcliffe have been doing what so many young men before him have done—simply gone to the East End to slake his baser sexual appetites?'

'He wasn't like that,' Blackstone said stubbornly.

'Oh, you knew him, did you? I wasn't aware that you moved in such exalted social circles.'

'I didn't know him when he was alive,' Blackstone admitted. 'But I've got to know him since he was murdered. And I rather admire the young man.'

The Commissioner shook his head in exasperation. 'Let us assume for a moment that there is a remote possibility that I am right and you are wrong. Charles Montcliffe goes to a brothel, stays rather later than he should have, and on his way home gets his throat cut by a thief. Isn't that possible?'

'It wouldn't explain what happened today.'

'Are you talking about the servant girl disappearing?'

'Yes.'

'Do you know for certain that her disappearance is connected with young Montcliffe's death?'

'As you pointed out yourself, sir, she's nothing more than a servant girl. Why should anyone go to so much trouble to snatch her unless there was a connection with the murder?'

'Of course, if you'd been there yourself to oversee the operation, Inspector, it's possible we'd never have lost her,' the Commissioner said, suddenly changing tack.

'As I've already told you, sir, I couldn't be there because Molly would have recognized me,' Blackstone said. 'Besides, I had confidence in the two men I'd assigned—'

'That was certainly well placed, wasn't it?'

'—who would have successfully accomplished their task had it not been for the outside interference.'

The Commissioner sighed theatrically. 'You're a very good detective, Inspector Blackstone,' he said, 'but you're going to come badly unstuck over this business. And when you do, don't expect *me* to pull you out of the mess you've landed yourself in.'

'Does that mean I'm still on the case, sir?' Blackstone asked, feeling a relief that surprised even him.

'Yes, you're still on the case. And I'll tell you why. One: you're still on it because I'm not yet convinced you've completely crossed the line—though as I said a moment ago, I have no doubt that you will. And two: because I can't think of another detective in the Yard who I wouldn't have to *coerce* into taking over your investigation.' The Commissioner waved his hand dismissively. 'You can go now, Blackstone.'

'Yes, sir,' Blackstone said. 'And may I take the opportunity to thank you for the confidence you've shown in me.'

The Commissioner frowned. 'You know that line I mentioned, Inspector?' he asked.

'Yes, sir?'

'You've just edged a couple of inches closer towards it.'

TWENTY-THREE

The designers of Slater's Restaurant on Piccadilly must have had shares in a decorative wrought ironwork factory, Blackstone thought. It was everywhere—forming a canopy over the bar, as a guard around the steps down to the tearoom, and as a banister on the stairs that led to the domed glass skylight.

There was other evidence of modest opulence, too—the waitresses all wore smart uniforms, the restaurant was carpeted throughout, and in every possible alcove and cranny the management had placed a palm plant in a round brass pot.

It was a more expensive place than Blackstone would usually have chosen to dine in—the economy-priced establishments run by Lyons and the Aerated Bread Company were usually good enough for him—but he'd argued to himself that after all the work Hannah had done for him, she deserved a real treat. Now, sitting across the table from her, he decided he'd made the right decision, because—dressed as she was—she would have looked out of place even in the fairly smart ABC.

She was wearing a blue patterned dress, with godets of contrasting, lighter coloured material down the sides. The dress had puff sleeves and a low neckline that revealed the beginnings of her firm bosom. Her hair gleamed, and she had artfully placed silk flowers in it. Blackstone could not imagine how any woman could ever be lovelier.

'One and threepence a pound,' the Russian woman said.

'I beg your pardon?'

'If you are thinking of buying me—which, from the way you have been so carefully examining my every flaw and failing, you must be—then I'll cost at least one and threepence a pound.'

Blackstone felt himself start to colour. 'I'm...I'm sorry,' he stuttered. 'I don't mean to stare.'

Hannah laughed. 'Don't worry about it, Sam,' she said. 'I am not one your typical English women who dress to attract—and then are completely scandalized when they catch someone looking at them. I am flattered when I see in a man's eyes that he wants me.'

I *do* want you, Blackstone thought. More than I can ever remember wanting a woman before.

The waitress arrived with the menus.

'What will you have?' the Inspector asked his guest.

Hannah laid her menu aside. 'I think 1 would rather prefer to leave the choice up to you.'

With the confident air of a man who knows his food, Blackstone ordered veal in a cream and mushroom sauce for both of them.

'Will you be having wine with your meal, sir?' the waitress asked.

Would they? He supposed so—but he had never ordered wine in his life, and had no idea what to choose.

'If you don't mind, I'd like to select the wine,' Hannah said.

'No, I don't mind at all,' Blackstone replied, fully aware that they both knew the Russian woman was rescuing him from an embarrassing situation.

When the waitress had left them, Blackstone said, 'Do you think that Count Turgenev is some kind of diplomat?'

Hannah laughed. She seemed to laugh a lot, Blackstone thought, but while the laughs sometimes seemed to have a bitter edge to them, this one was filled with genuine amusement.

'Have I said something funny?' he asked.

'You're always the policeman, aren't you?' Hannah replied. 'Here you are, out with a beautiful woman—and I am beautiful, aren't I?'

'Yes,' Blackstone said. 'You're beautiful.'

'Out with a beautiful woman, and all that you can think about is your detective work.'

Blackstone grinned ruefully. 'You're right,' he admitted. 'I just can't help it, I suppose.'

Hannah clucked in mock disapproval. 'Very well then. We will get the business out of the way now, so that after that we can converse like normal people. I know nothing of Count Turgenev but what I have seen with my own eyes. I know that he gambles heavily and is not assured enough of his own safety to walk the streets alone. Beyond that he is a mystery to me.' She paused. 'Can we talk about something else, now?'

'Of course,' Blackstone agreed, suddenly feeling awkward. 'What subject shall we choose?'

'Tell me about Afghanistan.'

Blackstone shook his head. 'There's nothing more boring than ex-soldiers recounting old hardships.'

'You misunderstand me,' Hannah told him. 'I want to know what you learned from it.'

'You mean, what I learned about the country?'

'No, not what you learned *of* it—what you learned *from* it. How it changed you as a man. If, that is, it did.'

'Oh, it did,' Blackstone said sincerely.

'Then tell me about that.'

'All right,' Blackstone agreed. 'But if it's going to make any sense, then first I'll have to tell you one of those war stories you'll find boring.'

'I'm sure it will be worth it in the end.'

'We were on the march from Kabul to Kandahar,' Blackstone said. 'General Roberts was forcing quite a pace—well, I suppose he had to, really, at least by his lights—and inevitably some people got sick and fell behind the main column. And once they did that, they were slaughtered by the Afghans who'd been hiding in the hills. This went on for a number of days, then a few of us fitter lads got permission to detach ourselves from the column and stay with the walking wounded. That way we could protect them, and they'd have a fair chance of catching up with the column once the general had called a halt for the day.'

Hannah smiled. 'Whose idea was that?'

'I think it might have been mine,' Blackstone confessed. 'Anyway, one day we came under attack from a bunch of Pathan bandits. It was all hand-to-hand fighting. Very messy. I'd just killed one of them, and I turned round to find that another one was standing on a rock a few yards away. He had his musket raised, and he was pointing it at me. The thing was, he was very slow and clumsy, and I knew there was a good chance I could shoot him before he shot me. But I didn't take my chance.'

'Why ever not?'

'Because he couldn't have been more than nine or ten years old.'

'Did he fire at you?'

'He didn't get the opportunity. One of my comrades picked him off.' Blackstone laughed, though without much humour. 'So, you see, it was a pretty empty gesture on my part.'

'I think it was a beautiful gesture,' Hannah said.

'That's when I realized I'd learned a lesson about myself,' Blackstone told her.

'And what lesson was that?'

'That I don't want to die, but there are things I simply will not do in order to stay alive.'

The waitress brought their food and they ate in companionable silence, savouring the rich sauce and the tender meat. Nor did they say very much over the sorbets that followed, either, and it was only when they were drinking their coffee that Hannah suddenly slammed down her cup and said, 'Damn!'

'What's the matter?' Blackstone asked.

'I think I'm catching Blackstone's Disease,' the Russian woman replied.

'Blackstone's Disease?'

'I'm starting to become as obsessed with this case as you are.'

She paused for a second. 'If I asked you a question about Charles Smith—assuming that's his real name—would you give me an honest answer to it?'

'I'd like to, but my instructions from the Commissioner are that—' Blackstone began.

'He's dead, isn't he?' Hannah interrupted.

'What makes you say that?'

'An important policeman like yourself would not be spending so much of your time on the case if he wasn't.'

'Perhaps I'm not quite as important as you seem to imagine,' Blackstone countered.

Hannah reached across the table and took his hand in hers. He felt a tingle run up his arm.

'I am willing to help you in any way I can, Sam, but you must be honest with me,' she said earnestly. 'We have to learn to trust each other.'

This was a test she was giving him, Blackstone realized, and if he failed it, she would walk out of his life for ever. Out of his investigation, he corrected himself. She would walk out of his *investigation* for ever.

'You're right in thinking that Charles Smith is no more than an alias,' he told the Russian woman, 'but however much you press me, I simply can't tell you what his real name was.'

'If you say that, I must accept that you have very good reasons,' Hannah said. 'But perhaps there is *something* about him you can tell me. You talk about him in the past tense. Does that mean that he *is* dead?'

Blackstone hesitated, then saw that in his very hesitation, he was telling what she wanted to know. 'Yes, Charles Smith is dead,' he said heavily.

'How did he die?'

There was no delicate way to phrase it. 'A few nights ago someone slit his throat and dumped his body in the river.'

Hannah shuddered. 'Poor Charles!'

'Were you very fond of him?' Blackstone asked, noticing that she was still holding his hand.

'Not *very* fond.' Hannah replied. 'He was nothing but a child when compared to you. But I *did* like him, and even if I hadn't, I don't like to think of anyone being killed in such a terrible way.' Another pause. 'You suspect Count Turgenev is behind the murder, don't you?'

'Yes, I do,' Blackstone admitted.

'Then he is much more than the degenerate aristocrat he appears to be. He is a very dangerous man—and you would be wise to tread warily.'

'Are you saying that you think I should stop asking questions about him?'

'That would certainly be a start.'

Blackstone shook his head. 'I can't do that. I've always followed any leads in an investigation I've conducted to their natural conclusion, and I'm too set in my ways to change now.'

'What is it you English say?' Hannah asked. '"There is no fool like an old fool"?'

Her words stung him more than he could have imagined they

would. But he was forced to acknowledge that she was right. Compared to her, he was old—and in pursuing Count Turgenev, he was probably a fool.

Hannah squeezed his hand. 'Don't look so downhearted,' she said in a soft, silky voice. 'There is something very appealing about an old fool.'

TWENTY-FOUR

Dusk was falling as Thaddeus Tompkins left the pawnbroker's shop where he worked and headed for his lodgings.

He was a far from happy man. The meeting with the detective that morning had made him very nervous, and the phone call that followed it had done nothing to allay his fear. Perhaps he should leave London, he thought. But to do that he would need money—and the only source of that was the man he would be running away from.

He felt a sudden chill run through his body. He looked around wildly. To his immediate right were the Royal Courts of Justice—the Old Bailey. To his left, just down Middle Temple Lane, were the Inns of Court. He was at the very heart of the British system of law and order, he reminded himself, so why should he be afraid? Besides, what had he done that was so wrong? Told one small lie! Said that a certain person had been to see him, when, in fact, that certain person hadn't! And even if he was scared of the man who had put him up to it, surely, having done the job properly, he no longer had anything to fear.

A four-wheeled cab that had been travelling down Fleet Street at a fair trot suddenly came to a stop next to him. The door swung open and a man's voice said, 'G'day, Mr Tompkins. Would you like to get in?'

The moment he heard the Australian accent, the pawnbroker's clerk was overwhelmed by a sense of dread.

'I'd...I'd prefer to walk, Mr Seymour,' he said.

'That's what I always told myself when *I* was poor,' the other man replied. 'Now I'm rich, I like to travel in style. So get in, Mr Tompkins. We have business to discuss—accounts to settle.'

'Send the money to the office,' Tompkins croaked.

The other man chuckled. 'That wouldn't be a very intelligent thing to do, now would it? Anyway, l don't just want to talk about our past dealings—I may have some new work for you.'

'I...I don't want to help you any more.'

'I wouldn't really think you'd got any choice in the matter,' the other man said, some of the geniality leeching out of his voice. 'Besides,' he added, his former jovial tone returning, 'what have you got to worry about, Cobber? Do you really think I intend to do you some harm? If I did, would I try it on right in the centre of your own city, with a London cabbie—the salt of the earth— as a witness? You must have a very low opinion of one of us if you can imagine that, Mr Tompkins.'

The pawnbroker's clerk licked his dry lips. 'I only wanted to clear my outstanding debts,' he said.

'Of course you did,' the man inside the cab agreed. 'Just as any honourable man would. But now I am giving you the opportunity not only to clear your debts, but to walk away from them with a substantial sum in your pocket. Get into the cab, Mr Tompkins.'

Slowly—reluctantly—the pawnbroker climbed into the cab. 'I'm no danger to you, you know,' he said, as he sat down.

'Course I know that, Mr Tompkins,' the other man said. 'Why don't you just sit back and relax?'

'Where are we going?'

'We're going to meet a man—a very influential man—who could make you rich, and me even richer than I am already,' Seymour said.

Then he knocked on the roof with his stick, and the Russian who was sitting behind the horse eased the animal forward.

*

Hannah told the driver of the hansom cab to stop midway down Commercial Road.

'So this is where you live,' Blackstone said when he'd paid the cabbie his fare.

'Why should you assume that?' Hannah asked.

'Because I can't see you walking far in that outfit,' Blackstone replied prosaically.

Hannah smiled. 'My parent's are very liberal, even by Russian standards,' she told him. 'But I doubt if even they would welcome a gentleman caller at this time of night.'

'Well, then?'

'I keep a small private apartment over the greengrocer's. I thought we would go up there for a nightcap.'

'Where's all this leading?' Blackstone asked.

'You English!' Hannah said. 'You must always think of the

future, rather than experiencing the present.'

'Don't you ever think of the future?'

'I had friends in Russia who were killed by a drunken mob,' Hannah said. 'I had other friends who were arrested by the Okhrana—'

'The *Okhrana?*'

'The Tsar's secret police. I don't know if you have no such thing in England, but in Russia they are everywhere.'

'I see,' Blackstone said. 'And you've had friends who were arrested by them.'

'And never seen again! That teaches one a valuable lesson. Of course you must think about the future. But you must also seize the gifts of the present, because you can never be sure for how long those gifts will he available to you.'

'Is that what I'm to see you as?' Blackstone asked. 'A gift? A toy to play with while I've got the chance?'

'Perhaps it could turn into more,' Hannah said. 'But for the moment, would it be so wrong to see the two of us as being gifts to *each other?*'

'You offered me a nightcap. What have you got to drink up there?' Blackstone asked.

'I can't remember,' Hannah said. 'Does it really matter?'

'No,' Blackstone admitted. 'It doesn't really matter.'

*

'Why are we crossing the river?' Thaddeus Tompkins asked

anxiously as the four-wheel cab made its way along London Bridge.

'To get to the other side?' his companion suggested, with a thin smile playing on his lips.

'You didn't say anything about crossing the river when I got into the cab,' Tompkins fretted.

'No, but I did tell you there was someone I needed you to meet. And that person is waiting for us in Bermondsey.'

'Who is he? What does he want?'

'He'll tell you that himself. Just be patient.'

The cab turned on to Tooley Street. Lights blazed in the pubs, and there were a few costermongers trying to sell the last of their stock before it rotted on their barrows, but other than that, the street was deserted.

'I don't like this,' Tompkins said weakly.

'No one cares *what* you like.'

The cab turned off Tooley Street, and made its way down a canyon between rows of tall warehouses. When it reached Cotton's Wharf, it came to a halt. Another cab was already parked there, and there were a number of lanterns glowing on a barge in the river.

'Get out,' the man sitting next to Tompkins said, as if he would be more than glad to see the last of him.

The clerk climbed down, and found himself facing a large man who seemed to emanate pure menace.

'We hired you to tell the police that Thomas Grey was a thief and a gambler,' the man said, with a slight foreign accent. 'You were supposed to convince them that his gambling was the reason Grey had disappeared.'

'I did just as I was told,' Tompkins whined.

'The policeman you talked to didn't believe you,' the other man said coldly. 'Or, if he did, his boss didn't believe *him.*'

'This morning, you were an asset to us—a rather poor one, but at least an asset. This evening, you are nothing but a liability.'

Tompkins had not heard the cab driver climb down from his seat, but now he felt the man's left arm clamp tight around his chest as the right hand dragged a razor across his throat. The pawnbroker's clerk gurgled, blew a bubble of blood from the gash—and died.

Another man appeared from out of the shadows, and helped the assassin to fling the body of the dead clerk into the waiting barge.

'You are to weigh him down, and throw him into the river,' Count Turgenev told the man on the barge. 'But you are not to do it until you are well away from London. I do not want there to be even the slightest chance of the police finding out about this until next Wednesday—after which it will not matter what they find. Do you understand?'

The man nodded. 'Yes, sir.'

Satisfied, the Count turned back to his bodyguards. 'We still have one more thing to do before our night's work is complete,' he said.

'Kill the policeman?' one of them asked.

'Exactly,' Turgenev agreed.

TWENTY-FIVE

That a single woman should choose to fill so much of the small room with such a large bed told Blackstone that he was not the first man Hannah had invited back to her apartment. Lying there naked, on that same bed, he tried to feel resentful over the fact—and found that he couldn't. The normal rules of conduct just did not apply to Hannah, he decided, and what would have cheapened other women only seemed to further proclaim her a free spirit.

She stirred slightly, next to him.

'Are you awake?' he asked softly.

'I've never been asleep.'

'You certainly *seemed* asleep.'

'When I have made love, I like to lie still and relive the experience over and over again. You will understand that when you know me better.'

Was she saying that this was just the beginning? he wondered.

'You will stay the night?' she asked.

He shook his head. 'I can't.'

'Because of your police work?'

'Because it would be a big step—a step which would raise my

hopes—and I'm not sure I'm brave enough to take it.'

Hannah laughed, but not cruelly. 'You're afraid you might fall in love with me?'

'I'm afraid I might have already.'

'And perhaps, if you stay, I might fall in love with you,' Hannah said, then, noting his reaction, she put her hand to her mouth in mock horror. 'Oh, I'm sorry. Was I supposed to say that I thought I had already fallen in love with *you*?'

'It would have been nice,' Blackstone said.

'There is nothing *nice* about love. Love is like a wild animal, which might snuggle up to you at one moment, yet the next might rip you apart with its claws. That is why it is so wonderful—because it is also so dangerous.' Hannah paused. 'What would you do if I said that if you left now, I would never see you again?'

'I'd go anyway,' Blackstone said firmly.

'Out of a misplaced sense of pride?'

'No. Because if I stayed, I would no longer be my own master.'

Hannah nodded seriously. 'You are a man of spirit, even if that spirit has been thoroughly soaked by your English drizzle. Go back to your lodgings if you must, Sam. I will see you in the morning.'

*

Blackstone descended the stairs from Hannah's small apartment and stepped out on to the street. He looked around for a cab, but since it was the only time of night when that part of London really slept—two hours after the pubs had shut their door to the late-night revellers, two and a half hours before they would open those doors again to the men who had to make an early start—there were none to be had. He didn't mind. For a man who had marched from Kabul to Kandahar, three or four miles of London streets—even after the most energetic lovemaking he could ever remember—was no problem. Besides, it would give him time to think.

He had gone less than a hundred yards when the conviction started to grow in him that something was seriously wrong. It was the shape in the doorway that first alerted him—the obviously *human* shape. Why would a man—by nature a creature drawn to the light almost as strongly as any moth—choose to position himself at a point equidistant from the two nearest gas lamps? Unless, of course, he wanted to remain concealed for as long as possible!

Nor was the man ahead the only problem. He could hear at least two sets of footsteps behind him—soft, slithering footsteps. He knew what caused the slithering sound. The men who were following him stuck strips of rubber to the soles of their boots— just as police constables did in order not to wake up residents when they were on night patrol in middle-class areas. But when he glanced over his shoulder, he saw no reassuring pointed helmets.

Blackstone came to a sudden halt, and, half a second later, so did the men behind him.

'I'm a police officer,' he said in a loud voice. 'Harm me, and you'll have the full force of the law coming down on you.'

One of the men behind him gave a dry throaty chuckle.

Blackstone's blood ran cold as he realized the three men already knew exactly who he was—and had been waiting to get him in just this situation.

Three against one were not good odds, especially since he had no weapon and they almost definitely did. His feverish brain working at double speed, he ran through his options. He could try to escape, but they had sprung their trap so well that he knew he would never make it. He could stay where he was, and wait for them to come to him—but that would only be giving all three of them the chance to attack him at the same time. So clearly, there was only one course of action he *could* take.

Drawing a deep breath, he broke into a run towards the man who was waiting ahead him. Yet even as he felt his feet pounding the cobblestones, he knew that he was making no more than a pointless gesture.

The man in the doorway stepped out to block the pavement, and from the stance he adopted it was obvious that he was holding a knife in his hand. The two men behind had already broken into a sprint to match Blackstone's. In a minute or so it would be all over, the Inspector thought. In a minute or so, he would have no more life in him than Charles Montcliffe had.

He could see himself stretched out on the coroner's slab, a subject of morbid curiosity—or perhaps revulsion—for the twelve men who would consider the evidence, and rule that he had been murdered by a person or persons unknown.

Enough of that! he ordered himself. Stick to the matter in hand! If they're going to finish you off, at least don't let them do it without a fight!

The man ahead of him was making slashing motions through the air with his knife, but Blackstone did not slacken his pace. He was five yards from the man. Then three. Then two. He was a yard and a half away when he pulled up short and lashed out with his right leg.

He felt the toe of his boot connect with his enemy's groin and heard the other man's agonized grunt as the air was forced out of him. The man fell forward, but instead of just collapsing in a useless heap as he was supposed to, he grabbed Blackstone's leg as he went down, so that both of them ended up sprawling on the ground.

It did not take the Inspector long to break free from his injured opponent's grip, but it took him longer than he could afford—and he was only half-way back to his feet when a heavy boot slammed into his chest.

Blackstone went down again, and this time—he was sure — it would be for ever. So this was how it ended. After surviving the Afghan campaign, after tracking down some of the most dangerous criminals in London, he was about to be slaughtered like a pig on the street.

A pair of powerful hands pinned his shoulders to the ground. He lashed out with his legs, but it did no good. He could see a man standing over him, the razor in his hand glinting against the light of the nearest gas lamp. Well, he thought, at least with professionals like these, it would be a quick death.

There had been four of them there, enacting this little drama, but suddenly there were seven. The new men moved with speed and assurance, two of them creating a human shield between Blackstone and the man with the razor, the third tackling the man who was pinning the Inspector down. It could scarcely have been called a fight at all—the rescuers arrived on the scene, the attackers took to their heels and fled.

One of the rescuers knelt down next to Blackstone. 'Will you be all right?' he asked.

Blackstone nodded—then, as pain coursed through his body, wished he hadn't. 'I'll be fine,' he gasped.

'What do you intend to do with *him*?' the rescuer asked, pointing to the man Blackstone had kicked in the groin, and who was still lying on the ground, groaning.

'I intend to arrest him.'

'Do you need any help?'

Blackstone painfully raised himself on one elbow. 'No,' he said. 'I'll be back on my feet before he will—and I've got a set of handcuffs.'

'Good,' the other man said.

He turned to his companions, and spoke to them rapidly in a language that, from his recent experience, Blackstone was almost certain was Russian. The two men disappeared down the alley from which they'd so recently emerged.

'You will have our protection until you leave Little Russia,' the rescuer said. 'You will not see us, but we will be there.'

'Who are you?' Blackstone asked. 'Why are you helping?'

'You already know who had Charles Montcliffe killed,' the other man said. 'Now what you have to find out is *why.*'

And then he was gone, swallowed up by the darkness of the alley.

Blackstone climbed painfully to his feet. He had not got a really clear look at the man who had saved his life, but he hadn't needed to, because he had seen him before—twice on the night he had gone to the fight with Hannah, and once again when he had visited the Russian Library.

*

Sergeant Patterson stifled a yawn, then took a gulp of strong coffee from his enamel mug. An hour earlier, he had been sleeping peacefully in his bed, and now he was back at the Yard, in the company of his chief and the man who had tried to kill him.

He looked at the Russian, who was handcuffed to a sturdy chair. The man's face showed neither fear nor anger. Instead, he appeared to have accepted what had befallen him with complete indifference.

Patterson glanced across at the window, where his boss was standing, looking out over the Thames. Given the attack on him, Blackstone should have been a mass of ragged nerves, yet he seemed strangely calm. Perhaps that was his military training. But his training didn't explain away the other changes in the Inspector. Patterson had never seen him look quite as he did at that moment—and it suddenly occurred to the sergeant that, for the first time in their partnership, his superior was *happy.*

Blackstone turned and caught Patterson staring at him. He coughed embarrassedly, the mantle of happiness fell from him, and he was hard-bitten police officer once more.

The Inspector walked over to the Russian. 'This is nothing but a complete waste of time,' he said. 'You'll tell us what we want to know eventually, so why not come clean now?'

The prisoner continued to stare straight ahead, as if Blackstone had not spoken.

'In this country, you can be hanged for the attempted murder of a policeman,' Blackstone told him. 'Do you want to hang?'

Still the Russian said nothing.

Blackstone walked over to his desk and sat down. 'I've had enough of him for one night,' he said to Patterson. 'Get one of the uniformed lads to take him down to the holding cells, will you, Sergeant?'

'When I've done that, can I go home for a couple of hours?' the sergeant asked hopefully.

'I'm afraid not,' Blackstone told him. 'I've got another little job I need you to do for me.'

'What's that, sir?'

'Since we seem to he getting nowhere with the monkey,' Blackstone said, looking across at his prisoner, 'I think it's about time we had a word with the organ grinder.'

PART THREE

SOUTHWARK STREET

TWENTY-SIX

It was a quarter to six in the morning, and already much of the city was wide awake. Scarlet mail vans dashed down the road, heading for Liverpool Street Station and the early trains. Milk carts were already returning from the same station, and as the horses' hooves clip-clopped against the cobblestones, the metal churns on the backs of the carts banged furiously together.

Blue and yellow trams carried workmen from south of the river to the more prosperous areas further north. The butchers' and greengrocers' shops were already open. All-night coffee stalls were still serving their cheap, almost tasteless brew, though they were losing most of their trade now that the pubs had opened their doors. The loafers were out in force; the beggars had taken up their favourite positions. And a police van—a Black Maria, as most people called it—was just entering Little Russia.

The Black Maria came to a halt in front of one of the more prosperous houses. Three men got out, two uniformed constables and a detective sergeant.

It was Patterson who knocked loudly on the front door, then knelt down to shout, 'Police! Open up!' through the letterbox.

It took perhaps two minutes of constant hammering before the door was opened by a broad young man still dressed in his nightshift.

'*Da?*' he said sleepily.

'I want to see Count Turgenev,' Patterson said. He held out a piece of paper in front of him. 'I have a warrant here for the Count's arrest.'

The other man shrugged indifferently. '*Niet gabaresh pa-inglesi.*'

'The Count!' Patterson said, raising his voice. 'I have a warrant here for his arrest.'

The Russian looked at him blankly.

'We have to come inside,' Patterson said.

He took a step forward, but the second he'd begun to move, the sleep disappeared from the Russian's eyes, and now he shifted so that he was blocking the doorway.

'We have to come in,' Patterson said exasperatedly. 'If you try to stop us, you'll be taken into custody.'

'Can I be of some assistance, officer?' said a rich baritone voice from the hallway.

On hearing the voice, the Russian in the nightshift immediately stepped aside, and Patterson was able to see a very tall man in a silk dressing gown standing at the foot of the stairs.

'I'm looking for Count Ivan Turgenev,' the sergeant said.

'You have found him. It is I. What seems to be the problem?'

'As I've just explained to your manservant here, I have a warrant for your arrest.'

If the Count was in any way shocked by the news, his face

certainly did not show it. 'On what charge am I to be arrested?' he asked.

'The attempted murder of a senior police officer.'

'That would be the intrepid Inspector Blackstone,' the Count said.

'You admit it?' Patterson gasped. 'Just like that?'

'I admit nothing,' the Count replied. 'Since I am suspected, I assume the attack took place somewhere near here, and the only senior policeman who has appeared in the area recently has been Blackstone. It is a simple matter for anyone with a brain to put the two things together.'

'I'd like you to come along quietly, sir,' Patterson said.

'I will give you no trouble,' the Count promised. 'Though I would appreciate it if you would give me a few minutes to get dressed.'

'Of course. But you'll have to have one of my men with you at all times,' Patterson said.

'While I do my toilet? Certainly not. He can wait outside my dressing room door.'

Patterson shook his head. 'I'm afraid that won't do, sir.'

The Count fixed him with hard blue eyes, which felt to the sergeant as if they could burn their way through a glacier.

'It is as below my dignity to attempt to escape through a window as it would be for me to dress under the gaze of a common policeman,' the Russian said. 'Your man can wait outside. Are we agreed on that?'

And almost as if someone else were working his mouth,

Patterson heard himself say, 'Yes, sir. We're agreed on that.'
*

Blackstone looked across the table in the interview room at Count Turgenev, and reflected on the strange fact that though the Russian had become central to his inquiry, the two of them had not—until now—exchanged a single word.

'Why haven't you objected to being dragged out of your bed at an ungodly hour of the morning?' the Inspector asked.

Turgenev shrugged. 'Your sergeant produced what he said was a magistrate's warrant. There seemed to be no point in arguing.'

'But you'd have argued if the same thing had happened to you in Russia, wouldn't you?'

A thin smile came to the Count's lips. 'In Russia, it would *not* have happened. In Russia, I could have killed one of my *muhziks* in front of a thousand witnesses, and everyone would have pretended that the murder had never occurred.'

'So you're admitting that you tried to kill me?'

'There is nothing in what I have said which could lead you to draw such a conclusion.'

He was a cool bastard, Blackstone thought. Nine out of ten men in his position—and probably nine hundred and ninety-nine out of a thousand aristocrats—would have been expressing their complete outrage at being dragged to Scotland Yard. Yet the Russian count was choosing to treat the whole situation as nothing more than an amusing incident.

'Three men tried to kill me last night,' the Inspector said.

'I am sure that is very important to you, but why should it be of any interest to me?'

'We have one of them in the cells. He's a Russian. According to his papers, his name is Boris Kamanev.'

'You still fail to engage my curiosity.'

'I still fail to engage your curiosity, do I?' Blackstone demanded. 'Despite the fact that you know him? Despite the fact that he just happens to be one of your bodyguards?'

Turgenev laughed. 'One of my bodyguards?' he repeated. 'I don't have any bodyguards.'

'Then who are those hard, watchful men who seem to go everywhere with you?'

'Ah, you are referring to my personal attendants.'

'And is it just a coincidence that one of your *personal attendants* took part in the attack on me?'

'Are you suggesting that Boris has implicated me in the attack?'

'I'm not prepared to disclose exactly what Kamanev has told me under interrogation. But let's just say that I found it very interesting indeed.'

The Count laughed again. 'Never bluff when you have an absolutely bust hand, Inspector. Boris has told you *nothing*— and, whatever you threaten him with, he will continue to tell you nothing.'

'Most men will say almost anything to ensure their own survival,' Blackstone countered. 'They'll even sell their own mothers down the river if they believe it will reduce their own punishment a little. How can you be so sure that Boris Kamanev has not sold *you* down the river?'

'There is nothing you could subject Boris to that would be anything like as harsh as conditions he has already endured without complaint. I remember he was once taken prisoner by tribesmen in Af—'

He stopped, as if he had suddenly realized that in boasting about the loyalty of his man he was giving too much away.

'In Afghanistan,' Blackstone supplied. 'You were about to say he was taken prisoner by tribesmen in Afghanistan.'

'Perhaps I was,' the Count agreed. 'What of it?'

'And since he was probably working for you at the time, that means that you were in Afghanistan, too.'

The Count shrugged, unconcernedly. 'Over the years, I have visited many distant places.'

'But why *were* you in Afghanistan?' Blackstone pressed. 'Were you on *official* business?'

Turgenev shook his head. 'I am too rich—and far too easily bored—to have ever entered government service.'

The Count took a flat tin out of his pocket, extracted a long black cigarette, and lit it up.

'It is thought that it was in Afghanistan that the Mongols invented polo,' he said. 'But it wasn't played in quite the same way as it is now. Instead of a ball, they used a live—bound—prisoner, who they would pick up and hoist across their saddles. The other players would then attempt to pull him away. The prisoner rarely survived the game.'

'I'm sure some people would find that fascinating,' Blackstone said, 'but I don't see what it's got to do with—'

'You asked me what I was doing in Afghanistan, and I am telling you,' the Count interrupted. 'The modern version of the game, which the natives call *buzkhazi*, uses a headless calf soaked in brine instead of a prisoner, but it is still a ferocious sport in which both rider and mount must be ruthless to succeed. I happen to be a keen polo player, so that is why I went there—to buy myself a string of ponies.'

'I don't believe you,' Blackstone said.

'You must believe or disbelieve as you like, but I *am* interested to know why you refuse to accept a perfectly truthful story.'

'Polo is a civilized game,' Blackstone said. It has strict rules and well-disciplined horses.'

'The ponies I bought in Afghanistan *were* well-disciplined,' Turgenev told him. 'But they were not formally disciplined, as are the horses available in Europe. My Afghans reduced all the other mounts on the field to nervous wrecks in a matter of minutes.' He paused. 'Do you understand what I'm telling you, Inspector?'

Yes, I do, Blackstone thought. You're telling me that you play hard and you play unfairly, and that if I have any sense at all, I'll take the lesson of last night's murder attempt to heart and get away from London as quickly as I can.

'Do you know any of the Montcliffe family?' he asked.

'I move in all sorts of social circles and know all manner of men,' the Count replied.

'You haven't answered my question.'

'I believe that I have met Earl Montcliffe on one or two occasions. Perhaps even as many as three.'

'What the hell does that mean—you met him?' Blackstone demanded. 'Did you dine with him? Did you go shooting together?'

The Count shook his head. 'Nothing like that. We met at functions. I don't suppose we exchanged more than a few words, but even such a slight exchange was enough to tell me that he is what you English would call "a complete bloody fool".'

'If he's a bloody fool, why does he have such a key role in the Jubilee celebrations?' Blackstone wondered aloud.

'He is a bloody fool from a noble family. That is usually enough to bring a man to eminence in most of Europe.'

'But not in Russia?'

'Most certainly in Russia. Our own Tsar would make a very good English lord.'

Did this man believe in *nothing*? Blackstone asked himself. Or was all this an elaborate act?

'What about Hugo Montcliffe?' he asked, staring straight into the Count's eyes. 'Have you met *him* at functions?'

'No,' the Russian said, blinking slightly.

'But you have met him somewhere,' Blackstone persisted.

For a moment, it looked as if Turgenev was about to tell him to go to hell, then the Count said, 'I came across him a few years ago—in Australia.'

'What were you doing there?'

The smile returned to Turgenev's lips. 'I had never shot a kangaroo before,' he said.

'And what was your impression of the Viscount?'

'That not only was he as stupid as his father, but he had some rather distasteful habits.'

'What kind of habits?'

The smile was still in place. 'One gentleman does not discuss another gentleman's habits with a social inferior.'

At least half of what the Russian said was a calculated attempt to taunt him, Blackstone realized—to make him so angry that he lost control of the situation. Well, it wasn't going to work.

'There is one member of the family we still haven't discussed,' he said.

'Is there?'

'You know there is. What can you tell me about Charles Montcliffe?'

'Who is he?'

'The Earl's youngest son.'

'I don't believe I've ever met him.'

'That's strange—because Charles seems to have been spending a great deal of his time in Little Russia.'

'Perhaps so,' Turgenev said, almost lazily, 'but as far as I know, our paths never crossed.'

He was so sure of himself he wasn't even bothering to make his lies sound sincere, Blackstone thought.

'Why are you in London, Count Turgenev?' he asked.

'I am in London for much the same reason as I have visited many other places—because it amuses me to be here.'

The door suddenly flew open, and standing in the gap was a furious-looking Commissioner of Police.

It was a bad sign that he'd come personally, Blackstone thought. A very bad sign.

'I want to talk to you, Blackstone,' the Commissioner shouted. 'Out here! Right now!'

As he rose to his feet, the Inspector noticed the smirk that had formed on the Russian's lips.

I'll have you, you bastard! he promised silently. Whatever it takes, I'll have you.

There would normally be a number of officers walking along the corridor at that time of day, but apart from the Commissioner— whose rage seemed to have grown ever more intense since he'd ordered Blackstone out—it was completely deserted.

People always keep clear when the shit's about to fly, Blackstone thought. He supposed he couldn't blame them.

'I don't know what idiot of a magistrate you got to sign that arrest warrant for you,' the Commissioner said, 'but when I find out who he is, I'll have his balls on a plate!'

'The magistrate was only doing his duty,' Blackstone told him. 'There is strong evidence to link—'

'I don't give a damn about any evidence—strong or otherwise. I've had both the Home Secretary and Earl Montcliffe on the phone to me within the last fifteen minutes. They're furious.'

'Why should Montcliffe be furious? Doesn't he want me to solve his son's murder?'

'Well, of course he bloody does, you damn fool! But not at the expense of causing a diplomatic crisis. Do you know how important the Count's family is in Russia?'

'No, I don't,' Blackstone admitted. 'It didn't seem at all relevant to my inquiries.'

'A count is the equivalent of an English earl,' the Commissioner told him. 'And you wouldn't think of arresting an earl, would you?'

Oh yes, I would, Blackstone thought. If I could prove that Earl Montcliffe or his son had anything to do with Charles' death, I'd have them behind bars before you could say 'landed gentry'.

'Do you know what I'm going to have to do now?' the Commissioner demanded. 'I'm going to have to go into that room and apologize on behalf of the Metropolitan Police and the British government. I'm going to have to humble myself—and I don't like doing that.'

'What about me?' Blackstone asked.

'You?' the Commissioner said.

'Do you expect me to apologize to Count Turgenev, too—because I won't do it.'

The Commissioner looked at him as if he were a madman. 'No, I don't expect you to apologize, Blackstone—because your apologies aren't worth anything any more.'

Blackstone felt his stomach turn over. 'What do you mean by that, sir?' he asked.

'As of this moment, you're suspended from the Force,' the Commissioner said. 'But that's only a temporary state of affairs—as soon as we can convene a board of inquiry, you'll be kicked off it completely!'

TWENTY-SEVEN

Positioned on Park Lane, just opposite the Montcliffe mansion, Blackstone felt as if he were standing knee-deep in the shattered remains of his own career.

He had been fired! He had lost the only job he'd had since the Army—the only job he'd ever really cared to do. What was left for him now but casual labouring on a building site or down at the docks? What was there to look forward to but ending up in the workhouse—with two meals of gruel and bread a day, and the time between them spent unpicking oakum?

He had been fired! Not because he had been doing his job badly—but because he had been doing it too well. It seemed inconceivable to the Commissioner that aristocrats could ever commit a crime, yet a study of their ancestors would reveal a long line of robbers and murderers.

Well, he wasn't going to take it lying down. He might have lost his position on the Force, but that didn't mean he couldn't see this investigation through to the bitter end.

He glanced across at the steps that led down to the servants' entrance of the house. If he knocked on it now, they would refuse to let him in, but if he waited until one of the tradesmen arrived and followed him down, then the door would already be open.

And the butler would be there! Hoskins would be there because it was his job to see that none of the staff told the visitor about Charles Montcliffe's mysterious disappearance—his job to protect the Family from outside influences, to insulate them in their own world of certainties.

A butcher's wagon rattled down the street and came to a halt in front of the mansion. The driver's mate dismounted, walked around to the back of the van and took out a large side of meat wrapped in sacking. Blackstone waited until the man had disappeared down the steps, then rapidly crossed the road.

The driver's mate had stepped through the door when Blackstone pushed him roughly to one side and grabbed the butler by the lapels of his jacket.

'We need to talk,' he said.

''Ere, what's goin' on?' the deliveryman demanded. 'Police business!' Blackstone told him. 'Put down that meat and clear off—or you'll be in big trouble.'

'Mr 'Oskins...?' the driver's mate appealed.

'Do as you're told,' the butler said calmly. 'Nothing's going to happen here that I can't handle myself.'

The deliveryman shrugged, propped the side of meat against the wall and headed back up the stairs.

The butler looked down at Blackstone's hands. 'I don't like being manhandled,' he said.

'And I don't like being buggered about,' Blackstone told him.

'I've got some questions, and I want them answering.'

'With the Earl's permission—'

'To hell with the Earl,' Blackstone said, tightening his grip on the butler's lapels. 'His son's been murdered! You know that, don't you?'

'For God's sake keep your voice down!' the butler hissed. 'Yes, the Family has shown the confidence I'm held in by telling me of Master Charles' fate. But the rest of the servants do not—and must not—know.'

'And have they also told you about that bastard Hugo?'

'The Viscount?' Hoskins asked, sounding genuinely surprised. 'What do you know about the Viscount?'

'That he didn't want Thomas Grey found. And the reason he didn't want him found is because Thomas knows exactly what part Hugo played in his brother's murder.'

Hoskins shook his head. 'You don't understand the situation at all,' he said. 'If you'll release me, we can go to my parlour, and I'll explain everything in civilized surroundings.'

The butler's parlour was furnished with articles considered no longer good enough to be above stairs, but it was still far more luxurious than anything a police inspector would ever be able to afford, Blackstone thought.

Would have been able to afford, he reminded himself. Now that he'd lost his job, he could afford *nothing*.

The butler poured them both a glass of port wine, and took a seat opposite Blackstone.

'Why do you think the Viscount was involved in his brother's death?' he asked.

'A few days before Charles Montcliffe died, he and Hugo had a fight and Hugo gave his brother a black eye. You're not going to deny that, are you?'

'No,' Hoskins said quietly. 'I'm not going to deny it.'

'Then after Charles died, I came up with a plan to find Thomas. Lord Dalton put it to the family. Hugo vigorously opposed it, and then—when it was plain that the Earl would give his consent—he leaked the details to his friends outside.'

'What are you talking about?' the butler asked. 'Which friends?'

'Friends he first met in Australia. And what's happening now is that there's a conspiracy afoot to protect the heir to the precious Montcliffe title at whatever the cost—a conspiracy that you're probably a part of. But it won't work! If it's the last thing I do, I'll see Hugo Montcliffe swings for his brother's murder.'

The butler shook his head, almost pityingly. 'You've got it all wrong, Mr Blackstone.'

'So put me right.'

'Very well,' the butler agreed. 'But I must be allowed to explain things in my own way.'

'All right.'

'As butler to this household, it is my duty to protect the Family from any unpleasantness—' Hoskins began.

'Get on with it,' Blackstone said impatiently.

'Part of my job is to ensure that the Family are not exploited by any of their servants. But I also have a responsibility to my staff. I must ensure that they, too, are not exploited—either by each other or...' he lowered his voice, '...or by anyone from above stairs.'

'Are you saying—'

'There have been times during my buttling career when a pretty parlour maid has caught the eye of the master I was serving, or—more often—one of his sons. I have always seen it as my job to ensure that such an attraction is not allowed to develop into a situation.'

'How've you managed that?' Blackstone asked.

'Oh, there are ways,' the butler said. 'A raised eyebrow. A subtle word. They soon come to understand that to cross the forbidden line will be degrading both to the girl and to themselves.' He permitted himself a ghost of a smile. 'The upper orders are not *always* as stupid and insensitive as you seem to think they are, Inspector.'

'How does Hugo fit into this? Are you saying that he was attracted to one of the servants?'

'Yes.'

'Was it Molly?'

'No,' the butler said softly. 'Regretfully, I have to tell you that it was Thomas who had caught his eye.'

What was it Turgenev had said about Hugo? Blackstone asked himself.

That not only was the Viscount as stupid as his father, but he also had some distasteful habits!

'You're telling me the Viscount is a sodomite?' he asked the butler.

'I would not put it in quite such stark terms,' Mr Hoskins replied, 'but I have to admit that the Viscount did become obsessed with Thomas. He would find excuses to be alone with his brother's valet, and would brush his body up against the poor man. It soon became plain to me that nothing I could do or say would stop him, and the situation could only get worse.' The butler sighed heavily. 'And so I was forced to do something I have never had to do before in all my years of buttling. I asked a member of the Family to intervene on Thomas's behalf.'

'Charles!' Blackstone said.

'Master Charles,' the butler agreed. 'He was outraged when I told him what was going on. He had a fierce argument with his brother, and the Viscount, who has always found it easier to think with his body than with his mind, knocked him down. So you see, there is no dark conspiracy to protect a murderer. Thomas did not run away because he knew who had killed his master—he did it to escape the unwanted attentions of his master's brother. And the reason the Viscount does not want Thomas found is because he is afraid of the scandal that might create.'

*

As Blackstone made his way slowly up the servants' steps on legs that felt as if they were made of lead, his mind was in turmoil. He had been so sure—so very sure—that while it would not be easy to prove his case, he at least had a case to prove. Hoskins had put an end to all that. The butler was probably wrong when he said that the only reason Thomas had fled the house was to escape the attentions of Viscount Montcliffe. The valet *had* to have known something about the story Charles was working on, or Turgenev would never have made such elaborate efforts to track him down. But the butler had probably been *right* when he'd claimed that the reason Hugo did not want Thomas found was because of the potential for scandal.

So where did that leave the investigation? A prime suspect had been eliminated—a suspect Blackstone had intended to use as the key to open the whole can of worms. And without that lead, where could he go next? He no longer had the resources of Scotland Yard at his disposal. He didn't even have the authority to question suspects any more. He did not want to give up—but he simply didn't see what else he could do.

He was dimly aware of the sound of horses' hoofs, and of the coach, bearing the Montcliffe family crest, pulling up beside him. He found himself watching—without much real interest—as the coachman opened the door and Lady Emily climbed out.

'Inspector Blackstone!' she said. 'I've been to Scotland Yard to look for you, but they said you'd been suspended.'

'And so I have,' Blackstone agreed. 'The Home Secretary and your father joined forces to see to that.'

A shocked look came to Lady Emily's face.

'But that's terrible! Apart from William and myself, you seem to be the only person interested in finding out who killed Charles.'

A question suddenly appeared, unbidden, in Blackstone's mind. It shocked him to find it there. It was not the kind of question he would have come up with before his night of passion with Hannah, he recognized. And it was not the kind of question he should be putting to someone like Lady Emily. Yet, he badly wanted to know the answer.

'Do you love Lord Dalton?' he asked.

Lady Emily looked down at the pavement. 'William is the kindest and most considerate of men,' she said.

'We both know that's no answer,' Blackstone said softly.

Lady Emily lifted her head again, and looked him in the eye. 'The most important word in my family is not "love",' she said. 'It is "duty". Duty to the Crown—and duty to the Montcliffe name. That is why two of my brothers are serving with Her Majesty's forces overseas, and why I...and why I...'

'Why you're marrying Lord Dalton?' Blackstone supplied. 'Out of duty to the family?'

'I will learn to love William over time,' Lady Emily said determinedly. She reached into her bag. 'I almost forgot,' she continued. 'The reason I went to see you at Scotland Yard was that I have something to give you.'

She produced a crumpled piece of paper and handed it to him. On it, written in a handwriting that looked very like Charles Montcliffe's, were a few hastily scribbled notes.

Empire Livings Pictures, 37 Fenchurch Street: are they involved?
Pro: Why has Turgenev told 'Seymour' to give them money if they're not?
Anti: Don't see how they fit into the scheme.
Need to talk to someone else. William? The Police?

'Where did you find this?' Blackstone asked.

'In Charles' room. I...I go there sometimes. I find it a comfort. The last time I was there, I walked over to the fireplace. I don't know why. The fire was laid, though, of course, it hasn't been lit for months. I noticed that amongst all the pieces of balled-up newspaper, there was one sheet which was plain. It was this note that Charles had written to himself. What does it mean? What are living pictures?'

'It's the latest novelty,' Blackstone said. 'They flash thousands of pictures, each one slightly different from the one which preceded it, on to a screen. It gives the impression of movement.'

And Charles Montcliffe had suspected that this particular living picture company was involved in a plot with Turgenev—had believed it so strongly, in fact, that he had been considering taking his suspicions to either Dalton or the police. It would have been a wise move to have done just that, Blackstone thought, and if he'd followed it through, he might still be alive.

'Is it of any use to you?' Lady Emily asked anxiously.

'I don't know,' Blackstone admitted.

But already the fires of hope—fires that had been all but extinguished a few minutes earlier—were burning brightly again.

TWENTY-EIGHT

In many ways, it could have been any normal weekday morning on Southwark Street. Trams, carrying their penny passengers, were rattling up and down the road as they always did. Wharfingers in frock coats scurried self-importantly along the pavements with wads of shipping manifests tucked under their arms. A bill-sticker was pasting an advertisement for the latest show at the New Savoy on to a convenient wall. A beer boy was weaving his way in and out of the stream of foot traffic and using the pole from which his cans of beer hung as an encouragement to other pedestrians to clear a way for him. Yet there was also a new excitement in the air—an excitement born out of the fact that the Queen, who had probably never even been to the East End before, would soon be passing—in state—along this very street.

The preparations for her procession were well underway. Line after line of brightly coloured bunting had been strung across the road, photographs of Her Majesty were on display in every window—and two young men in worn suits watched anxiously as a gang of workmen erected wooden scaffolding in front of a second-hand clothes shop.

Blackstone tapped one of the two young men on the shoulder. 'I'm looking for the owners of the Empire Living Picture Company,' he said. 'The girl at the office said I'd find them here.'

The men turned to face him. 'I'm Mr Dobkins,' said the shorter, stockier of the two, 'and this—' indicating his tall thin companion—'is Mr Wottle. And who are you?'

'Police,' Blackstone said.

Wottle, who had a naturally pale complexion, went even whiter. 'We've got written permission from the council to put the platform up,' he said. 'I can show it to you, if you like.'

'That won't be necessary, sir,' Blackstone told him. He looked up at the scaffolding. 'So that's where you'll have your camera, is it?'

'Our *two* cameras,' Dobkins said, his tone somehow suggesting that he felt slighted by Blackstone thinking they'd use only one. 'This is going to be the greatest living picture ever filmed.'

'Expect to make a lot of money out of it, do you?' Blackstone asked.

'We expect to make a fortune,' Dobkins replied, the aggression still in his voice.

'There are millions of people flocking into London for the Jubilee,' Wottle said, 'but there are many millions more who *can't* come, and they'll want to see it as much as everybody else does.'

'We'll be able to sell the living pictures to every music hall in the entire country,' Dobkins said. 'Anyway, what can we do for you?' he continued, ostentatiously checking his pocket watch. 'Please be brief and to the point, because—as you can see—we're very busy men.'

'I'd like to know if either of you have ever had any dealings with a journalist called Charles Smith,' Blackstone said.

'We've talked to him,' Wottle admitted.

'Where?'

'He came to our office.'

'How long ago?'

'I think it was a week yesterday.'

'And what did he want?'

'He *said* he was interested in writing a piece on living pictures,' Wottle replied.

'But that was a complete bloody lie!' Dobkins added. 'He had no real interest in them at all. When I was explaining to him how they are going to change the world, I don't think he was even listening.'

The manager of the Ghetto Bank had said pretty much the same about Charles Montcliffe's lack of interest in what *he* considered to be the big story, Blackstone thought. Charles Montcliffe might have been good at collecting facts, but he'd certainly had no idea of how to handle people.

'So if he wasn't interested in living pictures, what was he interested in?' the Inspector asked.

'He wanted to know what dealings we'd had with some Russian chap,' Dobkins said.

'I think his name was Count Turgulev—or something like that, anyway,' Wottle added.

'And what did you tell him?'

'The truth,' Wottle said. 'That we've had no dealings at all with any Russian, let alone with a count.'

'Did he seem happy with your answer?'

Dobkins snorted. 'Far from it. He had the impertinence to question us further. Asked if we had a partner.'

'And what did you tell him?'

'I told him exactly what I'll tell you—that whether we have a partner or not is no one's business but our own.'

'I could *make* it my business,' Blackstone said. He reached out for one of the scaffolding poles, and shook it. 'Now that doesn't seem very stable to me. I think there's a real danger it might fall down and hurt somebody. Maybe I'd better have a word with the local coppers about it.'

'We *do* have a partner,' Wottle said hurriedly. 'His name is Mr Seymour.'

Are they involved? Charles Montcliffe had scribbled down on his piece of paper. *Pro: Why has Turgenev told 'Seymour' to give them money if they're not?*

'Tell me more about this Mr Seymour of yours,' Blackstone said.

'He's filthy rich, but he'll never be a gentleman,' Dobkins replied.

'He can he a little blunt and direct,' Wottle explained, 'but I expect that comes from being Australian.'

'How long has he been your partner?'

'He first came to see us a few wee—' Wottle began.

'Why should that possibly interest you?' Dobkins interrupted.

Because it had interested *Charles Montcliffe*, Blackstone thought.

But aloud, he said, 'It would be a real pity if that scaffolding *did* have to come down, now wouldn't it?'

The two young men exchanged questioning glances, and then Dobkins gave Wottle a reluctant nod.

'Mr Seymour came to see us a few weeks ago,' Wottle told Blackstone. 'He said that he'd had a very good idea, but he didn't have the technical skill to see it through himself.'

'And what was this good idea of his?'

Wottle pointed to the scaffolding. 'This. Making a living picture of the Jubilee procession.'

'I see,' Blackstone said. 'But what I don't understand is why, once he'd told you his idea, you needed to take him on as a partner.'

'He had money and we didn't,' said Wottle ruefully.

'You were in debt?'

'Up to our necks. It wasn't just that we owed rent on the office. We'd fallen behind on the payments for the equipment. Another couple of days, and we'd have lost everything.'

'So he paid off your bills for you in return for a share of the profits of this living picture?'

'That's right,' Wottle agreed.

'What percentage is he actually getting?'

'Twenty!' said Dobkins, who seemed to have the ability to make even a simple answer seem like an act of defiance.

'And how much would you have given him if he'd pushed you?' Blackstone wondered.

'Twenty percent was very fair,' Dobkins said.

'We'd have given him fifty percent,' Wottle said candidly.

'Perhaps even more.'

'Can you give me an address for this Mr Seymour of yours?' Blackstone asked.

The two young men looked blankly at him.

'No, I'm afraid we can't,' Wottle confessed.

'But you must have been to his office, surely.'

'He always comes to ours.'

Blackstone sighed. 'All right, I'll have to find him the hard way,' he said. 'Give me either the name of the solicitor who drew up the deeds of partnership or the name of Seymour's bank.'

'There were no deeds of partnership,' Wottle told him. 'Mr Seymour was quite happy with a handshake. He said they often did business that way back in Australia.'

'His bank, then,' Blackstone said impatiently. 'The place you got the credit drafts from.'

'I can't help you there, either,' Wottle said. 'Mr Seymour always prefers to do his business in cash.'

TWENTY-NINE

The public house was called the Eagle and Child. It was a poky, uncomfortable place, with both the walls and the ceiling stained a dark nicotine brown. Most of its customers were dockers who had failed to find work that day but still had enough money to get noisily drunk. It was not an establishment Blackstone would normally have chosen to drink in, but on that particular day it had one distinct advantage—it was not an establishment that anyone else from New Scotland Yard would choose to drink in, either.

Blackstone sat at a table in the corner, studying the legacy Charles Montcliffe had left behind him. It wasn't much to go on—two pieces of paper, one stolen from Lord Dalton, the other given to him by Lady Emily Montcliffe. Worse yet, the two documents—if they could even be called that—seemed to have very little in common. The one that had been part of a larger sheaf of notes was so bland it could almost have been a schoolboy's homework, the Inspector thought, whereas the other hinted at a dark conspiracy.

The pub door swung open, and Patterson walked in. The sergeant looked cautiously round the room, did a double-check, then made his way over to Blackstone's table.

'By rights, I shouldn't be here, sir,' he said. 'As far as the top brass back at the Yard are concerned, even to be seen talking to you is to be considered a capital crime.'

'Well, you'd better bugger off then, hadn't you?' Blackstone said.

For a moment, the expression on Patterson's face showed his relief at being let off the hook so easily, then his jaw set firm and he sat down opposite his boss.

'No, I won't just bugger off!' he said. 'You want to stay on the case, and *I* want you to stay on it. So sod the stuffed shirts who think they know how to run a police force! Sod the lot of them.'

Blackstone nodded gratefully. 'D'you want a drink?'

Patterson glanced across at the crowded bar. 'No,' he said. 'By the time they'd have pulled it for me, I'd have to leave anyway.'

'What's happening back at the Yard?'

'They're running round like headless chickens looking for your warrant card. You should have handed it over to the Super when you were suspended.'

Blackstone grinned. 'I know I should. It must have slipped my mind.'

'So where is it?'

Blackstone patted his breast pocket. 'In here. And I'll tell you something else—I've got my revolver as well.'

Patterson shook his head mournfully. 'You're not making things any better for yourself, you know, sir,' he said.

'I'm finished at the Yard, whatever happens now,' Blackstone said. 'At least this way, when I meet two or three Russians down a dark alley, I'll be prepared for them.' He took a sip of his pint. 'How's the case developing?'

'One of the foot patrols found Thomas Grey and Molly the parlour maid in an abandoned house in Southwark about two hours ago.'

'Dead?'

The sergeant nodded. 'They'd both had their throats slit. It's impossible to say for certain, but the police surgeon thinks from the nature of the slashes that they could have been killed by the man who murdered Charles Montecliffe.'

'Well, of course it was the same man!' Blackstone said exasperatedly. 'And he killed them for the same reason—because they knew too much.'

'Knew too much about what?'

'That's where I'm stumped,' Blackstone admitted. 'But whatever it is, I'm sure now that Hugo Montcliffe isn't involved in it—and a couple of living picture photographers are.'

'What are you going to do now, sir?'

'I'll probably sit here until I get a blinding flash of inspiration,' Blackstone said. 'As for you—you'd better get back to the Yard before you're missed.'

Patterson glanced down at his pocket watch. 'You're right,' he said, standing up. 'See you at the same time, same place, tomorrow?'

'Same time, same place,' Blackstone agreed.

Patterson grinned. 'At least I won't have any trouble getting served tomorrow,' he said.

'Why's that?'

'The pub will be empty. Everybody'll he on the streets for the Jubilee procession.'

Blackstone watched his sergeant walk out of the door, then turned his attention back to the two pieces of paper in front of him—one which read like a schoolboy's homework and the other which seemed like the thoughts of a real investigative journalist. They simply didn't square up to each other. It was almost as if they had been written by two different people.

The Inspector slammed his hand down hard on the table. 'I should have seen it before!' he said, in a loud voice. 'I should have bloody well seen it before!'

*

He had to visit four more public houses before he found the man he needed to talk to. It was in the Green Man that he finally tracked down Inky Harris. The old forger was sitting alone, nursing a gill of dark ale. The sight of Blackstone seemed to make him nervous, and the nervousness grew when the policeman crossed the room and sat down opposite him.

'I ain't done nuffink wrong, Mr Blackstone,' he said. 'I'm straight now—honest I am. I wouldn't be drinkin' 'alf pints of porter if I was still workin' an' money in me pocket.'

'You might have retired, but in your time you were the best there was,' Blackstone said, with a hint of admiration in his voice.

'I'm *still* the best,' Harris said, sounding offended. 'If I went back into the business, there's not one of these young blokes whose work would come up to the same standard of mine.'

Blackstone shook his head doubtfully. 'The years do tend to take their toll, you know.'

'I tell yer, I could be as good now as I ever was.'

'Prove it,' Blackstone said, slapping the two pages of Charles Montcliffe's notes down on the table in front of him.

'What am I s'pposed to do with these?'

'Look at them—and then tell me something about them that I don't already know.'

The old man bent over the sheets and read quickly through both of them. Then he began again—slowly and laboriously—to go through them line by line. Finally, he pushed them both to one side.

'You're meant to fink they were both written by the same bloke,' he said. 'But they wasn't. One of 'em's a forgery.'

'You're sure of that?'

'Course I'm sure. Look at the loops on them "g's". 'Ere an' 'ere —' Inky indicated two points on the notes Lord Dalton had produced—'they ain't *exactly* the same—they almost are. An' let's face it, nobody's writin' is ever a *perfect* match wiv what he's produced before—but this "g" 'ere,' he pointed to one on the sheet Lady Emily had rescued from the fireplace, 'ain't even close to the uvver two.'

'Which one is the forgery?' Blackstone asked.

'Can't say for sure, but I'd put my money on the one wiv more writin' on it. It's a lot more painstakin' an' clumsy than the uvver, like the writer was tryin' to copy somebody else's style.'

So the sheet Lord Dalton had brought him hadn't been written by Charles Montcliffe at all, Blackstone thought, but by someone attempting to imitate him. And suddenly, everything was starting to make sense.

THIRTY

The Queen, who had been staying at Windsor, was returning to London to spend the night before her Jubilee celebration in Buckingham Palace—and London went wild. A large crowd had gathered outside Victoria Station to await the arrival of the royal train, and hundreds of thousands of other loyal subjects—perhaps even millions—lined the streets that led to the palace. As the royal coach, under an escort of Life Guards, covered its route at a slow trot, the crowd waved and cheered and shouted itself hoarse.

Sitting inside the carriage, the little old woman who ruled a quarter of the world was deeply touched. In all her sixty years on the throne, she had never seen such a show of affection. It was more like a triumphal entry than a mere ceremonial procession, she told herself.

The crowds grew even bigger the closer the coach got to the palace. In Hyde Park, ladies and gentlemen who had sat on their dignity all their lives now sat on sloping roofs of the chalets in the hope of catching a brief glimpse of their monarch. Rich and poor rubbed shoulders, and did not seem to mind—or even notice. Even the pickpockets, who had had a golden opportunity handed to them on a plate, chose to gaze in wonder at their queen rather then practise their trade.

The procession reached the palace, but Victoria's busy day was far from over. She gave an audience to dozens of foreign princes, envoys and special ambassadors, then presided over a dinner at which to be a mere marquis was to be a lowly figure, and even some 'highnesses' found themselves far down the order of precedence.

As the Queen went to bed that night, it was to the sound of a muffled roar from the thousands upon thousands who had surrounded the palace, and were determined to stay there until she emerged the following morning.

*

It was nearly closing time at the pub on the edge of Little Russia. Blackstone and Hannah were sitting at a table near the door. They were not talking. They had not, in fact, exchanged a word in over half an hour. Blackstone was not even looking at the Russian woman. Instead, his eyes were fixed on the table.

'What is troubling you, Sam?' Hannah asked. 'Your suspension?'

Blackstone came out of his musings. 'No,' he said. 'It's the case that's bothering me. Do you think the idea of playing detective would amuse you?'

'Why do you ask that?'

'Because if it would, I might have a task for you.'

Hannah took a large slug of her vodka. 'What sort of task?'

'I want a man following. I thought you might do it.'

'Why can't you do it yourself?'

'Because he knows me.'

'When would you want me to do this?'

'Tomorrow morning.'

'And for how long would I have to continue following him?'

'I don't know.'

'So what you are saying is that you want me to act as your unpaid assistant, following a man who may—or may not—have committed a crime, for however long it takes for you to learn something interesting?'

'That's about the long and short of it,' Blackstone admitted.

Hannah stood up. 'I'll get us some more drinks,' she said.

Blackstone watched her walk over to the bar counter. She was a beautiful woman, and he had no doubt now that he was in love with her.

So how could he willingly put her at risk? he wondered. How could he even contemplate placing her within the orbit of men who had already killed several times—and would kill again without hesitation? Because, he supposed, almost without noticing it, he had turned into a police officer first and a man second.

Hannah returned with the drinks. She smiled. 'You have made your offer so attractive that I don't see how I can refuse it.'

'Thank you,' Blackstone replied, as he felt his stomach turn over.

'When I agreed, I expected you to look much happier than that,'

Hannah said.

'I don't want you to do it!' Blackstone blurted out.

'Why ever not?'

'Because it's far too dangerous.'

Hannah frowned. 'Will following this man help to catch Charles Smith's murderer?'

'There are no guarantees in my line of work.'

'But there is a strong possibility that it might?'

'Yes,' Blackstone admitted. 'And it might also uncover a great deal else as well.'

'Then I want to do it,' Hannah said firmly. 'In fact, I insist that I do it.'

Blackstone hesitated. 'You won't take any chances, will you? If you suspect they've spotted you, you'll run.'

Hannah laughed. 'In Russia I survived two pogroms. This should be what you English call "a piece of bread".'

'"A piece of cake",' Blackstone corrected her.

'That's right,' Hannah agreed. '"A piece of cake".'

THIRTY-ONE

Sitting inside her hansom cab parked a dozen yards down the road from Lord Dalton's town house, Hannah watched the coach emerge from the mews. Perhaps Sam Blackstone was wrong about Dalton, she told herself. But just in case he was right, she had come well prepared. She opened her bag, looked down at her pistol, and wondered—dispassionately—whether she would have to use it.

Dalton's coach was well clear of the town house now. Hannah banged on the roof of the hansom, and the driver set off at a steady pace, just as she'd instructed him to.

Hannah lit a cigarette. It had been a matter of luck that she had come across Blackstone on his first foray into Little Russia, she thought, but even if they hadn't met by chance they'd still have *met*—because once she'd heard about him she would have found some way to approach him.

The coach turned south, heading towards the river, and the cab did the same. Hannah found herself thinking of another river and another capital city—the Neva and St Petersburg. She had almost died there—and would have done so willingly—but instead she had survived to fight another battle.

The streets near Lord Dalton's house had been practically deserted, but the closer they got to the City, the more people there were around.

By the time Lord Dalton's coach stopped at the corner of Gracechurch Street and Cornhill, there was scarcely a free inch of pavement. That was all to the good, Hannah thought. Crowds provided a cover. Even a hunted man felt safe in a crowd.

Quarry and hunter made slow progress down Gracechurch Street, but then Dalton turned on to Fenchurch Street, where there were fewer people.

If he turns round now, he's sure to spot me, Hannah thought, putting her hand in her bag and fingering her pistol.

But Lord Dalton continued to move forward with the purposeful stride of a man who knew exactly where he was going.

Blackstone *had* to be right about him, Hannah told herself. A person with nothing to hide would not abandon his coach and brave the crush on the street.

Dalton crossed Philpot Lane, and came to a halt in front of a terraced house next to a butcher's shop.

Hannah stopped too, and became suddenly very interested in the window of the haberdasher's she had just drawn level with. As in the old days, she forced herself to count slowly to twenty before turning her head and looking up the street. When she did look, there was no sign of Dalton.

It was time for her to find a public telephone box and call

Blackstone, she decided.

*

The night had been uncomfortably warm and the crowd outside the palace uncommonly noisy, but the old queen had still managed to get some sleep. When she awoke it was to the sound of tramping feet, as regiment after regiment of both colonial and British troops marched past the palace.

It was a breathtaking display of strength and number—a column so long that it was still passing after she had finished her breakfast. The Queen stood at the window for a while, and watched these soldiers—who were *her* soldiers, sworn to fight and die in the pursuit of *her* interests. She had never *quite* realized before the awesome weight of empire that pressed down on her ancient shoulders.

*

The proprietors of Empire Living Pictures were in the corner of the room, carrying out a final inspection of their equipment, when they heard the door click open and a familiar voice say, 'G'day to you, cobbers.'

The two young cameramen turned to look at the man who had just closed the door behind him.

'We never expected to see you here today, Mr Seymour,' Dobkins said.

'A man's got a right to protect his investments, hasn't he?' Lord

Dalton asked sharply.

'O...of course he has,' Wottle said, in a placatory manner. 'It's just that it came as a bit of surprise, that's all.'

Dalton frowned. He didn't know which of the two men he disliked the most—the stocky, abrasive Dobkins or the thin, stuttering Wottle. To think, he had had to force himself—a peer of the realm—to shake hands and be amiable to this dross. But there had been no way around it. He had needed them at one particular point in the plan, and so had forced himself to be pleasant. But now that phase had passed and he didn't need them any more. In fact, like Thaddeus Tompkins, the pawnbroker's clerk, they had become a definite liability that would have to be dealt with.

'Is everything ready?' he asked

Wottle nodded, and Dobkins just pointed to the cameras.

He would have instantly dismissed any of his servants who had acted so casually in his presence, Dalton thought—and the fact that these men did not know he was a lord didn't make their attitude any easier to take.

He walked to the corner of the room and inspected the cameras. 'They look heavy,' he said.

'It's a bit of a struggle moving them around,' Wottle admitted, 'but we usually manage.'

'Well, you won't have to manage today,' Dalton told him.

'And why's that?'

'Because I've hired some men to come down and help you on your way,' Dalton said, allowing himself a slight smile at the ambiguity of the last few words.

*

For her great day, the Queen had put on a black silk dress with panels of grey satin. It had been suggested to her by some of her advisors that she wear a crown, but she had politely refused, and chosen instead a bonnet trimmed with creamed white flowers and white aigrette. She had decided that her only jewellery should he a diamond chain, which had all the more value to her because it was a gift from her younger children. Now, examining herself in the full-length mirror while she was fussed over by half a dozen attendants, she was well pleased with the effect.

She had one more task to perform before she left the palace. An electric button—which was something that had not even existed when she'd been born—had been installed, and when she pressed it, it sent a telegram to every corner of her vast empire.

It was a simple message. 'From my heart I thank my beloved people,' it read. 'May God bless them.'

And Victoria meant every word of it.

She had found the weather rather unpleasant earlier—quite dull and sticky. But as she was being assisted into her open landau, which was to be pulled by eight magnificent cream horses, the sun burst through. Fancifully, she thought of it as God smiling down on her.

The Queen looked at the carriage that already contained her eldest daughter, Vicky, and sighed. She would have liked her beloved daughter to ride with her in the landau, but precedence would not allow them to sit side by side, and as Empress of Germany, Vicky could not possibly sit with her back to the horses.

The Queen sighed a second time. It was sometimes hard being royal, she thought.

At exactly 11.15 the twenty-one gun salute boomed out—signifying the start of the procession—and the coaches began to roll forward. The greatest celebration of the greatest empire the world had ever known was beginning. A shudder—which may have been anticipation or may have been awe—ran through the crowd that was tightly packed around the palace.

*

Blackstone paced fretfully up and down a short strip on the Embankment in front of the public telephone box.

Why didn't she ring? he asked himself for perhaps the hundredth time. Why didn't she bloody ring?

Because she might already be in trouble, a nagging voice in the corner of his brain whispered. Because she might already be *dead*!

The screech of the telephone bell cut through the still air, and shook him to the core. He flung the door of the kiosk open, and grabbed at the receiver.

'Is that you, Sam?' asked a voice at the other end of the line.

'It's me.'

'You were right about Dalton. He left his coach and walked on foot to an office on Fenchurch Street. It's—'

'It's the Empire Living Pictures Company,' Blackstone interrupted.

'How did you know?'

'That doesn't matter now,' Blackstone said. 'Listen very carefully, Hannah. I want you to get away from Fenchurch Street as fast as you possibly can. Go somewhere you know you'll be safe. A friend's house—someone Turgenev isn't likely to know about.'

'But why—?'

'Just do it!' Blackstone snapped.

He slammed the mouthpiece of the telephone back on to its cradle, cursing his own stupidity.

The purpose of Turgenev's trip to Afghanistan all those years ago. The Jubilee celebrations. And Empire Living Pictures. They all fitted together so perfectly that he should have seen the pattern the moment he'd talked to Dobkins and Wottle.

But he hadn't. Only now did he understand the enormity of what was being planned—and he was far from sure that he would be in time to stop it.

THIRTY-TWO

As the hour of the Thanksgiving Service drew ever closer, the few people who had been on Fenchurch Street drifted away towards St Paul's, and by the time Blackstone reached Philpot Lane the street was completely deserted—save for the attractive woman with black eyes and black curled hair who was standing a few doors up from Empire Living Pictures.

'What in God's name are you still doing here?' Blackstone gasped angrily. 'I told you to find somewhere safe to hide!'

'The situation has somewhat changed since I rang you,' Hannah said, her voice eerily calm. 'You no longer have just Lord Dalton to deal with. Turgenev and two of his henchmen are here now. You will need help.'

'From you?' Blackstone asked incredulously.

'From me,' Hannah confirmed.

Blackstone shook his head. 'You have no idea just how dangerous these people are. There'd be nothing you could do against them, and you'd only get in my way when I tried to do something.'

'Do you have a gun?' Hannah asked.

'Yes.'

'So do I. And I am an excellent shot.'

'Those men in there are not targets on a range. You'd never be able to bring yourself to—'

'To kill them?' Hannah interrupted. 'There was a man in Petersburg who thought I would never pull the trigger. They buried him the next day.'

This was insane, Blackstone thought. It was as if he were only now seeing the real Hannah. And he didn't have the time to deal with it—didn't have time to come to terms with the fact that this woman whom he loved had turned out to be a complete stranger.

'If I let you come in with me, you must promise to stay near the door,' he said.

'All right.'

'And to get out if anything goes wrong.'

'If I am with you, nothing *will* go wrong,' Hannah said confidently.

Blackstone sighed. 'Then if we are going to do it, let's get it over with,' he said.

*

The royal procession turned down Constitution Hill. Seven times, in her long reign, there had been assassination attempts on the Queen, and twice they had taken place on Constitution Hill.

The first had also been on a June day like this one, June 10th 1840. She had been three months pregnant with Vicky, and she and Albert had been driving to Belgrave Square to see her mother. They'd been in an open droshky when they'd heard a loud explosion, and turning their heads, they'd seen a small man holding a pistol in each hand. Albert, dear Albert, had pushed her to the floor of the carriage, so that the second bullet had flown over her head, and the would-be killer had soon been surrounded and rendered harmless by passers-by. Dark rumours circulated that Edward Oxford—for that was the man's name—had been hired by the King of Hanover, who would have succeeded to the British throne if Victoria had died, but the police found no evidence of such a link, and the man was judged by the courts to be criminally insane, then locked away in a lunatic asylum.

The second attempt came two years later, and the would-be killer—John Francis—selected almost the same spot as Oxford had chosen. He too, pleaded insanity, but had been sentenced to death—a sentence that was later commuted to a lifetime of transportation.

The Queen doubted that either of them had been insane. They had been nothing more than hateful little men with a grudge against society, which they thought they could assuage by killing their monarch. Victoria brushed aside thoughts of such unpleasant incidents, and turned her mind, instead, to the way Constitution Hill looked on that very special day.

The hill was lined with raised seats, on which the rich and powerful would have paid a fortune to sit. But those privileged to witness the start of the procession were neither rich nor powerful. One section of seats was filled by the Queen's servants and personal attendants—as well as those from other royal households.

Another section was occupied by the Chelsea Pensioners, old or disabled soldiers who lived in the Royal Hospital established as a home for them in 1682 by Charles II. And then there were the children—pupils from the Duke of York's and Greenwich schools—who waved their Union Jacks furiously and cheered her at the top of their thin voices.

Later the Queen would pass in front of the National Gallery, where a special stand had been erected so that the peers of the House of Lords—dressed in their ermine and coronets—would have their chance to show as much enthusiasm as the children had done. Later still, after the service in front of St Paul's, she would cross the river to the poorer part of London.

Victoria approved wholeheartedly with the way things had been planned—she was the queen of the whole nation, from the highest to the lowest, and it was only right that the whole nation should get the opportunity to see her.

Standing in front of the offices of Empire Living Pictures, Blackstone glanced quickly up and down the empty street. There was not a soul in sight. No one to be alarmed by what he was about to do—but no one to *raise* the alarm if anything went wrong, either.

He turned to Hannah. 'I'm going to kick the door in,' he whispered. 'While they're still in shock, we should have about two seconds to make our move. Don't waste them!'

'I won't.'

Blackstone tensed himself. It was vitally important to smash the lock with the first kick. Because if he failed, the men inside would he forewarned and ready for them—and both he and Hannah would be as good as dead.

He slammed his boot into the door, and felt the lock give way. In the moment it took the door to creak its protest and swing open, he corrected his balance and stepped into the room.

Blackstone quickly scanned from side to side—assessing the situation, deciding where danger was most likely to come from. It wouldn't come from Wottle and Dobkins, that was for certain—men with their throats slit rarely cause trouble. But as Hannah had told him, there were four *other* men in the room.

Dalton and Turgenev were standing in one corner, as if, a moment earlier, they had been deep in a private conversation. Turgenev's two thugs were bending over the workbench, adapting the cameras to the task for which they were to be used.

'If anybody moves, I'll kill him!' Blackstone shouted.

He sensed—rather than saw—Hannah slip into the room, and move slightly to his right.

'I've got the two with the cameras covered,' she said.

The Count turned towards her, and a look of total amazement came to his face.

'You!' he gasped.

'Me!' Hannah replied, with a note of triumph in her voice.

Something was terribly wrong here, Blackstone told himself. Why should Turgenev be shocked to see Hannah with him, when he'd already seen them together at the boxing match? But he hadn't, had he? All he had seen had been the Inspector and a woman wearing a veil!

'How is it you know each other?' he demanded.

'I am a member of the Okhrana—the Russian secret police,' Turgenev told him. 'Back in St Petersburg, we have an extensive file on this woman. She is a well-known criminal.'

Blackstone wished he could turn to look at Hannah's face, but he dared not take his eyes off Turgenev and Dalton even for a second.

'Is this true, Hannah?' he asked, out of the corner of his mouth.

'I am a well-known *revolutionary*,' Hannah replied. 'And this man is no longer a member of the Okhrana. Even that foul organization did not have the stomach for his methods. He was expelled over a year ago.'

Lord Dalton had been looking very calm for a man whose complicity in at least three murders had just been uncovered, but this fresh news seemed to shake him.

'You never told me you were kicked out!' he said to Turgenev.

'Why should I have done?'

'Because I am as involved in this operation as you are, and I have the right to know!'

'I did not tell my washerwoman, either,' the Count said scornfully. 'I pay her—just as I pay you—and *that* is all she needs to know.' He turned his attention back to Blackstone. 'You appear to have the upper hand for the moment, Inspector. How are we to resolve this situation?'

'We resolve it by me arresting you,' Blackstone told him. The Count shook his head. 'That is not a good idea—and you know it. You tried arresting me once before. Remember?'

'This time, I have solid evidence.'

The Count laughed. 'Evidence!' he repeated. 'What good do you think your *evidence* will be against the word of a Russian count and an English lord?' He paused for a second to let this thought sink into Blackstone's mind, then said, 'I think I have a better solution to our little difficulty.'

'And what might that be?'

'If you were to walk away now, and pretend to have seen nothing, I give you my word as a gentleman that when this is all over, I will see to it that you are paid ten thousand pounds.'

Blackstone felt outrage welling up inside him. 'Is that what you paid him?' he demanded, glancing at Dalton.

The Count laughed again. 'Oh no. Much more than that. A noble lord has far greater needs than a humble police inspector does.'

But the noble lord did not look so noble any more. Since Turgenev had shown his contempt by comparing the other man with his washerwoman, Dalton's shoulders had slumped and his face was set into a mask of misery.

'Yet even though you would not make as much out of this as Dalton has, with ten thousand pounds in your pocket you could still live like a king for the rest of your days,' the Count continued. 'You'd be a fool not to take it, don't you think?'

The contemptible offer was not even worthy of an answer, and instead, Blackstone turned his gaze—and his growing anger—on Lord Dalton.

'For all your talk about honour and dignity, you're no better than a common prostitute, offering yourself to the highest bidder,' he said.

'I wouldn't expect a man like *you* to understand what a man like *I* will do for love,' Dalton replied, regaining a little of his old spirit.

'Will someone here please tell me exactly what's going on?' Hannah demanded.

'They were planning to kill the Queen,' Blackstone said.

'Why?'

'In Dalton's case, it's for the money.'

'And Turgenev?' Hannah said. 'Why should he want to assassinate your queen?'

'Why don't you tell her, Count?' Blackstone suggested.

'Why not?' Turgenev agreed. 'Victoria is the glue which holds the British Empire together. To some of her subject peoples she is almost a god.'

'But gods don't get killed at the moment of their greatest triumph,' Blackstone said. 'Take away the mystery, and the colonies—especially India—would revolt.'

'And even the lily-livered scum we have running Russia now would be forced to intervene on the side of the Indians,' Turgenev said. 'We could not do it openly, of course, but even our *covert* help would be enough to ensure that once the British were kicked out, we would be welcomed in as honoured guests. We would achieve our dream at last—the dream which has driven us for hundreds of years. We would own the keys to our house.'

Blackstone had sensed Hannah shifting as Turgenev spoke. Now he felt the barrel of her pistol pressing into his spine.

'Hand over your gun to Count Turgenev,' the Russian woman said, in a voice which somehow managed to combine sadness with authority.

'Hannah—' Blackstone protested.

'Hand it over now, or I will kill you.'

This was no bluff. Blackstone was as sure as he'd ever been of anything that she meant every word she'd said. He held out the pistol, and Turgenev, looking perplexed, stepped forward to relieve him of it. Only when the Count had retreated again did the pressure of Hannah's gun against Blackstone's spine cease.

'I want you to walk slowly to the far end of the room, Sam,' the Russian woman said. 'When you get there, you will face the corner, raise your arms above your head and place the palms of your hands flat against the wall. My pistol will be covering you at all times, and if you make the slightest wrong move, I will pull the trigger.'

Could this really be the charming, amusing woman he had spent most of the last few days with? Blackstone asked himself as he followed Hannah's instructions. Was he such a fool as to have been completely taken in?

'What has made you change sides?' Turgenev asked Hannah.

'As long as you get what you want, does that really matter?' Hannah replied.

'I suppose not,' the Count said. 'But it does seem strange that a revolutionary like you—'

'You have already wasted five minutes,' Hannah interrupted him. 'If you are to succeed in your mission, you'd better move now.'

'What about him?' Dalton asked, pointing at Blackstone, prone against the wall.

'I'll take care of him,' Hannah said.

'He knows too much about my involvement in all this,' Dalton said. 'He has to die.'

'I am well aware of that,' Hannah answered. 'And as I have already told you, I will take care of him.'

THIRTY-THREE

The closer the royal procession got to the cathedral, the slower it moved. Several times, when a particular section of the crowd broke out into 'God Save the Queen', it stopped completely. Queen Victoria did not mind the delay. After sixty long years of putting her country first, it was gratifying to now be harvesting that country's tribute to her.

When the procession finally did reach the square in front of St Paul's, the sight before her almost took the Queen's breath away. Around the perimeter stood rank after rank of colonial troops. Indians, Canadians, Australians, Africans and Polynesians—there was not a race which was not represented. Mounted on horseback closer to the cathedral were senior officers from the Queen's regiments—Royal Scots Greys in their busbies, Lancers and Royal Horse Guards in their plumed helmets, Hussars wearing their curious fur hats.

Victoria turned to look at the cathedral itself. There were perhaps a thousand people standing on the steps—dignitaries on the left and right wings, the massed choir and musicians in the centre. Beefeaters from the Tower of London, looking splendid in their crimson uniforms, were providing the honour guard, and both the Bishop of London and the Archbishop of Canterbury were in attendance to conduct the proceedings.

It was a short service, as Victoria had requested, and because she was too lame to mount the cathedral steps, she stayed in her landau throughout it. A Te Deum, especially written for the occasion was sung, and the Queen found the Lord's Prayer so beautiful that she was almost moved to tears. Then it was all over, and to the sound of renewed cheering the procession set off again for the Mansion House, where the Lady Mayoress would present the Queen with a silver basket full of orchids.

And after that, it would finally be time to show the people of Southwark their monarch.

*

From his position in the corner of the room, Blackstone had twice tried to talk to Hannah, but the Russian woman had ordered him to be silent—and since she was the one with the gun, silence had prevailed.

Now, after what he estimated had been more than three-quarters of an hour, he heard Hannah say, 'You can turn around now, Sam. But please do it very, very slowly.'

He turned. Hannah was standing in the centre of the room, and had her pistol pointed directly at him. He calculated his chances of making a sudden dash at her and grabbing the gun—and quickly decided that he would be dead before he got halfway there.

'Why, Hannah?' he asked. 'Why are you going to let that madman get away with it?'

'Because, for once, his interests and ours coincide,' the Russian woman said simply.

'Ours?'

'The group to which I belong.'

'It can't help *you* to have Britain lose India,' Blackstone said.

'No,' Hannah agreed. 'But there will be other consequences to the assassination.'

'What other consequences?'

'Once your government learns that a Russian was behind the death of your queen—and I will make sure that it does—there will no choice but for your country to go to war with mine. It will be a long and bloody war which will all but destroy both of them.'

'And hundreds of thousands—perhaps even millions—of innocent people will die,' Blackstone pointed out.

'Yes,' Hannah agreed. 'But it is a necessary sacrifice. The Revolution cannot succeed until the state has been brought to its knees.'

'You were using me right from the start, weren't you?' Blackstone demanded.

'Yes, I was using you,' Hannah admitted. 'I needed to find out what Turgenev was up to, and setting you on him seemed the best way to do that. But when I went to bed with you, it was because I wanted to. You said you thought you were falling in love with me. Well, I have fallen in love with you.'

He noticed a tear running down her left cheek. 'But you're still going to kill me, aren't you?' he asked.

'I have to,' Hannah said, with a choke in her voice. 'I have been standing here ever since the Count left, trying to find an alternative. But there is none. You must die, Sam.'

'Why? Because it's what Dalton wants?'

'No. Because you know that Turgenev is not acting for the Russian government, but only in the interests of his own fanatical group. That knowledge could prevent the war.'

'The Russians will deny that he was working for them, anyway,' Blackstone said.

'True,' Hannah agreed. 'But without your testimony, no one will believe them.'

'You do realize that once this is all over, they'll kill you, too.'

Hannah nodded. 'That is probably true. But it doesn't matter. I am only a tiny cog in the machine. I will be easy to replace, but by my death I will have allowed the Revolution to take a giant step forward.'

So this was it, Blackstone thought. This was how it all ended. He had failed in his duty as a policeman, and he was about to lose his life at the hands of the woman he loved.

'Shall we get it over with?' he suggested.

Another tear ran down Hannah's cheek.

'If you would like to close your eyes—' she began.

'Oh no,' Blackstone interrupted. 'When I die, I want to be looking at my murderess.'

Hannah was crying in earnest now. 'I really do love you, you know,' she said.

'Do it!' Blackstone said harshly.

Hannah nodded again, and raised her gun slightly.

A chest shot, Blackstone thought. If she had gone for the head, he might have stood a chance, because there was always the possibility she would miss and he'd have time to make a move. But she was too professional for that. A bullet to the chest might not kill him, but it would take him down—and once he was down she could finish him off at her leisure.

Hannah's finger was wrapped around the trigger, and even from a distance, Blackstone could see it tightening. He looked into her eyes, hoping to find some sign that she couldn't go through with it. But beneath a deep sadness, there was an even deeper determination.

He heard the shot, but felt no pain—no searing agony as the metal tube tore its way through his body. But something had happened to Hannah! The top of her head had exploded, sending an obscene fountain of blood and gore high into the air.

Blackstone swung round to face the door, and saw a man standing there with a smoking pistol in his hand. He recognized the new arrival. The last time they had met had been on a nighttime street in Little Russia, when this man had saved him from certain death at the hands of Count Turgenev's thugs.

Hannah's legs collapsed beneath her, and she crumpled lifelessly to the floor. Blackstone rushed across the room, knelt down, and cradled what was left of her head to his chest.

'You've killed her!' he sobbed.

The man in the doorway shrugged indifferently.

'There was no choice,' he said. 'Perhaps if I had arrived earlier there might have been a way to spare her, but the agent I had on your tail did not tell me where you were until a few minutes ago.'

Even as he knelt there—even as the blood of the woman he still loved was soaking into his clothes—Blackstone felt the policeman deep inside him begin to reassert himself.

'Who are you?' he demanded. 'What are you doing here?'

'My name is Vladimir Bubnov, Inspector Blackstone, and I am what Count Turgenev *used* to be.'

'A secret policeman?'

'Yes, I am a member of the Okhrana. As to what I am doing here—we suspected that the Count and a few like-minded men were involved in some lunatic scheme, and I wanted to find out what it was.'

And just like Hannah, you used me to do that, Blackstone thought. But it didn't matter *who* had used him, or why—the only important thing was what he had found out.

He laid the bloody pulp that had once been Hannah's head gently on the floor, and stood up.

'Turgenev's men are planning to assassinate the Queen,' he said.

The Russian paled. 'My God!' he gasped. 'But they can't!'

'On the contrary,' Blackstone said, 'unless we can stop them, they have an excellent chance.'

'Do you know where this assassination attempt will take place?' the Russian asked.

Blackstone stripped off his bloodied jacket, threw it on the floor, and strode rapidly towards the door. 'Just follow me,' he said.

THIRTY-FOUR

Count Turgenev looked out of the window at the platform in front of the greengrocer's shop across the street. His two men were already in place, standing behind the cameras that concealed their snipers' rifles. What fools the British were to allow him such an opportunity to kill their queen.

'If all is still on schedule, the procession should be leaving the Mansion House now,' he said to the other man sitting at the table behind him.

But Lord Dalton did not hear the words. Instead, he was reliving the long struggle he had endured to get what he wanted finally.

He had first met Lady Emily Montcliffe when she was fifteen, and had immediately fallen in love with her. But he had not been such a fool as to announce that love, because he knew that, as things stood, the Earl would never allow his family name to be allied with that of the *nouveau* aristocracy. And so he had gone about things another way—by making himself useful.

The Earl would not dirty his own hands by indulging in commerce, but he had been quite willing to let others make money for him. And at first, that was just what Dalton had done.

Then there had been the trip to Australia that he had made with the Viscount. What a triumph of cunning and manipulation that had been! It had helped, of course, that Hugo was such a fool that it had been easy to persuade him that investing in worthless shares had been entirely his own idea. But to come out of the whole disaster perceived not as the destroyer of the Montcliffe family's finances but as its saviour was still nothing short of a masterstroke.

After that, it had been easy. He who pays the piper calls the tune, and when Dalton had asked the Earl for his daughter's hand in marriage, Earl Montcliffe had had no option but to agree.

That was how it should have ended, Lord Dalton thought—with he and his one true love living happily together for the rest of their days. But then he had made some bad investments himself—not as disastrous as the ones he had steered Hugo into, but damaging enough. Ruin had been staring him in the face, and he was well aware that the loss of his fortune would also mean the loss of Emily.

He had been in a desperate state when Count Turgenev had turned up to renew their Australian acquaintanceship. It hadn't taken the Count long to let Dalton know that he'd found out about his problems—and to offer him a way out of it.

Dalton had been horrified at first, but the horror had not lasted long. What did the life of one old lady matter—what did India matter—as long as he could have his Emily?

He looked up at the Count, who was still staring out of the window. When they had been in Australia together, they had got on well. But since he had taken the Count's money, the relationship had changed. Turgenev had become more and more off-hand, until, not an hour earlier, the Count had compared the man he had once treated as an equal with his washerwoman.

New nobility was a fragile thing, and Lord Dalton's had been very badly bruised. He burned with shame that he had ever associated with a man who should treat him with such contempt—and realized that he would continue to burn until he had had his revenge.

THIRTY-FIVE

Blackstone, and the Russian who said his name was Vladimir, sprinted across London Bridge, watched—as an unexpected entertainment—by the thousands of spectators who were being held back by soldiers and policemen. Blackstone had lost count of the number of times he had shouted out 'Police! Emergency!' when some official looked as if he were about to challenge him, and his arm was already stiff from holding his warrant card high in the air.

As he ran, his mind grappled with the problem of what to do once he and the Okhrana man were within reach of the platform where the assassins would be waiting. They both had pistols, but if they used them they would panic the dense crowd, and in the stampede that followed, scores of people would lose their lives.

Yet what other way was there of dealing with killers?

He reached the end of the bridge and he stopped for a second to catch his breath and look over his shoulder. The Queen's procession was still on the other side of the river, but it was gaining on them. By the time they reached the camera platform on Southwark Street, it would be almost at their heels.

Perhaps he should give up trying to stop the assassins and stop the procession instead, he thought desperately.

But what were the chances that the soldiers who were forming the Queen's bodyguard—and who would be no protection at all against a sniper's bullet—would ever believe a discredited policeman when he said the monarch was in danger?

He and the Russian had reached Southwark Street, but Blackstone still had no plan. The crowd here was packed even tighter than it had been on the bridge. Costermongers—who so hated authority that it was almost a badge of honour to have gone to gaol for beating up a policeman—stood wide-eyed, waiting for a monarch who could not even begin to imagine how harsh and brutal their lives were. Women who worked in their front parlours for up to sixteen hours a day, gluing hat boxes or making paper flowers, had for once given themselves a little time off and stood crushed together, awaiting a spectacle they would remember for the rest of their lives—and would go to their graves counting themselves fortunate for having seen.

Whatever their failings or however much their passivity sometimes exasperated him, Blackstone told himself, these were *his* people—and he couldn't let them down.

He could see the camera platform ahead of him, surrounded by onlookers. If he tried to storm it, he was sure that the Russians would have no qualm about firing down on him and the dense crowd. There had to be another way!

He looked up at the rooftops. In the more prosperous parts of the city, wooden seats had been erected on the roofs so that the spectators might sit in some kind of comfort. But here, south of the river, the house owners had merely rented space, and those who had paid out the few coppers they could ill afford clung precariously to the apex of the roofs and to the chimney stacks.

But how had they got up there?

They'd gone up ladders—like the one he could see just ahead of him, propped up against the side of an end terrace house!

And in a flash, Blackstone knew exactly what he had to do.

He came to a sudden halt. 'Inspector Blackstone. Scotland Yard,' he said to the policemen who were holding back the crowd. 'Make a path for me into Great Suffolk Street! Now!'

One of the constables frowned. 'Don't know whether we can, sir,' he said. 'The crowd's tightly packed, an' the Queen's due any minute.'

'Do it!' Blackstone ordered him. 'I don't care how you manage it—just bloody do it!'

The constables began to manoeuvre the people back down Great Suffolk Street. As he stood there bursting with impatience, Blackstone fancied that, even though he knew it would have been impossible over the excited buzz of the crowd, he could hear the click of horses' hoofs as they pulled the royal landau ever nearer. People who had been standing there all day for one glimpse of the Queen complained and grumbled as they were pushed back, but a gap wide enough for Blackstone and the Russian to squeeze through was eventually cleared. The Inspector started to climb the ladder, with the secret policeman right behind him.

He was just at the top of the ladder when the people on the

roof broke out into an ear-shattering cheer. Blackstone took a quick glance over his shoulder. The royal procession had almost crossed the river. It was close enough to make out the plumed helmets of the escort shining in the sunlight, and the white parasol that the Queen held over her head. He did not have long to act—and there was no room for mistakes.

The easiest and safest way to cross the roof would be along the apex, but every inch of it was occupied by spectators. He would have to make a run for it—gamble on his momentum counteracting gravity.

He pulled himself on the roof and felt his legs start to slip from under him. Quickly, he twisted his feet so they were at an angle to the incline and placed his left hand—palm down—on the rough slates.

'Oy!' someone shouted, 'I paid frippence for this spot. I want to see the Queen, not your 'ead.'

Ignoring the man, Blackstone edged forward, and heard the scarping sound of the Russian's feet behind him.

'Ready?' he asked.

'Ready,' the Okhrana man said.

Blackstone launched himself forward, arms spread out to provide what balance they could.

Ahead of him, he could see the platform. It looked wider from above than it had seemed from the street. The two men standing on it—Turgenev's henchmen—were crouched behind the cameras that hid their rifles. They had positioned themselves at opposite ends of the platform, thus taking advantage of the maximum number of firing angles available to them. Two rifles aimed at one little old lady in a slow-moving coach—they couldn't miss.

Behind him, he heard the sound of feet desperately trying to maintain traction and a grunted curse from Vladimir. Then the scraping stopped, and a second later there was a pained roar from the people below. Vladimir was gone. He had fallen off the roof and plummeted into the crowd. So now it was one police inspector—gone soft with the years of easy living since he'd left the Army—against two trained assassins.

Blackstone felt his feet slipping, just as Vladimir's must have done. He stopped moving, and wobbled to try and regain his balance. One foot was already over the edge when he twisted round and flung himself flat against the roof. His fingers reached out and grasped the edges of a couple of slates. He prayed that on a dilapidated building like this one, they would not give way.

'What the bloody 'ell do you fink you're doin'?' an angry voice called to him from the apex of the roof. 'Why can't you just sit still an' watch the Jubilee, like everybody else?'

Blackstone raised himself to a kneeling position, then gingerly stood up. From the street, the sound of cheering was growing in intensity, which could only mean that the Queen's procession was getting close. Blackstone broke into a cautious trot.

He covered the roofs of three houses and was almost directly above the platform when he felt the soles of his boots start to lose their grip again. And this time was worse than the last. This time, he wasn't sure he was going to make it.

And suddenly he *knew* he wasn't! His feet slipped more, and he was on the very edge of the roof. There was no space to twist this time—no room left for manoeuvre. He tottered there on the lip, waving his arms as a young bird flaps its wings while it is wondering whether it dare take that first leap into the void.

He was going to fall! Whatever happened, he was going to fall! All he could do, he thought in that split-second while thought was still possible, was to snatch what advantage he could from the situation.

He could have gone straight down, landing on the crowd below, but instead he dived forward, heading for the platform.

He was flying through the air—and if he carried on travelling at the same angle, he would hit the platform headfirst. He twisted his body frantically in a desperate attempt to ensure that he landed on his feet.

He almost made it!

*

'Blackstone!' Count Turgenev exclaimed.

'What?' Lord Dalton asked.

'Blackstone,' the Count repeated. 'He is not dead, as he is supposed to be. He is on one of the roofs, only a short distance from the platform.'

Dalton rushed over to the window. Yes, there was no doubt about it. The tall, thin figure who had just slipped off the roof—and was now flying through the air towards the camera platform—was undoubtedly Sam Blackstone.

He should never have trusted the Russian woman, Dalton told himself. He should have seen to it personally that the policeman was no longer a threat. But it was too late to think about what might have been. Blackstone *was* there. True, he was only seconds from death. But through his death, he could well stop the procession. Which meant that the Queen would not be assassinated! And he would not get the money that would save him from ruin!

At least there was now nothing to restrain him from doing what he had been itching to do for the last hour. He took a few steps backwards, placed his hand in his frock coat and ran one finger along the blade of the knife that was resting there.

*

The Russian closest to the falling man was crouched over the camera—pretending to film the crowd closer to Blackfriars Bridge—when the Inspector's knees slammed into his back. The assassin screamed in shock and agony, then pitched forward.

Blackstone sprawled on top of him, his chest covering the Russian's head. His knees were sending sharp shooting pains up to the tops of his legs, and he was sure that he would never walk again.

As the Inspector wriggled free from the fallen man, the other Russian quickly swung around the camera that concealed his rifle. His haste was a mistake—the tripod collapsed and the camera crashed to the floor.

Blackstone—his knees giving him hell—struggled into a

crouching position. The Russian glanced down at the camera—as if he were still considering the rifle as his first choice of weapon—then reached into his pocket and pulled out a glinting cut-throat razor.

The impact of two men hitting the floor of the platform had startled the people pressed down below, and several of them shouted comments: 'What's goin' on up there?'—'Has there been an accident?'—'Need any help?'

'Police!' Blackstone bawled back. 'I need the police.'

But even as he spoke, he knew there would not be enough time for anyone on the ground to come to his rescue. He was on his own.

He glanced down at the man he had landed on. He was twisted at an unnatural angle and lying perfectly still.

Dead! Blackstone thought. Or at the very least unconscious and with his spine broken. So that was one bastard he didn't have to worry about.

The second Russian—his arms widespread, with the razor in the right one—was making his way across the platform. Most men would have rushed at him, Blackstone thought, but this one was a professional. His approach was cautious—and when he struck it would be to maximum effect.

'Why kill me when you've no chance of getting away?' Blackstone said. 'Do you *want* to hang?'

The man with the razor laughed loudly, revealing his huge, irregular teeth. He hadn't understood a word, Blackstone thought. Or if he had, he didn't care. He was a creature of instinct—and his only concern at that moment was to eliminate his immediate enemy.

Blackstone forced himself into a standing position, and wondered how long his knees would hold out. The Russian was in striking distance now, but instead of attacking himself, he was waiting for his opponent to make a wrong move.

Blackstone feinted with his left arm, then twisted and swung with his right, but the Russian had anticipated just such a move, and the razor was already slashing down at his throat.

Blackstone blocked the attack just in time. The razor missed its target, and he felt a searing pain as it cut a deep gash in his right arm.

A one-armed man who was rapidly losing blood did not have long to land a decisive blow, he told himself through the pain— and as the Russian pulled back the razor to strike again, he lashed out with the edge of his left hand.

More by luck than judgement, he struck the other man's Adam's apple. The Russian gurgled and froze. Blackstone kicked him just below the kneecap, and the assassin went down. But only for a second! Despite the blow to his shin—despite the fact he was still fighting for air—he was already rising to his feet when Blackstone slammed his boot into his face.

The Russian's face was covered with blood. He had dropped his razor, but he was still far from beaten, and Blackstone did not know how much longer he himself could remain conscious. They had taught him in the police to use his judgement to decide the minimum force necessary to restrain a suspect—and he used the judgement now, as he picked up the razor and drew it roughly across the Russian's throat.

The Queen's mounted escort was only yards away, and behind it stretched a caravan of carriages led by Victoria's landau. Blackstone took one look at it, and then passed out.

*

The Queen was overcome by the reception she was receiving from some of her humblest subjects. How they loved her! How deep their feelings were! And to think, there had been a time when she had actually been booed in public!

Her landau had almost drawn level with an unusual wooden platform that had been erected in front of one of the terraced houses. The Queen looked up. Lying at the edge of the platform was a man. His arm was hanging over the side, and he did not seem to be moving.

Dead drunk! the Queen thought in disgust. And no doubt when he woke up he would tell himself that he had got into that disgraceful state to celebrate her jubilee. Well, she did not wish it to be celebrated in that way. She much preferred the cheers of her loyaler, *soberer* subjects.

If she had been a little closer, she might possibly have noticed that the man's arm was bleeding, and that drops of blood were falling, like the first signs of rain, on the ecstatic crowd below him.

THIRTY-SIX

It was eleven o'clock on the evening following the Queen's triumphant jubilee parade. Blackstone and Patterson were sitting opposite each other in the Rifleman's Arms, a pub conveniently close to New Scotland Yard. It was a place they'd often gone to when they'd solved a case, but that night there were none of the good spirits that usually accompanied a successful result.

'Cheer up, sir,' Patterson said, after they'd been sitting in silence for several minutes. 'It's not really a bad day's work to have saved the Empire.'

'I'm not sure it was that worth saving,' Blackstone said gloomily.

'What?!' Patterson asked.

'There are those who say we've brought civilization to the world,' Blackstone told him. 'But I'm not that convinced. How can we *export* civilization when half the people in Britain haven't even got it.'

'Not got it? There's nobody as civilized as we are.'

'Then why do people within a short walk of here wake up in the morning not knowing whether they're going to have enough to eat that day?' Blackstone asked. 'Why can a costermonger in

Lambeth expect to die by the time he's thirty-one, whereas a clerk from Peckham might live well into his sixties? You can't talk about civilization when—for so many people—life's no more than a struggle to get by.'

'Perhaps you're right,' Patterson said, though his patriotism would not allow him to sound completely convinced.

'Besides, are we really doing all those people who live in the Empire any good?' Blackstone continued. 'We've taught them to depend on us. However, will they manage to stand on their own feet when we pull out?'

'When we pull out!' Patterson repeated incredulously. 'We're *never* going to pull out.'

Blackstone shook his head. 'You've not been there like I have. If we hold on to the Empire for even another fifty or sixty years, it'll be a miracle.'

'Do you want to talk about the case, sir?' asked Patterson, who had decided it might he wiser—both for himself and his boss—to change the subject.

'Why not,' Blackstone agreed. 'What do you want to know?'

'I can understand how Lord Dalton became involved, if what you say about his businesses going bust was true,' Patterson said. 'Count Turgenev was probably offering him a lot of money—'

'A hundred thousand pounds at least, I'd guess. Maybe even more.'

'—but what I don't see is why the Count was prepared to hand over that kind of money?'

'That's easy,' Blackstone told him. 'He needed someone—

someone English—to do the groundwork for him.'

'But even so, he could surely have got the help he needed for much less than a hundred thousand pounds.'

'Dalton had one major advantage over anyone else. It was an advantage that was well worth paying a fortune for.'

'And what was that?'

'He was connected to the Montcliffes, of course.'

'So what?'

'So Earl Montcliffe was heavily involved in planning the Jubilee celebrations. Through Dalton, Turgenev learned well in advance what the route would he. That information was invaluable. And if there'd been any last-minute changes, he'd have found out all about that, too. Later on, of course, though they hadn't planned it that way, Dalton was useful again—keeping Turgenev informed of how my murder investigation was going. That's why the Count decided to have me killed—because Dalton told him I was getting a little too close for comfort.'

'What about Charles Montcliffe?' Patterson asked.

'What about him?'

'Was he killed because he found out about the plot?'

Blackstone sighed. 'Yes. And he probably told his valet about it—which is why Thomas went into hiding and was eventually murdered. But I don't think Charles Montcliffe started *out* investigating Count Turgenev.'

'So who *did* he start out investigating?'

'Lord Dalton. Charles Montcliffe was very close to his sister. And very protective! He wanted to find out what kind of man

Lady Emily was marrying. So he started looking into Dalton's background—and that's what led him to Turgenev and the plot to kill the Queen.'

'How long do you think it'll take them to catch Dalton?' Patterson asked.

'They'll never catch him.'

'What? You're not seriously saying that the finest police force in the world can't—'

Blackstone held up his uninjured arm to silence his assistant. 'Dalton is probably already out of the country. And even if he isn't, that's the way he'll be heading. He has no choice.'

'But if the police are watching all the docks—'

Blackstone sighed again, even more heavily this time. 'You still don't understand, do you?' he asked. 'They don't *want* to find him.'

'I beg your pardon, sir!'

'There's enough evidence available that if they do find him, they'll have to put him on trial. Think about it, Patterson—a member of the aristocracy in a plot to kill the monarch! That hasn't happened for over three hundred years. It'd be an embarrassment to everyone. But there is an alternative.'

'And what's that, sir?'

'Dalton is allowed to escape abroad. The story goes around that he's fled because of his debts. It's a scandal, but it's nowhere as big as the other scandal would have been. After a while, whatever evidence I've collected conveniently disappears—and as far as anyone's concerned, the assassination attempt never happened.'

'But people saw—'

'People saw three men fighting on a platform. At the time, they might have believed it was an assassination attempt, but they were in a very excitable mood, and they could have got it wrong. And later, when no one in authority says anything about it, they'll easily accept that they were mistaken—that it was nothing more than a drunken brawl between two rival sets of living picture cameramen.'

'So no medal for you, then, sir?'

'I'll be given my job back, but for me to get a medal on top of that, the Queen would have to know what went on,' Blackstone said. 'And as far as the people around her are probably concerned, she should never know.' He laughed. 'And possibly they're right. What would be the point in spoiling the old lady's big day?' He stood up. 'Time you were getting off home to your family, Sergeant.'

'And what about you, sir?'

'Me?' Blackstone said. 'I think I'll take a little stroll.'

Blackstone walked slowly along the Embankment, his knees spasmodically sending out warnings that he was taking more exercise than was advisable, his arm maintaining a dull throb that suggested that he would be better off in bed. He didn't care. He was alone now—but not as alone as he would be back in his empty room.

Thoughts of Hannah came—uninvited and unwanted—to his mind. He had loved her for such a very short time, yet he was certain that the ache that her death had left him with would never go away.

Look on the bright side, Sam, he ordered himself. You've saved some lives today.

And not just the lives of the people on the streets of Southwark. Or the lives of Britons in India and the lives of Russian and English soldiers. He had saved Lady Emily Montcliffe from a life that would have been a fate worse than death—a life married to a man who, beneath the veneer of civilization, was little more than a monster.

He stopped walking, and looked down at the river. He could hear the gentle swish of its tidal waters. He could see the lights of ships anchored midway between the two shores. And he was tempted to walk down the nearest set of steps, and keep on walking. Until he was drowned. Until he had made himself at one with the heart of the city he loved.

'Do not turn around, Inspector Blackstone,' said a voice from not far behind him.

'Vladimir?' Blackstone asked. 'Is that you? Have you recovered from falling off the roof?'

'The common people below cushioned my fall,' the Russian said. 'That is, after all, what the common people are for—to cushion the fall of those who matter. But why do you call me Vladimir? Do you mean Vladimir Bubnov? How could I possibly be him, since he does not exist?'

'But you still don't want me to look at you?' Blackstone said.

'I have already exposed myself to you far too much for my liking,' the Russian told him.

'So now you're going to kill me,' Blackstone said, not entirely certain whether he cared one way or the other.

'No, I am not here to kill you.'

'But you've got your pistol pointing at me right now, haven't you?'

The Russian did not deny it. Instead, he said, 'My Tsar and my country owe you a debt. I am here both to give you information and to offer you a reward.'

'Before we go any further, let's make sure that things are perfectly clear between us,' Blackstone said. 'You do know that I'll never forgive you for killing Hannah, don't you?'

'But she would have killed you if l hadn't,' Vladimir pointed out.

'That's true, but it doesn't alter anything, does it?' Blackstone said.

And though he couldn't see the other man, he was sure that the Russian was nodding in agreement.

'I understand your feelings,' Vladimir said, 'but there is business to transact. I must first tell you that Lord Dalton landed in northern France just over an hour ago.'

'Should that be of any particular interest to me?'

'Yes, I think so. Because just as you cannot forgive me for killing the anarchist woman, I hardly think it likely that Lord Dalton will forgive *you* for destroying his life.'

'You're saying he'll try to get revenge?'

'As soon as he possibly can.'

It's not the first time somebody's wanted me dead,' Blackstone said indifferently. 'What about Count Turgenev? Was he with the noble lord when Dalton landed in France?'

'No,' the Russian replied. 'A short while ago some of your fellow police officers found his body in a house opposite the camera platform. He had been stabbed at least fifty times.'

A frenzied attack, Blackstone thought—like the one that Charles Montcliffe had been subjected to after his throat had been cut.

'Was it your handiwork?' he asked the Russian.

'No,' Vladimir told him. 'We would certainly have killed the Count, but someone got there before us.'

'Dalton,' Blackstone said, with conviction.

'He is the most likely suspect,' Vladimir agreed. 'But now let us get on to more important matters. Since you have undoubtedly saved my country from a ruinous war, I have been authorized to offer you a reward of five thousand pounds, provided, of course, that you agree to sign an undertaking to never again mention the name of Count Turgenev.'

'He offered me ten thousand pounds to let him go ahead with his plan,' Blackstone countered.

'Perhaps we could match that,' Vladimir said.

'And if I asked for fifteen?'

'That might he considered a little greedy,' the Russian said.

Blackstone laughed. 'You're already sighting your pistol at me, aren't you? There's no need for it. I promise not to tell anyone about Turgenev—but I don't want your money.'

'I did not take you for a fool.'

'I've been a fool all my life,' Blackstone said. 'But even a fool can learn his lesson, given time. I'm sick of the games you people play. Sick of being a pawn in them—and of the people around me being pawns. I'm tired of the whole pack of you.'

'Isn't there a saying in English that you must either run with the fox or the hounds?' Vladimir asked.

'Yes, there is.'

'The wise man will always choose the hounds.'

'The truly wise man will stay at home and tend his vegetables.'

'I am not sure my superiors will accept that,' Vladimir said. 'They would be much happier if they knew you were on our side. And the best way to prove that you are is to take the money.'

'I'm going to walk away,' Blackstone told him. 'There's no one around, so if you're going to kill me, now's the time to do it.'

He walked slowly along the Embankment towards Waterloo Bridge. It was a clear night and, looking up, he could see the stars—the same stars he had watched all those years ago in Afghanistan. He no longer felt like taking his own life. Instead, he had again become the young man he'd been on the long march to Kandahar—a young man who would resist death, but not at any cost.

He had put at least two dozen yards between himself and Vladimir by now. And still he heard no loud explosion. Still felt no searing pain and realized that he had been fatally wounded.

He turned around. There was no sign of the Russian. Vladimir had vanished into the night as if he had been no more than a dream.

Lightning Source UK Ltd.
Milton Keynes UK
UKHW010727270223
417728UK00005B/643